LEGACY OF THE SAIPH

Book 4 of The Saiph Series

PP Corcoran

PP Corcoran
Visit my website at www.PPCorcoran.com
Print Edition:
Printed in the United Kingdom

First Printing: August 2019

Castrum Press

ISBN-13 978-1-9123273-1-7

In Memory of Stuart Murray

6 May 1974 to 27 August 2018
A friend and colleague taken too soon.

PP Corcoran

TABLE OF CONTENTS

CHAPTER ONE

FOR THE GOOD OF THE EMPIRE

FORAM SYSTEM | THIRTY-SIX LIGHT-YEARS FROM ALONA

"Have we re-established contact yet?" Demanded General Lura in a low, grumbling voice for perhaps the tenth time in ten minutes.

Fresh beads of sweat formed on the communications technician's forehead as she steadfastly refused to meet the general's eyes and, instead, waited for her senior colleague to offer the commander, of all Alonan Imperial forces in the Foram System, an explanation as to why he could not speak to Captain Calan. The Captain Calan who, voluntarily, had entered the alien ship hovering serenely in the main holo display and filled the center of the cargo bay converted by General Lura into his command post for this operation.

"This was to be expected, General." Chief Scientist Kilor reassured the military man while running a hand across his brown, lightly furred head.

Though perhaps not friends, Kilor and Lura had come to understand each other's strengths and weaknesses, during their long months together, sequestered in the Foram System. They had overseen the construction of the industrial base, which built the shipyards, which in turn were to build the warships the Empire so desperately needed, if they were to reach parity with the Humans and their Commonwealth Union of Planets' allies. Then, a new and more deadly enemy revealed themselves, coined the Black Ships by the Commonwealth, these ships were crewed by ghosts, at least all believed their race to be dead, at the hands of the Others.

The Commonwealth had gotten one step ahead of the Empire and identified this *new* enemy as the Saiph, the race, if you believed the geneticists, that had tampered with the DNA of races throughout the galaxy, his Alonan forebearers included, to ensure their progeny became the predominant lifeform on their native worlds.

Lura mumbled something under his breath, which Kilor chose to ignore and he quashed any sign of his own irritation reaching his outward features.

Lura had every right to be worried. Ever since the discovery of the alien vessel the entire system had been on high alert.

Foram was the biggest military secret the Alonan Empire had and to find this ship, whoever it belonged to, slap bang in the middle of it had the general, and his bosses, on edge. It was all very well Kilor insisting that the vessel was not of Commonwealth, Turak or any other known races design, but that only raised the military's fears that it belonged to another potential enemy.

The fact that the rock had entombed the vessel for the better part of a thousand years, according to Kilor's best estimate, did not lessen the general's concern, hence five of the empire's most advanced cruisers hovered within weapons range.

"Alert Commodore Valak he is to lock weapons on the alien ship and -." Ordered General Lura.

"I do not recommend that, General." Interrupted Kilor.

Lura snapped his head around to face the scientist, eyes narrowed, his rising anger at the civilian contradicting him became obvious.

Kilor rushed to explain himself. "As you see, General." Kilor used one hand to indicate the holographic representation of the vessel, as he spoke more sections of the ship changed from gray to yellow, depicting the vessel's power emissions as detected by an array of Alonan sensors. "The entry of Captain Calan appears to have tripped some form of failsafe system aboard the vessel. If, and I hasten to say it is speculation on my part, if one of those newly activated systems detects Commodore Valak's weapon lock, then the vessel may have an automated defense system which -."

"May perceive Valak's actions as a threat and open fire." Lura finished Kilor's sentence. "Very well, Kilor." Lura turned to face a waiting communications technician. "Inform Commodore Valak he is to maintain a passive, and emphasize passive, weapon lock on the alien vessel."

As the technician rushed to obey the generals order, Lura leaned in close to his civilian counterpart, keeping his voice low. "If that ship so much as twitches, I will have it reduced to atoms."

Kilor simply nodded his head, not trusting his voice not to betray his own fears as to what might be aboard the alien vessel.

* * *

"You're a Saiph!" Calan blurted out.

The Saiph standing before him in his blue, one piece, uniform seemed startled by Calan's recognition of his species. Taking a step backwards its hand dropped warily to what Calan was sure was a weapon, holstered on a silver belt encircling the Saiph's waist.

Calan froze. Standing in an airlock, dressed only in a thin thermal inner suit, he really did not want to antagonize the one person who could, with a simple motion, slam the inner door of the airlock closed and open the outer one sending the unfortunate captain out into the freezing depths of space.

The Alonan slowly, in his most nonthreatening voice, repeated himself while pointing a finger at his uniformed host. "Saiph."

The Saiph cocked its head to one side for a moment, as if listening to an unseen entity, all the time keeping its eyes locked on Calan. Suddenly a hidden speaker by the airlock door boomed out. "Saippphhh."

Calan's mind whirled. *By the Gods this is happening! I am standing here talking to a real live Saiph and he hasn't killed me yet?* That thought brought Calan up short. *Now there's a question. Why hasn't he killed me? Everything we know about the Black Ships says the Saiph crew are genocidal maniacs.* Calan looked again at the Saiph stood not more than two meters from him trying frantically trying to work out what was going on in its head.

Is he as confused as me? We know this rock had buried this ship inside it for a millennium. Could the crewmembers have no idea what was going on in the wider galaxy? That the Empire is at war with the Saiph?

Well, I'm not going to find out, if I can only speak to him one word at a time, am I. Calan admonished himself. *Now, that I can do something about.* Keeping his hands in plain sight he bent slowly at the waist, reaching for the left arm of his limp pressure suit lying on the airlock floor.

"I'm just going to get my comms pack." Calan said slowly and calmly. The Saiph did not appear to object, well, at least their hand did not move any closer to their weapon, Calan noted encouragingly. Calan's fingers touched the still-cold plastic casing of the compact comms pack attached to the sleeve of his suit and deftly released it, holding it out in front of him so the Saiph could see the blinking lights on its control surface.

Moving the comms pack to the front of his face so he could see the control surface, Calan called the main menu. Designed for use in space by an armored gauntlet wearer, the small device required him to use an unexpected amount of pressure and he ended up pressing on the control surface hard.

Eventually, Calan found the sub menu he was searching for. The translation protocols. A thought occurred to him. The comms pack used software that the Empire had- procured from the Commonwealth. Its database incorporated each individual language encountered by the Commonwealth and hundreds of sub dialects. *What if the designers hadn't included Saiph in the database? Why would they? Everyone thought they were extinct, until the Black Ships debacle.*

He need not have worried, Calan sighed in relief as the software highlighted the word 'Saiph' on the screen. Tapping the accept icon the screen blinked on and off two times before displaying the word 'Ready.'

Well, here goes, thought Calan, clearing his throat.

"Hello." He said as clearly as possible ensuring the comms pack's translator software did not inadvertently mix the greeting with another word, like, say *bomb*.

The comms pack obediently translated the greeting into Saiph and produced the appropriate sound from its compact speaker.

Confounded by the little speaker addressing him in his own language the Saiph's jaw dropped open, wide enough to drive a starship into it and his eyes went wide as plates. Recovering quickly, the Saiph's lips moved and a chattering noise, came out. The translation software paused momentarily, for a second Calan thought the device was malfunctioning, before he remembered that no one had heard a live Saiph speak in its native tongue in a thousand years. Satisfied it had the translation correct the device activated its external speaker.

"Greetings."

Calan let out a breath. *Either this Saiph is the politest killer the galaxy has ever known, or he isn't going to kill me...*

"My name is Captain Calan of the Alonan Imperial Navy and I mean you no harm."

Dutifully the translator conducted its task and produced a series of chattering noises to which the Saiph replied.

"I am unfamiliar with this Alonan Imperial Navy that you are part of. I am Commander Okal of the progenitor ship *Savior*. I take your word that you harbor no hostile intent though -" The Saiph paused ensuring that he had Calan's full attention. "Actions speak louder than words. Perhaps, you could inform the warships surrounding my vessel to withdraw to twice their current distance."

"Commander," Said Calan delicately. "Perhaps you are... ah... unaware of current events -."

A high-pitched laugh escaped Okal which took him a couple of seconds to contain before he spoke. "Captain Calan, my crew and I have been in suspended animation for longer than your entire civilization's existence. So, forgive my ignorance. I assure you, however, that this ship is fully capable of defending itself against any aggressor."

Despite himself, anger flooded Calan's body. "Aggressor? It is you Saiph who are the aggressors. Only weeks ago you murdered the entire colony on Balat. You and your Black Ships!" Calan stepped forward closing the distance between himself and Okal, the Alonan's anger poured forth unchecked. "You are responsible for waging a war of genocide across the galaxy, wiping entire races from existence -" Calan leaned forward and ignored Okal's instinctive reaction to reach for his weapon at his waist.

"You are the aggressor here, Commander Okal." Calan was now close enough that the spittle from his mouth landed on the Saiph's face.

The airlock descended into silence.

Calan fought to control his anger when an awful thought entered his head. *By the Gods, I've signed my own death warrant!*

But, when Calan looked upon the face of Okal he saw the unmistakable look of horror plastered the Saiph commander's face. Okal staggered backwards and bumped into the frame of the airlock, which opened at his touch to reveal two more, identically dressed, Saiph standing in the corridor beyond. Their faces reflected the horror of their commander.

Okal spoke in a low, barely perceptible voice which Calan strained to hear. "What has the Leader done?" Calan's anger now dissipated, he sensed the despair in the Saiph's voice, as Okal repeated himself. "What has that mad man done?"

Calan stared at Okal, unsure of what to say and, when their eyes met, Calan found despair and- shame laid bare in Okal's.

"If what you say is true then the- the-." Okal struggled for the correct word. "The criminal who calls himself the Leader, a piece of filth responsible for the destruction of my home world, is still alive after all these years." Before Calan's eyes, Okal's face became hard as stone. "He and his followers must be stopped." The Saiph commander stated resolutely. "Your technology is not on a par with ours and therefore neither is his." Okal's spine stiffened as he came to a decision. "We will help you with that." The two Saiph standing silently in the corridor beyond the airlock flicked their heads to one side in unison. A move that Calan interpreted as agreement with their commander.

"I must speak with your superiors, Captain Calan, as soon as possible." Rushed Okal. "We've been asleep for an age with no contact with the outside world. By now the Seed Worlds should have come to fruition and, if your – sorry, what is your species' name?"

"Alonan." Calan said helpfully.

"Yes, yes. If you Alonan have attained this level of technology, then you have discovered the Library my crew and I established, in this sector, before entering hibernation." Okal paused expectantly.

"Eh… we have discovered no such library, Commander." Calan replied after a moment's hesitation, wondering how much of the current situation he should tell Okal.

The *Seed Worlds* that Okal mentioned must be planets like Alona, Earth, Garunda and Pars where the Saiph had altered the DNA of specific genetic lines. And, the library must be the underground knowledge repositories, like the Rubicon Cave the Humans discovered, which gave them a step up to their technology base.

Calan had eluded to a war raging among the stars with his angry outburst moments earlier. Now, though, with a calmer head, perhaps it was prudent to leave further discussions about the war to individuals well above his pay grade. He noticed that Okal watched him inquisitively.

"Yes, Commander?"

"If you have not discovered the Library in this sector, then why are your warships, according to our sensor readings, equipped with a version of a Saiph-designed gravity drive?"

Forced to think fast, Calan searched for the correct words. "We, ah, recovered an abandoned alien ship from the fringes of our system and luckily our scientists were able to reverse engineer the technology." The lie left a bad taste in his mouth and Calan realized it may be the first of many untruths.

Okal fixed him with unblinking eyes and Calan prayed that the Saiph commander did not notice the small beads of perspiration forming on his forehead.

After what seemed like forever, Okal gave that funny little twitch of the head that the other two Saiph crew members had done before and Calan allowed himself to breathe again.

"Very enterprising of your engineers, Captain Calan. If they are capable of reverse engineering an entire star ship then, with our help, I expect them to achieve remarkable things in a truly short space of time."

"Indeed!" Changing the subject quickly, Calan said, "Talking of my people, my lack of contact with them will be causing alarm and you said you wanted to speak with my superiors."

"Of course, of course." Said Okal as if only now remembering that he had made the request. Speaking aloud to an unseen individual who was, obviously, listening in Okal said. "Chera, disable the Interference Field and allow Captain Calan to use his communication device."

Almost immediately the small translation device burst forth with the urgent voice of the comms tech in General Lura's command post.

"...Calan. Captain Calan. Are you receiving me? Please respond."

"Command, this is Calan. I am safe and well and have made friendly contact with the crew of this ship."

A short series of muffled voices emanated from the speaker, before the commanding voice of General Lura emerged from the device. "Captain Calan, what is your situation?"

Calan flashed a look at Okal and carefully considered his next words. "Sir, I am standing with Commander Okal, the commander of this ship. He assures me he intends us no harm. In fact, he has made it clear that he wishes to aid us in our conflict with the Saiph."

There was a distinct pause before General Lura came back onto the radio. "Does he now?" The wariness in the general's voice hung in the air. "Then his species are familiar with the Saiph?"

Calan shared a wry smile with Okal who, in return, let out a small chattering sound that Calan assumed was a laugh. "Uh, yes, sir, you could say that. It would be wiser if I brief you in person, before you meet with Commander Okal. It would help, eh, prevent any misunderstandings."

In the command post, General Lura exchanged a confused look with Chief Scientist Kilor who responded to the general with the Alonan equivalent of a shrug.

"Very well, Captain." Said Lura. "I await your return before deciding on our next course of action." The general cut the connection before Calan replied.

Only then did Calan realize he had arranged to leave the ship without Okal's permission. Just because the Saiph commander indicated his intention to assist the Alonans, it did not mean that Calan was free to leave.

As if sensing Calan's confusion Okal reached into a pocket and produced a slim, translucent plastic card, etched with a thin gold-colored circuit, and held it against the side of Calan's comms pack.

The circuitry glowed briefly, before returning to its original state.

Seemingly satisfied, Okal returned the card to his pocket on his uniform's forearm. "I have taken the liberty, Captain Calan, of retrieving and copying this communication device's translation software. I will upload the program to Chera, my ship's artificial intelligence. It will make our future conversations more succinct." As if on cue, a gentle beep came from the speaker built into the airlock's inner door frame.

"Commander." Calan's ears heard a soft feminine voice say in perfect Alonan. "Translation upload is completed and assimilated. I am now fluent in Captain Calan's language and others contained in his primitive equipment."

"Primitive?" Blurted Calan.

Again, the chattering sound of Okal's laughter filled the airlock. "Please forgive Chera, Captain. She can appear somewhat aloof."

"Commander." Chera interjected. "I detect an Alonan small-craft maneuvering to dock with the outer lock."

"Ah." Said Okal. "That'll be for you, Captain." Okal stepped back through the inner airlock door. "I have downloaded a communication's frequency into your device. Chera will monitor it. When you've appraised your superiors, I will await your answer to our offer. Meanwhile, I must revive the remainder of my crew and ascertain the status of our embryo banks."

The inner door closed leaving Calan alone in the airlock, once more. Hurriedly, he re-dressed, double-checked the seals of his pressure suit and turned to the alien control panel covered in Saiph symbols.

He had no idea which sequence depressurized the lock and opened the outer door.

He need not have worried, either a crew member, or more likely Chera, had been surveilling him, for his suit's system reported:

AIRLOCK DEPRESSURIZING

As the airlock reached vacuum, the outer door slid to one side. A shuttle door hovered, only two or three meters beyond, and the outer door of its personnel lock lay already opened. Two suited figures hung from magnetic grips on either side of the open lock.

Upon seeing him they activated the maneuvering packs on their backs and glided effortlessly toward him. As they reached Calan, they pirouetted in unison and came to a halt on either side of him. Calan reached out and slipped an arm through the handling hooks on the rear of each maneuvering pack.

"Secure." He said over his suit's radio. Small thrusters on each suit carried Calan toward the waiting Alonan vessel.

Calan wondered how he would convey the news of his astounding discovery to General Lura.

* * *

The recording ended for the third time and the side room off the main control room, that General Lura had had cleared of all personnel, at the insistence of Captain Calan, descended into silence.

Chief Scientist Kilor, the only other person present, besides Calan and the general, struggled to keep the one thousand and one questions, that he wanted to barrage Calan with, in check. Instead, he remained silent, for the look on General Lura's face was one of profound thought.

Calan had stood while the communication device, he had carried while aboard the Saiph vessel, replayed his entire conversation with Commander Okal. Hearing that the alien vessel was of Saiph construction and real, live, Saiph were still aboard it had initially shocked Kilor. That shock had quickly turned to fear as he, like Calan, thought these Saiph were the same as those who had spread nuclear death over the Balat colony.

The revelation that the Saiph crewing the Black Ships were, in fact, enemies of *these* Saiph and *these* Saiph were willing to assist the Empire in its war against the Black Ships, had flung the scientist's mind into a whirlwind of overlapping possibilities.

Armed with Saiph weaponry the Empire could not only defend itself against the Black Ships, but it would be a generation ahead of the best the Commonwealth had to offer and would have a similar edge on anything the Turak had yet revealed on the field of battle. Lura spoke for the first time and ended Kilor's musing.

"Okal states that he has no connection with those of his race who are in control of the Black Ships?" He asked Calan.

Calan peeled his eyes from the rear bulkhead, where he had them fixed, as he stood to attention in front of the seated general and scientist to make eye contact with Lura. "That is what he stated, General."

Lura rubbed his bottom lip absently before asking his next question. "And he went as far as describing the leader of these Black Ships as a criminal and offered to assist us by providing the Empire with advanced technology to combat this *Leader*?"

"Correct, General." Answered Calan succinctly while wishing that Lura would stop asking him questions that he already knew the answer to because he had heard it on the recording twice. A spasm ran through Calan's left leg and he flexed his toes in order to shake the cramp off. Standing to attention while Lura and Kilor listened intently to the recording, twice, from their comfortable seats was taking its toll.

The captain's involuntary muscle spasm did not go unnoticed by Lura who waved a hand in the direction of a spare seat. "Sit down, Captain, before you fall down."

Calan gratefully sank into the proffered seat, as a wave of exhaustion swept over him. His body craved sleep, now, the adrenalin which filled his system during his encounter with Okal had drained from him.

"Mala!" Called Lura and, as if by magic, the general's aide appeared in the open doorway. "Fetch some gilon." Calan's ears perked up at the name of the expensive herbal beverage. Served hot and sweet, gilon's recuperative properties were almost legendary. His body may crave slumber but a large cup of gilon would keep him going until the opportunity to fall into his bunk arose.

"At once, General." Replied Mala with a curt nod before, once more, vanishing.

Lura returned his attention to his interrogation of Calan. "Okal claims he had no outside contact since he entered this- suspended animation?"

Calan nodded wearily.

"And as such, has no idea of the events that have unfolded in that time?" Pressed Lura.

"Correct, General." Answered Calan his voice beginning to betray his growing impatience at his superior simply repeating information that he already knew.

Kilor sat forward as he caught the tone of the captain's answer, nervously flicking his eyes in the direction of Lura who, either chose to ignore the implication in the tired, younger Alonan's answer or simply did not care. The General was, after all, the closest thing to the Emperor in this star system. Still, Kilor decided this might be an opportune moment to intervene on Captain Calan's behalf before the junior officer said something which would incur the wrath of Lura.

"Perhaps..." Began Kilor only for the door to open and the general's aide, Mala, to enter bearing a tray with a jug of steaming Gilon and three cups. The room lapsed into silence as Mala placed the tray on a side table and proceeded to pour three portions of the Gilon, its herbal fragrance subtly infused the room. Mala exited the room after he had served each of the occupants and the door automatically closed behind him, leaving the three men sequestered once more.

General Lura absently sipped at his gilon ostensibly oblivious to the presence of the other two, his eyes unfocused as his brain worked on something he had not chosen to share with the others. Calan was simply happy for the pause in the questioning and gratefully partook of his gilon, closing his eyes to savor the rich flavor. Kilor, on the other hand, held his cup in both hands without drinking from it. Watching Lura through the steam rising from the hot gilon he wondered what was going on inside the military man's head. Kilor knew better than to interrupt, so remained silent and waited for Lura to work through whatever he was considering.

Seconds stretched into a minute. The minute morphed into five minutes and the five minutes became ten. From Calan came the gentle sound of a snore and Kilor could not help the smile tugging at his lips, at the sight of the captain slouched in his seat, with the now empty cup precariously perched on the seat's armrest. *Hmm, gilon's miraculous recuperating effects are a myth after all*, thought Kilor as he stood as quietly as he could and retrieved the captain's empty cup before the inevitable happened and the cup tumbled and smashed on the deck. Gently, he prized Calan's fingers from around the cup and returned it to the tray that Mala had delivered them on.

"A wise move, my friend." Said Lura in a hushed voice, startling Kilor who nearly knocked over the cup he had so carefully retrieved.

"You will be the death of me one day if you keep creeping about like that." Joked the scientist as he caught the playful look in Lura's eyes. A look that in a single blink became serious again.

"I believe the good captain has presented us with an opportunity."

"How so?" Asked Kilor.

"By not revealing any details of the outside world to Okal during their initial meeting. We have the opportunity to construct a narrative which exploits Okal's stated desire to aid in the fight against the Black Ships."

Kilor pondered Lura's words for a moment. "You mean lie to Okal."

Lura shrugged as he reached to refill his cup. "Lie; Mislead; Forget to mention certain facts; Enhance the Empire's version of the truth. Call it what you will, friend Kilor. We tell Okal that we are the last remaining Seed World. Despite the victorious battle with the Others, the battle left –" Lura took a sip of his Gilor before continuing, "left the Seed Worlds' defense in tatters and made them easy prey for the Black Ships, who pounced on the now defenseless worlds and erased them from existence."

A loud "Hmm." Escaped Kilor. "Something which may still happen."

Lura pointed a thin finger at the scientist. "Exactly. A deception sprinkled with enough truth to make it believable."

A worry line appeared on Kilor's brow. "But to what end?"

"We reveal the truth about the purpose of Foram. Well, near as damn it- the Empire's last-ditch attempt to build warships capable of standing against the Black Ships. A shipyard hidden from prying eyes because we fear the Black Ships know the location of our home world after the attack on Balat."

"Mmm, and if Okal is truthful, he will give us access to his ships' technology. Technology which is at least equal to the Black Ships, never mind the Commonwealth and the Turak." Kilor found himself becoming caught up in Lura's scheme until the worry line on his brow transformed into a full-fledged frown. "But, how do we stop Okal from finding out the truth?

"The truth?" Lura asked with a chortle. "The truth as far as Okal is concerned is what we tell him. Given time I'm sure we will fathom Okal's reasoning for hiding in Foram. Meanwhile, we play the imperial security card and prevent him from leaving the system. For his own, and our, protection of course.

Only the Gods know where the Black Ships are, and the discovery of *this* shipyard would be disastrous. We must keep contact with Okal and his crew to an absolute minimum." Lura indicated the slouched form of Calan. "The good captain will act as liaison and will shadow Okal wherever he goes."

"And absolutely *no* access to navigational or intelligence data." Added Kilor.

Lura raised his cup in agreement. "Fabricate some excuse, like the new warships' information nets are kept clean until the last moment in case of capture or compromise. Look, these are all details we can work out as they present themselves."

"I'm not sure I like the idea of lying to Okal, though." Admitted Kilor.

"I can see no other way." Said Lura. "Are you willing to take the chance that Okal might offer to share his technology with the Commonwealth or the Turak?" Lura fixed Kilor with steady eyes.

After a moment's hesitation Kilor shook his head.

Satisfied, Lura raised his half empty cup of gilon. "For the good of the Empire."

"For the good of the Empire." Repeated Kilor to the gentle snoring of the sleeping Captain Calan who remained blissfully unaware of the part he was to play in Lura's plans.

✳ ✳ ✳

Okal prowled the metal walkways that formed the heart of the *Savior*. Ignoring the chill in the air caused by the banks of refrigeration units which filled every spare inch of the space. Okal was too restless to lie in his soft bed and sleep. The Saiph commander had done enough sleeping for a lifetime and his head still swirled from the news his meeting with the Alonan General Lura had brought.

The now familiar anger, no despair, swelled in Okal once more.

The images of death, on a scale he found difficult to comprehend, which the Leader and, his unwitting puppets the Others, had brought to the galaxy. The home world scrubbed clean of life in the name of Saiph superiority. The Seed Worlds hunted, one after another.

Thousands of years of intricate genetic manipulation laid waste under nuclear bombardment. Then of course there was the collateral damage. It seemed the Leader was not to be satisfied with destroying the Seed Worlds. The Others had seen to it that any civilization they had encountered suffered the same fate as the Seed Worlds. Worlds the Elders never imagined existed, died at the bidding of the Leader.

When Lura had finished telling Okal of the events that forced the Alonan Empire to hide their shipyard away what they called the Foram System, Okal shared with them his own journey which had led to him and his crew's presence here.

The attempted coup by the Leader, his subsequent confinement and escape as he and his followers fled the home world and disappeared among the myriad of stars that made up the night sky.

The Elders' realization that, one day, the Leader may return to threaten the intricate planning that had established the Seed Worlds. The Elders had decided long ago, after the disastrous encounter with a primitive early space-capable race that colonization of other worlds was not compatible with Saiph philosophy. Hence the abandonment of the colonization program. Something abhorrent to the Leader who advocated the superiority of the Saiph as a race and its predetermined place as the supreme being of the galaxy.

The Leader's escape and the threat he posed, forced the Elders to either amend their outlook or consign themselves and the Seed Worlds to whatever fate the Leader decided upon.

The progenitor ships became the Elders' answer.

Each ship was tasked to visit a star system close to a Seed World and establish a Library containing the accumulated knowledge of the Saiph civilization; then they would find another star system, this time devoid of life-bearing planets, their crew would enter artificial hibernation in safety and emerge, in a thousand years, in to a galaxy which had long since seen the scourge of the Leader and his followers turned to dust. With their precious cargo the *Savior* and her sister ships, carrying the Saiph, would survive as a race and be capable of rebuilding, perhaps even, of becoming a greater, more enlightened civilization than they were.

Okal rested his hands on a guard rail, his head bowed, eyes closed. The Elders' worst fears had come true, according to what the Alonans had told him.

The planet of his birth was no more and the crushing burden of the survival of his race now sat heavy upon his shoulders.

"Pardon the interruption, Commander." The soft voice of *Savior's* AI, Chera, broke into his dark thoughts.

Okal pushed himself upright. "Go ahead, Chera."

"All crew members are revived and have been examined by medical technicians. The crew are gathered on the mess deck in accordance with your orders, Commander."

"Thank you, Chera." Replied Okal. "And the search program?"

Okal detected a momentary pause before the AI answered. "There are no transmissions from other progenitor vessels at this time, Commander. However, the distances involved, and the background interference generated by the Alonans' communications and their ships' drives may hinder their detection. May I suggest a solution, Commander?"

"Of course, Chera."

"A drone launched into clear space, up to three light-years from here, will increase my chances of detecting one of my sisters' transmissions by 287.42 percent, Commander."

Okal dismissed Chera's solution, out of hand. "Not yet, Chera. Launching a probe, without clearing it with the Alonans, may lead to a few questions from our new allies."

"So, we are allying ourselves with the Alonans, Commander?" Asked Chera.

"For the moment. It's our best course of action." The first wisps of guilt entered Okal's thoughts. "If the Alonans are telling the truth, then we are responsible for the threat they face."

"You assume General Lura's information is, in fact, the truth, Commander."

"Yes, Chera, perceptive as always." A wry smile crossed Okal's lips. "It would be prudent of us to ensure the validity of the Alonan facts."

"The Alonan computer systems' firewalls do not represent a challenge to me, Commander" Chera stated.

"Subtle as a brick, Chera." Said Okal with a small chuckle, which drove the guilt away. The more pressing challenge of his primary mission came to the fore; their survival- his, his crews' and his races' to be precise.

"Very well Chera. With extreme caution, probe the Alonan's systems. Prioritize historical and navigational databases and search for any inconsistencies in the Alonan's story."

"Very well, Commander."

Orders given, Okal squared his shoulders and headed for the mess deck to brief his crew.

CHAPTER TWO

BOARD OF INQUIRY

TERRAN DEFENSE FORCE | NAVAL HEADQUARTERS | CARSON CITY | EARTH | SOL SYSTEM

The sharp sound of the ship's bell, rung by the presiding member of the inquiry board, cut across the dark oak paneled hearing room and caused John to flinch.

A commander from the Judge Advocate General's Corps sitting beside him did not notice his movements or, at least, she chose not to react to his involuntary start.

Commander Zeidler.

He had no idea what her given name was, she had never introduced herself as anything other than her rank or surname and by the time he understood that he needed a lawyer, it was too late to ask.

So, Commander Zeidler it remained.

Zeidler sat motionless. Her dress whites were free of blemish, so much so that they looked as though they had been freshly issued that morning, while the creases of her blouse and pants looked sharp enough to cut through battle armor.

The day after John's return to the Sol System, he received notification that his actions in the Guzman System would be subject to a formal board of inquiry and he was required to report to naval headquarters in Carson City, forthwith.

When his shuttle door cracked open, on the roof of the impressive skyscraper that was the home of the Terran Defense Force Navy, he was met with the sight of Commander Zeidler awaiting him. After the briefest of introductions, where she assessed him like a law enforcement interrogator rather than a defense lawyer, Zeidler escorted him to a pre-prepared briefing room and began her, for want of a better word, interrogation.

With no remorse the she had analyzed, second by second, every move John had made, again and again. With the aid of a wall-sized holograph projector they ran through the battle around the colony in Guzman, stopped at every decision point and gamed out what could have happened had he chosen differently.

As hours became days, John grew weary of every line of questioning.

Each evening, physically and mentally drained, he would return to his quarters wishing the inquiry would end. He dreamed of jumping on transport and returning to Geneva to be reunited with his wife. In reality, a video call at the end of the day was the most he could manage.

Seemingly sated, Zeidler moved onto more personal questions about John's relationship with his wife.

How is your home life?

Had you argued before your departure for Guzman?

Were you under any stress from home, that might have affected your judgment?

His anger had grown with each question, until, he exploded from his seat and barely restrained himself from grabbing the unemotional commander by the throat. After a few moments he regained his poise, the blood pounding in his ears gave way to the realization that Zeidler was baiting him; to see how, or if, he would react. *Played me like a world class pianist*, he had thought, before giving the lawyer grudging respect. Zeidler had identified the chink in his armor, now she could defend it.

And how he needed that armor.

The intense preparation Zeidler put him through felt like nothing compared to the actual Board of Inquiry; a solid two weeks of grueling, sometimes pointed, questioning of his actions in Guzman.

The navy had not treated him lightly.

They brought tactical expert after tactical expert.

Instructors from the Naval Advanced Tactical Course, retired admirals, civilian weapons' experts, even graduates from his own peer group.

After all, on paper, CSG *Itus* was vastly superior to the Black Ships that she faced. The cruisers attached to *Itus* should have been more than a match for the Black Ships, let alone the CSG's battleships and, not forgetting, TDF *Itus* itself; the first human-built carrier and home to seventy-two deadly Mosquito space-fighters. The odds must surely have been stacked against the Black Ships.

However, the Saiph cruisers had leveled the playing field with their Active Energy Shielding. That shielding forced John to close with the much smaller ships, to allow his Mosquitos and battleships to pound those energy shields flat, for while the shields were active the Black Ships fired back with impunity. The brave Mosquito crews had done exactly as ordered. They closed with the enemy, harassed them with missile and rapid-fire plasma cannon and they gave their destroyers the opportunity to race ahead of the lumbering capital ships, of CSG *Itus*, to add their firepower to the relentless battery.

The Black Ships had raced to clear the spheres of overlapping interference generated by equipment aboard John's cruisers, which prevented the Black Ships from activating their gravity drives and impeded their escape. In a fatal error the Black Ships abandoned their headlong flight to safety and turned to face the human destroyers. Perhaps their commander thought they could defeat them, make good their escape before the capital ships caught them, but they were wrong.

The destroyer's sacrifice was enough. The battleships closed to point-blank-range, firing missile after missile at the enemy, repeatedly battering their energy shields with mega-tonnes of nuclear blast. All the while, the fighters darted and danced in their hunt for the tiniest gap in the Black Ships' defenses.

When the enemy's shields failed and the onslaught of human missiles reached the battle armor skin of the cruisers' hulls, their fight was over.

Two of the enemy cruisers ceased to exist, except as rapidly moving gaseous elements.

A third, its drive impaired during its attempted escape, suffered an infliction of brutal damage from a pair of heavy cruisers; wrecking the Black Ships' ability to continue their fight.

And the fourth and final Black Ship? She was broken clean in half by the combined fire of six destroyers. The sight of the two tumbling chunks of ship trailing atmosphere, wracked by explosions as the thick brown atmosphere of a sole gas giant swallowed them up was etched into his mind.

The cost of victory had been high. All six of the plucky destroyers had been lost, along with thirty-eight fighters, five cruisers and two battleships. 2,384 men and women.

Nevertheless, he had weathered the Navy investigation with patience, answered their questions with forthrightness and remained calm in the face of their, sometimes, accusatory tones and today his fate would be decided.

Twice more the bell rung, sounding like the death knell of John's career. Not that his career was that precious to him, he was surprised to learn himself, after he understood the conflicted feelings that coursed through him on his return to Sol Systems Gateway Station.

He absently wondered if the officers and political hacks, filling the three rows of seats behind him, fathomed the depth of his grief at the loss of life. *Probably not.* The only person who did was Patricia.

Sitting right behind John, separated by a waist high wooden rail, Patricia Radford, nee Bath, absentmindedly worried her lower lip, before admonishing herself for displaying an outward sign of nervousness and forced her features into their default pose of complete self-control.

Patricia had borne witness to the toll that Guzman had taken on the man she loved. Over the years in which the bloody conflict with the 'Others' had dragged on; John's steadfast resolve was that he fought for something greater than himself and that resolve had been his rock. No matter how bloody the battle, how hard-fought the victory, the end result was always worth the cost.

Except for Guzman.

John had returned from that far-away-system a different man.

Patricia knew that a spark was missing from his eyes, a once bright light, symbolic of his warmth and playfulness was extinguished and replaced by shadows. Patricia was sure he still saw the world around him, but it was with a more cynical eye than before.

Beside Patricia, silent and unmoving as a rock in the middle of a storm, sat Admiral Ai Jing, Chairman of the Combined Joint Chiefs of Staff, Commonwealth Union of Planets.

It was most unusual for an officer of his rank and position to be present, never mind blatantly supporting, an officer who was subject to a board of inquiry.

Jing had ignored the whispered gossip in the corridors of power in Geneva and beyond. Each day the board sat in session Jing was found in this exact same seat, directly behind John. Never saying a word or expressing an opinion, for his presence alone spoke volumes and his presence acted as a signal to the rest of the fleet.

On the second day of the inquiry two flag officers took seats in the public gallery. Analisa Chavez Commanding Admiral of the Home Fleet and Admiral Abdul-Rauf Assaf, Chief of Naval Operations.

Over the following days the public gallery became a veritable who's who of Terran Defense Force flag officers.

By the close of the first week the politicos were so concerned about the media coverage of the board of inquiry, that bright and early on Friday morning, a none too subtle message was received by Admiral Jing's office. Signed by the Secretary of Defense a memo sought clarification on the current disposition of fleet and branch commanders. Scuttlebutt had it that when Jing returned to his office, during a brief hearing recess, he was overheard swearing in a number of languages, not all of which were human.

Jing was not a man who took to political interference; however, the wily old admiral had learned to play the game of politics at the feet of the man Jing considered to be the father of the modern TDF, Olaf Helsett, the Viking powerhouse himself.

On the Friday afternoon a signal was dispatched from Admiral Ai Jing, Chairman of the Combined Joint Chiefs of Staff; a thinly veiled snub to those politicians who were more afraid of the optics than in showing support for a man who, more than once, had laid his life on the line to protect them:

P 151826Z MAR
FM ADMIRAL AI JING CHAIRMAN OF THE COMBINED JOINT CHIEFS OF STAFF
TO ZEN/ALNAVFLEETCOM
INFO BUENAVCOL
BUENAVWPS
BUENAVDESG
BUENAVRECE
BUENAVSURV
WD GRNC
BT
SECRET TDF EYES ONLY
CCJSS CONSULTATIONS AT HEADQUARTERS TDF, CARSON CITY, EARTH COMMENCING 180700Z MAR.
ALL OFFICERS OF FLAG RANK TO ATTEND.
LIST OF ATTENDEES AND DAYS TO FOLLOW.
BT
NNNN

***

WHEN THE MONDAY MORNING arrived, true to his word, Admiral Jing hosted a breakfast in his private dining room on the top floor of the sprawling building of Naval Headquarters.

The Six attending flag officers enjoyed the commanding views of the city and the peaks of the Rocky Mountains beyond, through the floor to ceiling windows and over their hearty breakfast and steaming coffee, Jing chaired a free-flowing discussion of varying views on the colonization program, weapon's development and the shortage of personnel.

At 0850 hours Jing called a halt to the proceedings, thanked those attending and released them to enjoy the remainder of the day, before heading to the elevator which took him down forty-nine floors to where John Radford's board of inquiry was being held. Entering the room, he silently took his seat in the front row beside Patricia. No sooner had he made himself comfortable when six flag officers trooped in and ignored the hovering holo cams of the massed ranks of the media, arrayed in the press section, and the harsh glares of the handful of politicians who had, inaccurately, judged the savaging of a high ranking naval officer as an opportunity to forward their own lukewarm careers.

And so, proceeded each day of John's board. Until today.

Senior officer of the board, Admiral Kengi Kone, plucked from her usual position as the senior instructor at the Joint Naval Academy on Garunda, cleared her throat and the sound focused the suddenly quiet packed rooms' eyes upon her.

Patricia had met Kone only once, at some fancy shindig before John had relinquished command of Third Fleet and Patricia hadn't been able to put her finger on the 'something' behind Kone's polite yet superficial murmurings. However, when Kone's appointment to the board became public, whispered rumors of bad blood between John and Kone, finally, reached her ears.

Kone had, apparently, been in line to succeed John as Third Fleet's new commander once his rotation ended. But, following the brutal battering inflicted on Third Fleet at the Battle of Narath, the Joint Chiefs of Staff decided to rebuild Third Fleet from the ground up; with its constituent Battle Forces distributed amongst, what the Chiefs considered, higher priority units such as Admiral Chavez's First Fleet. The final nail in the coffin for Kone's aspirations for fleet command, came when the Garundans blindsided the entire Commonwealth by declaring their intention to offer *Yolva*, or succor, to the few remaining survivors of what had once been their most feared enemy; the Others. The ancient tradition of *Yolva* demanded that the Garundans care for and protect their defeated enemy as if they were family and Garunda had bent to the task with a will that had left the other worlds of the Commonwealth in awe.

Yolva resulted in the few remaining ships that could have been assigned to Third Fleet being re-tasked to assist the Garundans and crushed Kone's hopes of becoming its commander.

Patricia's attention came back to the here and now as she watched Admiral Kone lift her PAD and cast a hasty look around the room. Patricia suppressed the inklings of a shiver and steeled herself, unaware that she had reached out to touch Jing's hand and he had responded by placing his hand reassuringly atop hers.

If the flag officers, perched on the row of seats behind Jing, noticed this show of emotion from a man reputed to be as animated as a rock face, then they chose to ignore it.

"After careful deliberation and having examined all the facts before the Board –" Kone hesitated, eyes leaving whatever was written on the small electronic device and locking with those of John. Was it anger he registered in those narrowed eyes?

Disappointment maybe? John returned her gaze with unblinking, unflinching steadiness.

If Kone's intention was to stare him down, then she was onto a hiding to nothing.

The interaction between the two officers did not escape Jing; he resolved, there and then, that a certain Admiral Kone, for as long as he had influence within the naval forces of the Commonwealth, would never receive a fleet command.

"It is the view of the majority of the Board- a narrow majority, that the decisions of Admiral John Radford, Commanding Officer, Carrier Strike Group *Itus*, were not responsible for the significant losses inflicted on CSG *Itus* during the Guzman action. It is therefore the Board's recommendation that no -" The word seemed to make Kone want to gag. "Disciplinary action be taken against Admiral Radford or any of his officers."

The ringing of the bell, signaling the dismissal of the board, was drowned out as reporters raced each other for the exit, already pulling out their mini cams or tapping away on their PADs as they rushed to be the first to get the news out.

John was deaf to the raucous sounds around him. The weight on his shoulders evaporated, like the morning mist struck by the first warming rays of the new day's sun. Commander Zeidler lifted the stack of PADs on the table and placed them into her attaché case before standing and momentarily brushing away a piece of imaginary lint from her, as normal, immaculate, pressed uniform.

"I believe my work here is done, sir." Placing her cap upon her head her hand came up so fast he thought she would knock the cap flying. Instead, the edge of her fingers stopped on the peak of her cap as she saluted him.

Pushing himself to his feet John returned her salute.

"With your permission, sir?" Asked Zeidler.

For the first time in what seemed a lifetime a smile tugged at his lips. "Of course, Commander. And -" Zeidler was caught off guard as he stuck out a hand. Lowering her salute, the usually aloof and professional Zeidler took the proffered hand. "Thank you." Said John.

To his surprise Zeidler flashed the briefest of smiles. "My pleasure, sir." And with that she turned in place to face Jing. Snapping a salute to the Chairman which he returned before releasing her on her way.

"I don't know where you found her, sir, but I'm damned grateful you did." John said to Jing, only for the Chairman to let out one of his all too seldom short, barking laughs. John cocked his head to one side and his brow creased. Turning to Patricia he saw his confusion reflected in her face.

"Commander Zeidler has not been a serving officer for over a decade, though, she still holds a Naval Reserve commission which she requested I activate to allow her to represent you." The crease on John's brow spread to cover his entire forehead which seemed only to fuel the amusement that Jing was obviously relishing.

"I have no doubt that the good commander's decision to take unpaid leave from Geneva's top law firm came as a bit of a surprise to them too."

Patricia let out a loud, theatrical gasp as she rounded on Jing. "If you do not explain yourself now, Ai, then there shall be no tea for you the next time you call!"

Suitably admonished, by probably the only person on this side of the planet who would dare call Jing by his given name, Jing threw up his hands in mock defeat as he took a step back and allowed himself another brief laugh. "As the commander explained to me. She received a message from her husband," Jing tipped his head toward John. "A man, I believe, you served with at the First Battle of Garunda? The message indicated that you may require legal representation, so, she hopped on a sub orbital and, the next I knew, she was standing in my office offering her services."

John prided himself on knowing the names of everyone serving under his command, though, as he had reached the dizzying heights of flag rank, remembering all of those names become a near impossible task. However, he did know the name of every ship's captain and second in command, from the largest battleship to the lowliest cargo hauler. Racking his brain to remember any officer called Zeidler he found himself shaking his head slowly admitting defeat.

"For the life of me I cannot place the name Zeidler."

"I don't remember saying that the commander's husband was called Zeidler." Replied Jing mischievously.

"Oh, put him out of his misery will you, Ai." Scolded Patricia with a semi playful swipe at the diminutive chairman.

"OK, I'll give you a hint." Jing was enjoying watching him squirm but decided to bring his dilemma to a close. "*Dagger*."

John reached behind him; his hand found a table to steady himself against as his mind reeled at the sound of that single word. Patricia instantly threw him a concerned look as she leaned over the low wooden rail separating them with a reassuring hand.

"What is it, John? I don't understand."

"Zeidler is Engel's wife?" He managed in a strangled whisper.

He conjured the image of a lone destroyer, its captain and crew risking their all to stand between a planet and a fiery, nuclear-fueled destruction that the Others had decided was to be their fate. Engel had jumped his destroyer to the very edge of Garunda's atmosphere, in a desperate maneuver designed to halt a missile which had eluded the overstretched defenses of the Battle Force, as it fought the Others' fleet. Engel had known his decision risked the lives of every soul aboard TDF *Dagger*; for if he did not intercept the missile, with the destroyer's Close In Weapons Systems, his ship was in the missile's direct path, but, he understood the destruction of his own ship would assure the missile could never reach the planet's surface. Thankfully, Engel's gamble played out. The missile *was* intercepted and destroyed by *Dagger*'s

CIWS and Engel received Earth's highest honor, The Terran Medal of Honor, for his actions.

"Looks like that family is getting into the habit of rescuing me from tricky situations." Said John

"Indeed." Agreed Jing. "And talking of tricky situations, I think I have possibly stretched Patricia's good graces as far as I want to for one day, so let me make it up to her." Turning his head slightly so that both the Radfords were in his eye line he allowed himself a small smile. "I hereby order you to take one month's compulsory leave. Find somewhere you can recharge your batteries, John. Let somebody else worry about the Black Ships for a short while. I think we are all going to have to be on the top of our game for what is to come."

Patricia's evident happiness at the prospect of having her husband all to herself for a whole month was tempered by the grim look that formed on both John and Jing's faces.

This war was far from over and there would be plenty more losses like those suffered at Guzman before it ended.

CHAPTER THREE

RED STAR NOT FOUND

TDF *TYCHO BRAHE* | INTERSTELLAR SPACE | 1136 LIGHT-YEARS FROM EARTH

"DSDG fully deployed doctor." Reported the technician monitoring the Deployable Stellar Detection Grid, a truly massive array covering nearly 1000 square kilometers of space, the brainchild of one Doctor Sylvia Sarkisian. The DSDG was originally designed to detect the faintest of stars and provide scientists with unparalleled empirical data as to the formation of the universe it had however, been hijacked by the Department of Special Projects for a more pressing purpose. Operation Bright Star. The search for the home of the Creator. Sylvia Sarkisian did not doubt the necessity of the mission but is still riled her that her own purely scientific research had been side tracked and the elderly woman ensured that the only physical embodiment of the Department of Special Projects aboard the *Tycho Brahe*, one Lieutenant Terrance Wilson, was sure to know how she felt.

"Thank you Aife." Said Sylvia gracing the far younger female technician with a grandmotherly smile before turning her attention to another tech sat in front of a bank of holo displays. His eyes flicked from one holo display to another in rapid succession as tried to absorb and rationalize the information flowing across them. Seeing a deepening wrinkle of his brow Sylvia stepped over to him so she could see the displays herself. "How is it looking Arun?" She asked trying to keep any note of concern out of her voice.

Arun tapped a key halting the scrolling display on the left hand holo, lifting a stylus he highlighted a single line of code with a resigned sigh. "Same damn issue as before Doctor. Looks like one of the processing units is out of sync again. I've tried re booting it with no joy, looks like I'll need to go out there and do it manually or pull the whole thing and replace it. Sorry."

Sylvia felt a familiar sense of frustration building up inside of her. *Damn was right!* She said to herself. They were already nine weeks behind schedule and the data they had retrieved so far was only a fraction of what it should have been. Every time they deployed the DSDG it was one glitch after another. At first, she had tried to console herself that the DSDG was, after all, an experimental piece of equipment and she had expected there to be issues with both the hardware and the software. Now though, after seven deployments, it was the same issue time after time. The bloody processing units! Sylvia could have strangled the idiot penny pincher at the university who had given the contract to build the units to the lowest builder. In fact, she still might. The processing unit was responsible for not only collecting the data from each quadrant of the DSDG it ensured that the quadrant was aligned properly with the rest of the DSDG, essential if the gathered data was to be trusted as not overlapping with another quadrants data thereby giving false readings. The processing unit would then send the data up the chain to an area processor who double checked the alignment of the quadrants within its area before it in turn passed it to the central processor back on the *Tycho Brahe*. It all sounded fairly simple in principle but in practice, keeping the 10,000 individual quadrants looking at the same point in space at the same time while analyzing the data they captured took an immense amount of processing power. So much so that the entire forward cargo bay of the *Tycho Brahe* was one massive computer core that any university anywhere in the Commonwealth would have been proud of. As for the processing units that kept failing, if she had her way they would have turned the ship around and returned to Earth at the first sign of trouble and replaced the lot of them. Unfortunately, the DSP had classified this whole mission so they were forced to make do with what they had in spares or could hash together themselves.

It didn't really help that sitting quietly in the corner watching proceedings was Terrance Wilson. He hadn't said a word during the entire deployment stage, something which Sylvia's team had gotten down to a fine art, only taking four and a half hours now instead of the original entire working day that the first deployment had taken. *Which would be great if only the damn thing worked* Sylvia chided herself. Turning to explain herself to the young lieutenant Sylvia paused as she noticed that he had his head down and was tapping away on his PAD. Probably filing some slighting report to his bosses at the DSP she thought before chastising herself for being such an old woman. The lieutenant and his aide, Ensign Burkett, had been nothing if not polite and helpful while her team had wrestled to resolve the various 'hiccups with the DSDG. The engineering team had commented that Ensign Burkett's input into how to improve processing speed had been quite insightful and had asked her if she could approach Lieutenant Wilson to see if they could use the ensign on a more regular basis.

Something which Wilson had gladly acquiesced to, jokingly commenting that at least he wouldn't have to keep listening to Burkett going on about how he would do things if he had a chance.

Wilson's head came up and he started speaking catching Sylvia off guard. "The XO is prepping a boat with an Extra Vehicular Activity team now doctor, they should be ready to launch in the next twenty minutes or so. If you don't mind, I'd like to catch a ride? I've not been off the ship in weeks and could do with a change of scenery besides…" Wilson gave Sylvia a conspiratorial wink along with a slight nod in the direction of Ensign Burkett who was completely oblivious to what was going on around him as he worked on two PAD's at the same time. "It might be fun when he eventually realizes that I'm not here and goes running around the ship looking for me."

Despite herself Sylvia's lips twitched into a sly smile. She may not like having her strings pulled by the puppet masters of the DSP, but she just couldn't bring herself to dislike the affable lieutenant. "I'm sure whatever help you could be to the EVA team would be greatly appreciated lieutenant."

Flinging another sideways glance at the oblivious Burkett, Wilson eased himself off his seat and out the door.

✳ ✳ ✳

"The captain's pretty pissed that we have another one of these processor units failing again lieutenant." Said Commander Apter. "And I don't have to remind you that when the Captain is pissed then I get pissed and you know what happens then…"

Terrance Wilson gave the XO a knowing look before finishing the XO's sentence. "I get it in the neck." The two men shared a chuckle before Apter's mood changed to one of all business. In the time Terrance had been aboard the *Tycho Brahe* he and Apter had become as friendly as a junior officer could become with a lieutenant commander so he appreciated fully the pressure being placed on Apter and the captain from the higher echelons of the navy to come up with the location of the red star that the Others legends specified was the home of the Creator. The fact that the Creator had revealed himself to be the same person behind the Black Ships that had rout such destruction on the Alonan Empire's colony world of Balat, Garunda's Dagger Station and the Turak ships at Selene before ripping up Carrier Strike Group *Itus* at Guzman only for the Creator to be identified as non-other than a Saiph was a pressure that Terrance was glad was well above his pay grade even if it was his theory that had ended up with him, an intelligence analyst from a nondescript office on the 21st floor of the Office of Naval Intelligence in Carson City never having had a duty aboard ship before never mind a secret mission on behalf of the Department of Special Operations, a department of the navy so secret it only existed in rumors, deep in interstellar space. How many times in the past few months had he chastised himself for sharing his theory that the Creator's home was actually a Dyson Sphere constructed around a red dwarf star and if you traveled far enough out from the center of the spiral arm then you would actually be able to see the light from star being extinguished by the completion of the Dyson Sphere as it fully enclosed and eclipsed the star. Putting Wilson's theory into practice though was proving more difficult than either he, Sylvia Sarkisian, or the Department of Special Projects had thought.

Reaching the doors to the small craft bay Apter halted Wilson with a hand on the junior officer's forearm. Apter locked eyes with Wilson as if he was trying to communicate the importance of what he was going to say next.

"The Captain is considering returning to Gateway Station. In fact he has already requested permission from Brigadier Statham."

Wilson felt his breath catch in his throat as his eyes went wide with surprise. For the captain to go directly to the head of DSP, Brigadier General Earl Statham, with his request to return to Gateway Station only showed Terrance how serious the captain thought the situation was. Apter fully understood Wilson's reaction to the news. It mirrored his own disbelief when the captain had informed him not twenty minutes ago.

"The Captain feels that with the number of repeated technical failures the array is suffering that it would be better for us to call a halt now, return to Gateway, and fix the issues once and for all before heading back out."

First and foremost, Terrance Wilson was an analyst. Forcing his mind to concentrate on the problem in front of him instead of the feeling of failure growing in the pit of his stomach, Terrance let the cold, undeniable, logic of numbers play out. Weighing the amount of time the *Tycho Brahe* had spent deploying the DSDG, running system checks, then going live only to discover a faulty processing unit which in turn meant prepping a shuttle and EVA crew. Pulling the faulty unit and replacing it only to find another unit elsewhere amongst the thousands of sections making up the DSDG had failed forcing the repair crews to go through the whole process again.

Prior to the *Tycho Brahe* shipping out Sylvia Sarkisian, her team, and those at the DSP had estimated that the time required to fully deploy the 1000 square kilometer DSDG, gather the required data before securing the DSDG away again for transit to the next deployment location would take roughly seven to ten days. In fact, just to get the DSDG up and running on its first deployment had taken fifteen days. Fully 25 percent of the replacement processor units in stock had been eaten up before a single byte of useful data had been processed. Now, after seven deployments, only the superhuman efforts of the repair techs who had somehow managed to cobble together replacement parts for the never-ending number of faulty processors had kept the DSDG functioning. Four months in deep space should have by now been producing the results that the expeditions bosses back at DSP had hoped for instead all the crew had to show for it was bleary eyes and short tempers.

"The Captains right." Said Terrance grudgingly somewhat to Apter's surprise for the commander had anticipated the younger officer to have fought tooth and nail to see through a project which had been his brainchild after all.

"We should return to Gateway. Rip out all the processing units and replace them with an improved design based on what we have learned out here."

"Dr Sarkisian's not going to be happy." Said Apter.

"She will see the logic behind the decision." Terrance reassured him. "The good doctor and her team are as frustrated as we are. Give her the resources to fix the issues with the DSDG and she will give you something that will do what we need."

"Maybe we can temporarily detach Ensign Burkett to her team to help with the redesign. Might keep him out of our hair for a while." Joked Apter

Terrance let out a short laugh himself as he imagined Sarkisian's face when she heard that choice piece of news. "I would love to be in the room when you tell her that. Let's just say she treats our Ensign Burkett like one of her annoying grad students."

"He does seem to have an issue with knowing when to keep his opinions to himself." Agreed Apter before giving Terrance a conspiratorial wink. "I'll make sure I pass along your suggestion to the captain." Any reply Terrance may have made was cut off by the voice of the Duty Watch Officer booming out through the ships public address system.

"Commander Apter report to the bridge. Commander Apter report to the bridge."

"No rest for the wicked." Said Apter as he spun on his heel and headed off in the direction of the nearest elevator shaft to take him the four decks up to the bridge leaving Terrance standing alone in the corridor with his thoughts. The smiling image of his wife Maggie cradling a sleeping, four-month-old Richard Wilson, as he had left for the shuttle that would take him to Gateway Station and *Tycho Brahe*. Terrance had known at the time that Maggie's smile had hidden her unhappiness at being left alone to care for Richard. Unhappiness made only worse by Terrance's need to keep the true purpose of his tour of duty on the research ship a secret from her. As far as Maggie was concerned Terrance's tour aboard ship was a mandatory box ticking exercise which he needed to complete so that he could be considered for promotion. What sort of naval officer would he be if he had never served aboard a single ship Terrance had joked with her. His attempt at levity and her own fake laughter in response had done nothing to mask the truth. Terrance was hiding something from her, and she did not like it. Not one single bit. With any luck there would be time for a spot of shore leave when they returned to Gateway. A family trip to visit Aunt Elizabeth on Janus might be just what the doctor ordered.

Terrance pushed thoughts of family out of his mind as he slapped the door open pad and entered the small craft bay. The repair team were already well into their preparations to head out and retrieve the latest faulty processor. Seeing Terrance approaching a rating indicated an EVA suit hanging on a rack. Acknowledging him with a nod Terrance began unfastening his own uniform with a small sigh. Today was turning into a long day.

***

JSN *VIGILANT* | ORBITAL SHIPYARDS | JANUS | 4.7 LIGHT-YEARS FROM EARTH

"Now that is a thing of beauty." Said the woman dressed in the uniform of a vice admiral of the Terran Defense Force to the man fidgeting uncomfortably in his brand new, blood red uniform blouse and jet-black trousers. Shoulder boards of space black carried three bright yellow, seven pointed stars which, according to the new rank and insignia structure of the fledgling Janus Space Navy proclaimed him to be a full admiral and the highest-ranking officer of the JSN.

"That she is." Agreed Robert Lewis trying to run a finger inside his too tight uniform blouse collar without drawing attention to himself. Kaitlin Rocha suppressed a none too subtle chuckle at her former boss' obvious discomfort.

"Still getting used to the new uniform I see." She said in a voice low enough that it only carried as far as Robert's ears earning her a grunt in agreement.

"The designers obviously thought us spacers have the necks of scrawny chickens." Robert replied in the same low voice.

The final strands of the intricate web of gantries and mooring lines retracted to allow Robert and Kaitlin their first unobstructed view of the massive construct lurking in the largest dry dock to be found orbiting Janus.

Kaitlin eyed the warship within with appraising eyes. The latest innovative battle armor reflected the harsh yard lights, casting shadows across its bulk where the ships outer boxy hull, as opposed to the more conventional curved lines common to other races warships, was pot-marked with three rows of missile tube covers that ran the length of the ship. Raised carbuncles housed heavy grazers while smaller turrets contained a mix of close in defense lasers and high-speed anti-missile-missiles peppering the hull in painstakingly mathematical precision ensuring that not one single square centimeter of hull was left unprotected.

The throng of dignitaries from what appeared to Robert to be every corner of the Commonwealth and its associate members squashed into the hastily converted viewing platform let out a collective gasp as JSN *Vigilant*, the first true warship commissioned into the JSN, floated free of its moorings and glided gracefully into open space on its maneuvering thrusters. Kaitlin was not the only military figure in the room to appraise *Vigilant*. Robert spied Benii, Nilmerg, Persi, and Garundan naval officers scrupulously inspecting the warships unconventional boxy hull. While the other Commonwealth officers may have been eying the *Vigilant* with grudging admiration the sole representative of the Alonan Empire ensured that her expression remained completely neutral though Robert was sure she was soaking up every detail of *Vigilant's* outer hull.

Kaitlin caught the frown that fleetingly wrinkled Robert's forehead. "That your local imperial spy- sorry, Liaison Officer?"

"Yep." Replied Robert moving his gaze to somewhere else in the crowded room before the Alonan noticed she was subject of Robert's attention. "Arrived unannounced yesterday morning and virtually demanded a private tour. ONI nearly had kittens. They were running around like a bunch of headless chickens until they could find an escort of equivalent rank up here to play babysitter."

Looking beyond the Alonan major, Kaitlin spotted an uncomfortable looking middle-aged woman in the uniform of a major of the Janus Ground Forces. Its dark brown coloring sticking out like a sore thumb amongst the gathered naval uniforms though, thought Kaitlin with passing irony, the dark brown color of the ground forces officer was a near perfect match for the mud brown which was the standard uniform color of the entire Alonan military.

"I take it Elizabeth was not best impressed that her own people had not been able to give her a heads up to the Alonan's impending arrival."

Robert let out a small, snorting laugh. "If I know my wife, I think we can be fairly certain that the wording of the signal she sent off to Waypoint 4 would have left them in no uncertainty as to her displeasure."

Kaitlin's lips twitched into an involuntary smile as her mind conjured a picture of the sprawling Commonwealth naval station that had started life as a simple search and rescue base positioned on the long shipping route between the Commonwealth and the Alonan Empire. However, with the growing animosity between the two-star nations, Waypoint 4 had taken on a more militarized role. It was now the home of a Commonwealth Battle Force and all the support elements such a large group of warships required to sustain it as well as being a hub of commerce and immigration. As such, the Alonan Liaison Officer would have been processed through the station and should have immediately raised a red flag alerting their final destination as to their flight plans. For the Alonan to turn up at Janus without ONI being forewarned had been an oversight that Kaitlin was sure had earned some poor soul a few choice words screamed in whatever their particular species used as an ear drum.

"So, when do I get my tour of your new flagship Robert?"

In response Robert cocked his head in the direction of the prematurely balding figure of Thomas Crothers. "When my boss says so."

Thomas Crothers, President of Janus, was surrounded on all sides by clucking politicos from various Commonwealth nations while flanking him, attached by invisible umbilical cords, were Chin Lee, the Presidents Chief of Staff, and Rayner

Vargas. The imposing Janus National Security Adviser had somehow managed to displace his own Secretary of Defense who had every right to bathe in the spotlight at the launching of the *Vigilant*. Instead, said secretary was ensconced in an animated conversation with his opposite numbers from Pars, Garunda, Benii and, of course, Earth.

Robert and the rest of the fledgling Janus Space Navy were under no illusions that, although the Commonwealth navies were pleased to see Janus beginning to shoulder the burden of its own defense, Earth in particular was a little put out that Robert had insisted that their current Commonwealth partners have restricted access to the more sensitive areas of *Vigilant*. Inevitably this caused some ruffled feathers within the TDF as some asked who these upstarts thought they were. When Robert's decision had been escalated up to cabinet and finally presidential level Thomas Crothers had sided with Robert. As the President pointed out, the Commonwealth may be Janus' brothers in arms at the moment however, that may not always remain the same. To reinforce his point the President cited the TDF's decision not to share its Mosquito space fighter technology with the other nations of the Commonwealth. The JSN's Bureau of Design had implemented its own crash program to design and build an equivalent to the Mosquito based on the original Benii space fighter, the Freiba. Even with the aid of Benii experts the JSN was still months away from anything even resembling an initial production model. The TDF's decision was perhaps a minor inconvenience as the Benii were more than willing to share their fighter technology with other Commonwealth navies but the precedent had been set and Crothers had decided to use Roberts decision to make a statement to Janus' closest allies. Janus was no longer a colony she was the mistress of her own destiny.

A change of status that Robert was constantly forced to remind himself during his conversation with Kaitlin. A women Robert considered a friend however, as Robert's wife Elizabeth had pointed out on more than one occasion, Kaitlin was still an officer of another nations navy and it would be remiss of her not to squeeze, in the most polite of ways of course, every piece of intelligence she could about the *Vigilant* and her planned sister ships.

"In fact, Kaitlin." Said Robert as he focused on his fellow admiral. "Why don't you join Elizabeth and I for dinner tonight aboard. I've been wanting to show off my luxurious and extravagant admiral's quarters, and see if all the hype about my personal chef is true or just hot air. And, of course, it would be rude of me not to include a small tour."

Kaitlin raised her glass and gave him a mock salute. "Now how could I refuse an offer to compare my paltry quarters to your no doubt palatial rooms."

Robert's own glass raised in salute as they both let out a conspiratorial chuckle.

Beyond the triple glazed armor glass *Vigilant* maneuvered side on giving the thronging room its first clear view of the battleships side belt. Missile hatches, Close-

In-Weapon System hubs and the larger, bulbous protrusions with laser and graser snouts jutting from them like the spines of a porcupine. As Kaitlin's eyes ran the length of the ship, she gave a small grunt of admiration. Reaching *Vigilant's* stern her gaze fell upon the six projecting weapons pylons. An innovation of the JSN which her own TDF were examining closely for incorporation in their next generation ship the weapons pylons were inspired by those found on Turak warships.

Every Turak ship so far encountered by the Commonwealth had weapons pylons which extended away from the ships central core and, at their outermost point held heavy grasers which could be swiveled forward or aft depending on the threat axis. The JSN had tweaked the idea to suit their own needs. While retaining *Vigilant's* heaviest weapons on its outer hull like any conventional human warship, Janus had equipped the pylons with rearward facing missile tubes and CWIS providing *Vigilant* with an extremely effective aft defensive screen compared to standard warships which relied on what weaponry could be placed between the exterior plasma engine nozzles. A simple but elegant solution which many a ship designer back on Earth was kicking themselves for not thinking of first.

Where all these design innovations had a perfectly logical explanation Kaitlin's examination of the *Vigilant* inevitably drew her attention to the thing which had TDF designers baffled. Along both flanks of the *Vigilant* ran a series of equidistant doors. Ten to each flank with two matching doors at the root of the uppermost weapons pylons where they joined *Vigilant's* main hull. Each door was large enough to allow a medium sized shuttle craft to pass through. The TDF's intelligence services had concluded that these doors opened out into a cargo area beyond though, and Kaitlin agreed here with the egg heads in the Bureau of Design, nobody could explain why a battleship the size of the Vigilant would require so much cargo space. Standard operating procedure for the TDF and, it was assumed, the JSN would be for battleships to operate as part of a balanced force such as the TDF's own Battle Force. Battleships like the *Vigilant* formed the core heavy units, while cruisers and destroyers provided support and protection. A separate logistics train of collier and repair ships would round out the force for longer cruises otherwise the ships would simply return to their home port for repair and replenishment. Kaitlin could see no purpose in having what, to her eyes, was wasted space.

Whatever the reasoning behind these doors she was sure all would be revealed after dinner.

* * *

The elevator doors smoothly slipped aside, and Robert Lewis waved a hand beckoning his guest to proceed him.

"Ever the gentleman." Said Kaitlin Rocha graciously.

"I try my best." Replied Robert as he followed her out into another gleaming corridor.

The smell of cleaning products and fresh paint tingled Kaitlin's nose and she inhaled just that little bit deeper as she savored the smell and taste of a new ship. It was a smell that would quickly be replaced by grime and sweat of hundreds of crew men and women who would call *Vigilant* home and no matter how hard the atmospheric scrubbers worked they would never be able to replicate that first, unforgettable smell.

Kaitlin crossed the wide corridor halting in front of a window made out of thick armored glass. The window gave Kaitlin a bird's eye view of one of the cargo holds that had raised such interest with the TDF's own intelligence people. Before her was a space large enough to hold a couple of small shuttle craft. An overhead gantry ran perpendicular to the thick, battle steel blast doors while a track system was embedded into the floor. Ranged along the walls were various ports which, if Kaitlin was supposing correctly, were fuel and replenishment umbilicals for the shuttle craft the cargo bay was obviously designed to hold.

"You are undoubtedly wondering why we need so many cargo bays aboard a battleship aren't you?" Said Robert standing beside her after a few moments as he looked down upon the crewmembers scurrying about in the bay below moving large cargo pods from one side of the bay to the other under the watchful eye of a senior bosuns mate. Occasionally the senior sailor's mouth would enunciate a word which Kaitlin did not need to hear through the thick glass to know its meaning. In response a tardy junior rating would hustle a little bit faster hoping the bosun find someone else to berate.

"It is a bit odd Robert." Kaitlin answered without taking her eyes away from the view below. She would need to remember every detail, no matter how small, for her report when she returned to her own ship.

"Those so-called experts who signed off on *Vigilant's* final design forced it on me." Grumbled Robert.

That got Kaitlin's attention. Turning she gave her old boss a mock look of shock and surprise. In all the years that she had served alongside Robert she had never known anyone to force something upon him that he didn't actually want and was just pretending not to like. Kaitlin could not keep the disbelieving sarcasm out of her voice as she spoke. "Really?"

A rumbling laugh came from Robert as he turned away from the window and rested his rear against the corridors wall. "Well, if truth be known." A smile that would have done a fox proud spread across his face. "Those idiots who hold the navy's purse strings are more worried about the land grab that's going on at the minute than building a true fighting navy. They wanted to restrict the JSN to cruisers and spend the rest of the cash on cargo ships to service the privately funded colonization effort."

Robert shrugged his shoulders with a frustrated sigh.

"I came up with a compromise. We outfit *Vigilant* with extra cargo space which we can use to transport supplies to these new colony worlds if need be when we do our port visits, and I get my battleship."

"H'm, looks like we both have the same problem." Kaitlin agreed. "Central Command have been stripping away my cruisers for months and forming independent cruiser squadrons to head out and hold the hands of colonists who are worried the Black Ships are going to pay them a visit."

"Not that a few cruisers are going to do much good if what happened to CSG *Itus* at Guzman is any example." Said Robert solemnly.

Both officers remained silent for a few moments lost in their own thoughts. Pushing off the wall Robert straightened up. "How about a quick nightcap before you head back?"

Kaitlin graced him with a smile. "Now that, Robert. Is the best idea you've had all day."

The conversation turned to happier things as they made their way back to the elevator. As the doors closed behind them the senior bosun sounded a short blast from the comms unit at her waist. The shrieking sound resonated off the bay walls bringing all activity within to a halt.

"All right people let's get this crap out of here and stowed away wherever you got it from!"

Half an hour later the bosun cast a last eye over the now empty bay assuring herself that the bay was ready to receive its real cargo. Whenever that may be, she mused striding out of the bay, the armored doors closing with a heavy thunk behind her.

CHAPTER FOUR

RETURN TO COMMAND

CENTRAL COMMAND | MONT SALEVE | EARTH

The briefing room buried deep within Mont Salève, headquarters of the Terran Defense Force, held only a single occupant who sat silently, lost deep in thought.

A gentle hiss announced the briefing room doors separating, the bright lights of the corridor ensured whomever entered was cast in shadow, however, John Radford instantly recognized the outline of the diminutive figure, Chairman of the Combined Joint Chiefs of Staff, Admiral Ai Jing. John sprang to his feet assuming the position of attention only for the sound of a gentle chuckle and the wave of a hand inviting him to return to his seat.

"Please, John, sit, sit."

John was halfway back into his seat when the sound of a gruff voice, obviously engaged in a heated discussion with someone outside of John's earshot, caused him to halt. Instead, the first genuine smile since his return to duty after Jing's month-long enforced leave, tugged at the corner of his mouth. Jing noticed his smile and allowed a small smile of his own to creep onto his face.

"Perhaps, you could hurry the good doctor along, John, I have a meeting with the new Secretary of Defense in half an hour and she may think me a touch tardy if I'm late."

"My pleasure, Admiral." John's long legs ate up the short distance to the briefing room door. Stepping through, John emerged into the brightly lit corridor only to stop abruptly as he was confronted by the back of a slightly overweight, prematurely balding man, wearing a jacket that would not have looked out of place on a shipyard worker. There were literally more pockets than John could count, and each was stuffed with electronics; from a basic PAD to a strange device, that looked like a screwdriver crossed with a wizard's wand. Doctor Jeff Moore, head of the CUOP's secretive research and development base on the planet Zarminda, was oblivious to John's presence as he talked animatedly into his comm while reviewing information displayed on a PAD he held in his other hand.

"Look, Jerry, I don't care what the data says. The containment field needs to be a third of the size it is now. You tell professor what's his face that he can get off his fat academic ass and come up with a way to do it or I'll find someone who can. If the Saiph can do it, then so can we!"

John cleared his throat loud enough that Jeff could hear, however, the scientist did not turn nor did he pause in his conversation, as he held up the hand containing the PAD, flicking it dismissively.

The smile on John's face slipped into a more childish grin, as he deftly maneuvered his hand past Jeff's raised arm and tapped the disconnect button on the PAD before hurriedly taking a step back. Spinning in place, face flushing red with anger Jeff turned to confront whomever had been so presumptuous as to interrupt him. "What the hell do you -" Anger quickly turned to joy as he found John standing grinning at him.

Conversation forgotten Jeff stuck a hand out, remembering at the last minute it still contained a PAD which he slipped into one of his jacket's many pockets before extending his hand again, grasping John's and shaking it enthusiastically.

"Damn, John! Good to see you, good to see you. How's Patricia? I hear she and Madkin have had a few toe-to-toes since he took office." A loud chuckle reverberated off the corridor walls. "She always was one to make her opinion heard. And what about married life? Treating you well? I don't suppose you get much time at home these days, what with these bloody Black Ships and all, maybe -"

John broke into Jeff's never-ending stream of questions. "Which is exactly what we are here to talk about, Jeff." Canting his head toward the still-open briefing room door. "And I don't think it's a good idea to keep Admiral Jing waiting, do you?"

Jeff closed his still-open mouth with an audible click before nodding sharply. "Of course, you are correct. No time to waste." He said as he stepped past John and through into the room. With a slightly exasperated shake of the head, John followed the scientist and reassumed his seat. Jeff took the one opposite him, while Admiral Jing waited patiently for them both to settle, from his seat at the head of the small table. Jeff arranged a number of PADs on the table before him and ensured they were aligned perfectly straight. Satisfied he had everything he needed, and everything was in its correct place, he shifted his gaze to Jing who's features, as usual, betrayed nothing.

"Are you ready to begin, Doctor?" Jing asked without a trace of the irritation which John's frowning face failed to hide.

You might be one of my best friends, thought John as he regarded Jeff silently, *but your OCD can be pretty damned annoying.*

Like a scolded schoolboy Jeff mumbled "Yes, of course, Admiral, my apologies. I'm ready any time you are."

Turning to John, the chairman glanced at his own PAD before speaking. "According to your latest estimate, John, the Carrier Strike Group should be up to full strength by the end of next week."

John gave a nod of agreement which caused Jing to raise one questioning eyebrow.

"That's pretty impressive considering the losses you took."

John paused before answering Jing's question. "First Fleet have permission to release some of their reserves to bring us back up to strength, tonnage and type wise, while our damaged units have got priority in the yards."

"And what of the fighter squadrons?" asked Jing.

"Replacement crews and Mosquitos are either already embarked or are due to arrive over the next few days. My CAG, Captain Taw, has assured me she'll have them up to speed by the end of the month."

Jing steepled his fingers in front of his face and held John's eyes with his own. "And your honest assessment as to when *Itus* will be ready to fight again, if called on?"

John had known Admiral Jing long enough to know that the man appreciated honesty, above all else, no matter if that honesty meant bad news. "*Itus* and its ships are fit to go to war tomorrow, but if you want *Itus* to be operating at peak performance, I'll need three, possibly four months to bring it up to the well-oiled machine it was before Guzman." John took a deep breath steeling himself for his next words, for they had to be said. "Even then, Admiral, if *Itus* was to go up against a Black Ship force even half its size, I have no doubt that it would be a death sentence for my ships and their crews." John spared a glance for Jeff who had begun tapping the tabletop with a finger poised beside one of his PADs. John returned his attention to Jing. "As long as the Black Ships can hide behind their energy shields, we may as well be flinging rocks at them, and, God forbid we encounter any of their ships armed with the antimatter warheads that destroyed Dagger Station then..."

Jing understood John's unfinished sentence. The head of the combined Commonwealth forces knew that no matter how many ships and men he had under his command the Saiph and their Black Ships had an advantage in their combination of energy shields and antimatter warheads that was, for the moment, insurmountable.

"Doctor Moore." Said Jing cocking his head in the direction of the scientist. "I believe this is where you inform us that you have made a miraculous breakthrough and are able to supply the fleet with any number of extraordinary weapons to suit Admiral Radford's needs."

Jeff's cheeks blew out and he released an irritated sigh. "If only that were true, sir." Jeff entered a command into one of the multiple PADs arrayed before him and a wire frame schematic of a sleek, deadly looking missile snapped into holographic existence, hovering at head height in the middle of the table.

"This, Gentlemen, is our latest antimatter weapon. It is a variant of the test bed used by Admiral Glandinning in conjunction with a highly experimental, multi-frequency Gravity Drive to circumvent the areas of null space generated by the Others' Gravity Drive interference buoys. These buoys effectively prevented our forces from reaching Earth and reinforcing First Fleet during their assault."

"And a close-run thing that was." Muttered John whose comment earned a sage-like nod from Jing. Many a wannabe strategy expert had expressed the view that if Jing had not raced to the defense of Alona, taking the bulk of Earth's available forces with him, then those same forces would have been in a position to repulse the Others' attack with ease, and it was only luck that the Others had not scorched all life from the surface of humanity's home world.

Only with the staunch and unwavering backing of then President Rebecca Coston had Jing weathered the political storm which screamed for his resignation and indictment on charges of gross negligence.

Many a military man had thanked their god, that Jing had retained his position, for it was the wily old admiral who had orchestrated the Commonwealth's final victory over the Others and who now led the battle against the Black Ships.

"So, where are we with bringing this new wonder weapon into general use?" Asked Jing.

Jeff slouched back in his chair allowing an exasperated sigh to pass his lips.

That's not good, thought John as a frown creased his friend's forehead.

"The antimatter missiles deployed in that action where our entire stock." Said Jeff.

"I'm well aware of that, Doctor." Jing said allowing a hint of frustration to color his voice. "I asked where we stand now." The Chairman pointed toward the image of the weapon, still rotating slowly above the table. "How soon can we begin deployment? That weapon will at least put us on a more-even playing field with the Black Ships."

Jeff reached out and lifted a PAD angling it so he could read the small screen. "As of this morning we have ninety-eight weapons ready for immediate use."

John felt the muscles on his jaw go slack as it fell open. His mind struggled to comprehend what his friend had revealed. After a moment or two he managed to construct a coherent sentence.

"Ninety-eight? But..."

"John." Replied Jeff as he lent forward perching his elbows on the smooth tabletop. "The antimatter in those weapons took the scientists at Zarminda over three years to produce. Three years to equip a half dozen warheads."

Even the normally inscrutable features of Jing were showing signs of, not exasperation, more annoyance. "I presume your latest bid for expanded funding has something to do with the..." Jing searched for the appropriate word. "Lack, of volume."

Jeff pointed a chubby finger at the chairman as he once more pushed back into his seat. "You've hit the nail on the head, sir. The facilities which produced the original antimatter which equipped those warheads, are woefully inadequate for large-scale production.

The personnel there have done their best, hence, we have ninety-eight weapons ready to deploy. However, as you can imagine, handling such a volatile substance as antimatter is extremely dangerous. Damn, even the Saiph, in their scientific database, advised avoiding it or, at best, handling it well outside a populated area. And by populated area I mean the same planet."

"Tell me you have a solution, Jeff." Interjected John.

The scientist turned his head to face John with a fox like grin plastered on his face. "Well, of course I do."

"Doctor Moore." Said Jing, choosing to ignore the scientist's smug reply. "Would you care to share?"

Jeff retrieved a PAD and tapped at its controls. The image of the sleek missile was replaced by one of a roughly circular, heavily scarred surface of an asteroid. "This, Gentlemen, is NYZ390642 or, as the Corps of Engineers have begun to call it, the Warren. The engineers have, for the past eleven months, been burrowing and excavating megatonnes of rock to make way for an entire fabrication facility which-" Jeff gave Jing an ingratiating smile. "If the good chairman grants us the additional funding, will become our center, not only for synthesizing antimatter but, for the fabrication of the missile bodies and incorporation of the warheads."

"What about storage?" Asked John.

Jeff fiddled with the PAD again and alongside the image of The Warren appeared what, to John at any rate, looked like an atypical shipping container. "Even with a complete production line dedicated to these weapons, it will take a significant amount of time before we have the numbers to employ them en masse.

For the moment, Admiral Glandinning intends to outfit these shipping containers with their own independent power supply, ensuring the stability of the warhead's magnetic containment bottle, a neat little trick we, er, borrowed from the Benii -"

There was that sly smile on Jeff's face again, noted John.

"Then store ten completed weapons per container, along with a stock of ready deployment spares."

"You and Glandinning are worried about the stability of the weapons, aren't you?" Said John without removing his eyes from the floating shipping container. His mind already hard at work considering options for employing these super powerful weapons of mass destruction and, just as importantly, their safe transport and storage. He had that itch, the one on the back of his neck that told him these missiles were just as dangerous for his own people as they were for their enemy.

Jeff shrugged in resignation. "In a nutshell. Yes." The scientist admitted. "If the magnetic containment bottle fails, even for a microsecond, then you can kiss the ship carrying the weapon and everything within a thousand kilometers goodbye. A failure in a single warhead will cause a sympathetic explosion in nearby warheads, expanding the likely destructive effect to something like 5,000 kilometers."

The flickering light of understanding sparked in John's brain. "Gavin has kept the containers as small as possible, not only because he's worried about the possibility of a containment failure, but he knows that a shipping container of that size can be lifted by a ship as small as a Tanto. A Tanto, though, is not equipped with Gravity Drive, so, how is it going to deliver the weapons to the fleet?" John raised one eyebrow and by the look on Jeff's face he knew the wily scientist already had an answer.

"The shipyards are already working on an adapted Tanto design, a variant called the Fire Ant, which will incorporate a Gravity Drive and expanded crew quarters. It will be tight." Explained Jeff. "However, they have promised to deliver a vessel no more than an extra third of the size of existing Tanto models."

John did some swift calculations in his head before addressing Jing. "Hmm, still too big for anything smaller than a battleship or a carrier like *Itus* to handle but I'm sure we can work out the details."

Jing gave John an affirmative nod before his eyes zeroed in on Jeff from behind his steepled fingers as he picked up on something Jeff had eluded to earlier. "Expand on *significant amount of time*, if you would be so kind, Doctor?"

Jeff shifted uncomfortably in his seat under Jing's gaze and his Adam's apple bobbed as he cleared his throat before answering. "We anticipate six months to a year before we can begin mass production... more likely the year."

Jing sat back in his chair. Eyes hardening as the clinical, detached mind behind them weighed up his options. The room descended into an uneasy quiet as Jeff and John anxiously awaited the chairman's next words. After a long few minutes Jing's finger snapped out, zeroing in on Jeff's chest.

"Doctor Moore, you will get your funding."

The satisfied smile forming on Jeff's lips was dashed by Jing's next words. "However, I expect the weapons to be in full production within six months and the first delivery to the fleet within seven." Ignoring the burgeoning protests which were about to issue from the scientist's lips Jing turned to John.

"John, get with your people. I want *Itus* ready to begin combat operations the same day it receives its first antimatter missile."

John curtly nodded his understanding, while Jeff desperately wanted to protest Jing's decision, but he knew fine well that once the chairman had made a decision you might as well argue with a stone wall.

Jing stood to leave bringing the other two men to their feet also. "Oh, and John."

"Yes, sir."

"Keep *Montu* and *Bastet* up to speed. Their carrier groups will follow your lead and you never know..." Jing lips nearly, but not quite, formed into a thin smile. "They might have some useful input."

Even though he had been working with the military for over a decade now, Jeff never quite got used to people being referred to by the name of their ships. On this occasion Jing alluded to the commanding admirals of the TDF's latest operation Carrier Strike Groups, modeled on John's *Itus* group which, in Jing's eyes and therefore the TDF's, had proved the concept of the carrier strike group by virtue of being the only force to have managed a victory, no matter how small, over the Black Ships.

Unlike other senior officers Jeff knew, John did not take Jing's thinly veiled order to involve his peers in operational planning of the deployment of the antimatter equipped missiles as a slight on his own abilities. In fact, John took from it the very opposite. Both *Montu* and *Bastet* were extremely capable commanders and having them available to war game against would only help hone John, and the ships under his command's skills. Following the beating *Itus* had taken at Guzman, Jeff knew they had to be at the top of their game the next time they joined the Black Ships in battle.

As the door slid closed with a gentle whoosh behind Jing, John allowed the mask of cool, military stoicism to slip. Jeff was surprised at the sudden, haunted look that his friends' eyes took on.

"Are you OK, John?"

Like the snapping of an elastic band John's eyes once more filled with the fiery determination that Jeff had always recognized in them as the heart and mind of a driven man, sure that he was on the side of righteous. White teeth flashed a wide, friendly smile and the crack that had allowed Jeff the briefest of glimpses into his friend's tortured soul disappeared.

"Sure." Replied John. "Now, why don't you run the specs of this new toy of yours by me and we'll see about kicking some Saiph butt with it."

The jovial laugh that followed did nothing to assuage Jeff's worries. Unfortunately, now was not the time to ponder on his friends' demons for there was a war to be won and John, like everyone else, had to play his part.

CHAPTER FIVE

THE SUPREME LEADER DELIBERATES

287 LIGHT-YEARS FROM EARTH

The Supreme Leader's hand struck the conference table and resounded through the room; the sound halted the hubbub of conversations from the gathered Saiph elite.

In deference, those around the table turned to face their leader whose hand rested on the metallic tabletop while he stared through the clear wall out onto the magnificent vista beyond.

The Supreme Leader's light brown eyes drank in the fruit of generations of work; golden crops tended by automated machinery and fields of thin stalks swayed back and forth in the gentle breeze; a random house, belonging to a worker, on the shore of a blue-green sea that stretched from horizon to horizon and red-hued light shimmered across the tops of the breaking waves.

The Supreme Leader's gaze travelled upwards to the life-giving star itself. So close he felt he could simply reach out and cup it in his hand.

The Supreme Leader spoke while continuing to gaze upon his creation. "Star Leader Foral, have you ascertained the reason for our cruiser's failure to complete their mission?"

"I have, Supreme Leader." Began Foral without hesitation. The commander of the Saiph fleet had been friends and a comrade-in-arms with the Saiph who rose to Supreme Leader for his entire career. If there was one thing he had learned over that time, it was that the Supreme Leader did not like sugar coated briefings.

"From the squadron's last received message; they arrived in the system, the humans call Guzman, without incident and detected only a pair of inferior human cruisers. The presence of these vessels is unsurprising as we know the humans have randomly dispatched small numbers of warships to their newly established colonies, while, we presume, holding their major fleet units close to their more heavily industrialized planets." Foral paused and turned to regard those sitting at the table. "This is an expected reaction following our successful strike on the Garundan space station, a move designed to allow us to dictate the terms of the fight while the humans and their Commonwealth allies are forced into a reactionary campaign."

"It appears the humans have other ideas, Foral." Commented Lorai. Foral pursed his lips while a number of heads around the table bobbed in agreement with the chief scientist's words.

Foral chose to ignore Lorai and continued. "We've concluded the human vessels detected our ship's arrival and were able to call reinforcements to ambush our cruisers. The data from our reconnaissance ship, which I dispatched to the edge of the system when our cruiser squadron failed to return, supports this assumption.

The data reveals a heavy fleet presence around the human colony and increased background radiation in the vicinity of the colony's major moon, indicative of the concentrated use of nuclear warheads.

Radar displays a fresh debris field that we've determined is a major recovery operation in the region of one of the system's gas giants. There is also a number of gravity drive nulling buoys deployed at various points in the system which makes escape from a superior force difficult, if not impossible, for our cruisers."

"And what is the aim of the recovery operation, you say, is happening around the gas giant?" Asked Lorai.

Foral reached out and tapped a control recessed into the conference table. Along one wall an image sprung into being. The streaked atmosphere of a gas giant filled the background. Its upper atmosphere forever obscured by clouds whose peaceful beauty belied the fact that they were moving at near supersonic speeds that could rip any vessel, deigning to descend into them, into pieces.

In the foreground, clustered around a massive box-shaped vessel darted smaller, nimbler craft. "Our reconnaissance ship recorded this image at what you can imagine was an extended range." A red circle superimposed itself around the larger vessel. "This, we believe, is a recovery and salvage vessel while these-" Yellow circles flashed onto the image around the small craft, "Are a variety of tugs and other various support ships." Foral touched another control and the image jumped forward in a series of time-lapsed images. The small craft repeatedly dipped in and out of the gas giant's upper atmosphere for short periods of time.

"What are they doing?" Queried Lorai.

Foral held one finger up and gestured to the scientist to have patience. A moment later the image showed first one, then a second, then another and another of the smaller vessels coming together in an ever-growing cluster, like piranhas homing on their prey, desperate to get their share before their prey was gone.

And, before their eyes, emerging from the murky clouds came a large, sleek section of a ship.

"That, my friends, is the bow section of one of our cruisers." Intoned Foral as a number of the gathered Saiph hierarchy let out murmurs and the odd suppressed gasp.

The Star Leader waited for the whispered conversations to subside before he spoke once more. "The cruisers we sent against the humans at Guzman were equipped with energy shielding, our latest armor, defensive and offensive weaponry." Foral aimed a soft furred finger at the rising shell of a once proud cruiser. "If the humans are as shrewd as we've assessed them to be, then in short order, they will reverse engineer our technology and significantly reduce our current warship's effectiveness against theirs."

A thought occurred to Lorai. "You make no mention of antimatter warheads, Foral."

The Star Leader gave a slow nod and chose his words carefully. "The deployment, to Guzman, of that weapons' system is deemed... *unnecessary* to meet our mission parameters"

"Well, at least we'll retain the advantage for the time being." Said Lorai.

"And time is the key factor which must drive our next move." The solemn voice of the Supreme Leader caused all eyes in the room to focus on his back, as he stood gazing over the magnificent landscape bathed in the star's red hue. "Until now we've used our fleet sparingly. Gauging our opponents' strengths and weaknesses. However, this turn of events forces us to change our efforts to eradicate the Half-Breeds and ensure we Saiph are victorious in the final struggle for supremacy."

The Supreme Leader turned to face them, taking the time to meet each one's eyes individually, to engage and bolster their faith in him and their mission.

"The time has come to show these lower lifeforms, dragged from primordial slime by the ill-conceived, ill-planned and poorly executed intervention of those who call themselves our Elders and our betters." The Supreme Leader sneered. "The Elders want nothing more, than for these Half-Breeds to regard them as benevolent gods, fawn over them and heap undying love on them for their kindness and generosity and for allowing these poor excuses for a civilization to even exist." The Supreme Leader placed both hands flat on the table and leaned forward as his voice descended into a low, feral growl. "Well, my friends, it is time the Half-Breeds learned what happens when their gods decide they've had enough of their polluting ways and decide to erase them from the galaxy."

The Saiph gathered around the table began to beat the metal tabletop with their fists, the rhythmic racket resonated around the room. The Supreme Leader raised himself to his full height, rested his hands on his hips and rejoiced in the admiration of his devotees. His saw his own fervent beliefs clearly mirrored in their faces and felt utter devotion and belief in his leadership in the sound of their beating their fists.

No one seated around that table was more enthralled by the Supreme Leader, and his goal, than the one who had not been among the Supreme Leader's group which fled the Saiph home world many years before. Instead, Geoll, the Caretaker of the Race was a direct descendant of those Saiph who had remained awake to ensure the Supreme Leader's plans blossomed while the elite slept their frozen slumber of suspended animation for years.

Geoll's parents, their parents before them, and their parents before them had sown the seeds, guided by the all-knowing artificial intelligence, which controlled the functions of the Dyson Sphere- the Dyson Sphere designed by Chief Scientist Lorai and the place the Saiph called home.

Those seeds had grown into a population of 1.8 billion purebred Saiph. A population which had built and would crew the mighty fleet that Star Leader Foral was to use to gain victory over the Half-Breeds.

From childhood, Geoll learned that the Supreme Leader, and the Supreme Leader alone, was the voice of descent. The lone voice that urged the Elders to curb their experiments. To stop the combining of Saiph DNA with those of lower life forms. The Supreme Leader had begged the Elders to recognize the manifest destiny of the Saiph to colonize every habitable world in the night sky, seize those worlds for the benefit of all Saiph and stop chasing the crazed and corrupt high-minded moralistic theology of sharing the Saiph's hard-won technical and scientific advancements with an artificially created half-Saiph, half-slime, inferior creature that was unfit to walk the same planet as, never mind dominate, the Saiph.

No, thought Geoll striking the table repeatedly with his balled fist, so hard he knew bruises would follow, but he did not for one moment care. The Supreme Leader was right. *Now is the time to bring forth the Saiph destiny. Now is the time to reinforce our position at the pinnacle of galactic civilization.*

The Supreme Leader bathed in the adoration of his inner circle and soaked up their love and devotion. They filled and energized him; now he was ready for the hard days which he knew were gathering like dark thunder clouds on the horizon.

Raising a hand, he waited for the rhythmic banging to slow and die.

"Friends," he addressed, in a warm voice. "My heart sings when I feel your loyalty." He clenched his fist and held it close to his heart, then his face hardened. "But now, we must steel ourselves. To assure final victory we will lose many. Death will come to those close to us; death will come to some of you gathered around this table right now." Heads turned to regard those sitting next to them. "Nevertheless, this price is one we must be prepared to pay. A price which will, undoubtedly, in the days ahead to question whether the cost is too great." The silence in the room as the Supreme Leader paused was palpable. "Star Leader Foram."

Foram raised his head, his spine ramrod straight. "Yes, Supreme Leader."

"Prepare the fleet for battle. Let us show our enemies the true power of the Saiph."

CHAPTER SIX

TURAK COUNCIL OF WAR

HOME | STAR SYSTEM 389267 | 28,109 LIGHT-YEARS FROM EARTH
The small craft with its distinctive scarlet band completely circling its boxy hull exited fold space and flashed into existence a scant 500 kilometers from the surface of a planet whose dense, murky clouds completely obscured the view of the surface.

The pilots took the few seconds required to orient their vessel and, aided by the on-board computers, they locked onto the homing beacon which guided the craft and its four passengers to their destination on the hidden surface.

On learning of their selection for the honor of piloting this mission, the small craft's crew had spent hours in the simulators preparing for what was ahead. For, in living memory, no-one had called upon Clan Orlak to visit this most sacred of places.

Following the beacon, the pilots dived headlong into the clouds and placed all their trust in the homing beacon; for in this most hallowed of places, ancient law disallowed active scans of any kind, even navigational radar.

Through the sea of clouds, the craft fell leaving the bright sunlight of the system's star behind. Acid rain pummeled the armored glass of the cockpit windows and hurricane force winds buffeted the craft as the pilots fought to retain control. Lightning flashes lit up the dense clouds for fractions of a second only to disappear and leave the craft in complete darkness once more.

Lower and lower until the craft breached the cloud base.

Visibility increased from a couple of meters to perhaps tens of meter as the pilots activated powerful lights mounted on the nose and extending wing roots.

The howling wind masked the high-pitched whine of the landing struts extending from the smooth hull. Still the pilots had no visual on their destination, they shared a nervous glance which turned relief as the homing beacon's tone changed to an ever-quickening beep.

On final approach and still the pilots could not visually confirm their height or destination.

Trusting in their training and the procedures, dating to the Clan's earliest recorded history, they pulled back on the power and slowed the small craft; keeping just enough forward and downward momentum to retain control of their ship against the gusts of wind and the relentless rain.

In their earpieces the homing beacon became one long, piercing tone and from out of the darkness emerged a landing pad its bright strobe lighting only now becoming visible. Faultlessly the pilots settled the craft dead center of the pad keeping the engine power up to hold them in place until they heard the reassuring clang of metal on metal as the landing pads claws securely locked around the crafts landing struts.

While beginning their shutdown procedure, the cockpit door slid to one side and Vek, Clan Lord of Clan Orlak, entered the cramped cockpit. Each pilot paused their movements and waited as Vek bent forward and looked out of the rain lashed windows.

Vek's grandfather had described this hostile world, they had landed on, to him as a child years before; though, his grandfather had retold the description Vek's great grandfather, the last summoned Clan Lord of Clan Orlak, had told him as a child.

No member of Clan Orlak had set foot upon Home in over a century.

Vek's intense red eyes stared out, piercing the gloom and pouring rain.

There, at the edge of his vision he made out a shape, a flash of lightning further illuminated the small craft and he saw the circling band of jade green around the hull.

So, Clan Akalu had heeded the summons of the Guardians. Another flash of lightning and he caught sight of more shadowy hull shapes, each secured firmly to a landing pad spaced equidistantly around a low, bunker like mushroom cap at the center. From the cap a hardened personnel access tube reached out connecting each craft to the cap allowing access without having to dress in protective clothing for the acid rain would strip any unprotected flesh from the bone which the howling wind would then spread among the boiling, dark clouds.

Reaching out Vek grasped the shoulder of each pilot with one salmon pink colored three fingered hand. "Can you feel the spirits of the dead crying out to you, brothers?" He asked. "Can you hear them demanding the clans set aside our fractious ways to fight our common enemy?"

Each pilot felt a chill run up their spines as they looked out upon the world which had been the cradle of the Turak civilization so many millennium ago desolated by their own hand, forcing the handful of clans that had survived the war to come together in peace, merging and sharing their pitiful resources to seek a new life among the stars where each clan could once more claim their heritage and rebuild their strength without ever forgetting the mistakes of the past that had so nearly seen the Turak become but a footnote in the never ending cycle of birth, death and rebirth among the countless stars.

Now, rather than allowing a dispute between clans to spiral into a war to threaten an entire clan's existence, they settled major disputes here; on Home, under the ever-watchful eyes of the Guardians, the clansmen who were randomly selected at birth from each clan and raised on Home.

The Guardians became the impartial arbiters trained to interpret the ancient laws and settle disputes; and they had the power of life or death, even over a Clan Lord such as Vek.

Today, however, Vek was not here to settle a dispute. He had appealed to the Guardians to gather the other clan lords to hear the troublesome news he carried.

Evidence that the Saiph scourge still existed.

Blinking red and white lights warned of the approaching personnel tube easing up to seal with his craft. Vek left the cockpit and joined the other two occupants of the craft.

Kal, his uncle, and his oldest and most trusted adviser, stood patiently by the airlock seemingly perfectly at ease. Dressed only in a gray colored, long sleeved top, and matching pants. His single adornment, a scarlet sash tied around his waist, identified him as belonging to Clan Orlak.

Vek's eyes moved to his second companion. Yue did not look as comfortable as Kal and this brought a slight, fang baring smile to Vek's otherwise flat face. His eldest son, future Clan Lord once Vek passed, had jumped at the chance of accompanying his father and great uncle to the fabled Home. Stood here now though in simple clothes and bare of any weapons. The youth's uncertainty was obvious for all to see.

"Fear not, my son." Said Vek "The Guardians ensure our safety, as they have since the time of the Great Conflagration. No clan *dare* bring weapons to Home; such an act would breach the ancient law founded by the Guardians and would sign their own death warrant. The Guardians would wipe the clan's name from our collective memory, they would strip the clan of all their goods and disperse the clan's people among our remaining clans."

Yue straightened his shoulders as he swiveled in the cramped aisle to face his father properly. "Please, Father, do not mistake anticipation for fear." The youth replied in a voice which did not quiver one iota.

Behind him Kal allowed a proud smile as he spoke. "Said like a true clan lord in-waiting, young Yue."

Yue gave his uncle a gracious bow from the waist. "And I wish that wait to be a long one, Uncle, for Clan Orlak could not be blessed with a more fitting head at such a pivotal moment in the history of the Turak."

Kal let out a bellowing laugh as he slapped the younger man's shoulder playfully while addressing Vek. "And such an eloquent speaker too, my lord. Perhaps, he should lead our delegation rather than two old battle-hardened warriors like us."

"Indeed." Said Vek. "I believe he's been practicing his wordsmith-ing on a certain daughter of Clan Lord Mynut."

Yue's face turned the same scarlet as his sash as he swiftly averted his eyes from those of his father. A high-pitched double beep saved Yue from further embarrassment, the alert indicated to the passengers and crew that someone was trying to gain their attention from the other side of the sealed airlock.

With the pilots under strict instructions not to leave the cockpit it fell to Kal to operate the locks mechanism. Both inner and outer doors parted in unison to reveal the imposing figure of a lone Guardian resplendent in his, Vek assumed the Guardian was male, form fitting slate gray full body armor which appeared to absorb the bright overhead lights of the personnel tube without reflecting a single erg of light. A ceremonial Boka blade hung in its sheath from his waist.

However, Vek was under no illusion that a simple single blade was the Guardians' only method of defense. Undoubtedly powered, the armor he wore multiplied the Guardian's natural strength a hundredfold; easily enough to rip Vek apart like a straw doll.

"Clan Lord Vek of the Orlak." Said the Guardian in a steady, unwavering voice. Respectful though not subservient. "Quarters have been prepared for you and your aides. Follow me." Without waiting for acknowledgment the gray armored Guardian spun on his heel and set off down the equally drab corridor.

Yue was aghast at the Guardian's perceived lack of respect for one of such high prestige as a Clan Lord however, a warning look from his uncle, stilled his tongue. His father appeared outwardly unperturbed by the Guardian's actions simply following a step behind the man. Yue flashed a questioning glance towards his uncle who raised a hand and indicated for the youth to proceed him. Setting his jaw, Yue stifled his anger and set off after his father's receding back.

The small group made their way along the corridor until they came to a junction where the single corridor split into four. At the entrance to three of the corridors stood a Guardian dressed and armed identically to their own escort. Pausing without turning the Guardian pointed one at a time to each of the guarded corridors before speaking. "You will not enter these corridors."

Again, the lack of respect shown by the Guardian to his father, a great clan lord, shocked Yue, and this time he could not hold his tongue as the blood raced to his cheeks. "How dare you speak-" The Guardian cut short his angry retort as he effortlessly stepped around Vek, drawing his Boka as he did in one easy motion. The razor-sharp edge of the Guardian's blade pressed into the side of Yue's throat. Yue had no chance to move aside.

"Forgive my son's disrespect, Guardian." Said Vek hurriedly. His father, to Yue's amazement, went to one knee and bowed his head in submission to the gray-armored Guardian. "The fault lies with me for not instructing him correctly before our arrival."

"You submit yourself to my judgment, Clan Lord Vek, in place of your clansman?" Asked the Guardian whose voice bore no indication that he held Yue's life in his hands.

"I do." Answered Vek without raising his head.

So quickly Yue could not be sure he witnessed it the Boka blade flashed in the corridors naked lights and returned to its sheath on the Guardian's waist. Yue swallowed heavily and released a small sigh before the small, bright red splashes of blood on the otherwise bare corridors surface drew his eyes. Blood which was dripping from a precise incision on his father's neck.

The heavy hand of his uncle, Kal, grasped Yue's arm preventing him from going to his father aide. "Stand still, boy!" Kal whispered harshly through gritted teeth. "Lest your ignorance bring forth your inheritance quicker than expected."

Vek remained kneeling with head bowed. Blood dripping from the barest of incisions precisely a centimeter to the left of the artery which, if severed, would have seen the clan lord bleed out in a matter of minutes without immediate medical attention. Yue's piercing red eyes fixed on the unmoving gray Guardian, its armored helm regarding Vek impassively.

"There shall be no second warning, Clan Lord Vek." The Guardian's head turned in the direction of the still restrained Yue and the voice was as equally impassive as its gaze though the words it uttered could not be mistaken for anything but a final warning. "If my blade is called to leave its scabbard again, it will show no mercy."

Conversation ended; the Guardian set off once more down the bare corridor. Vek followed, head held high, making no attempt to halt the slowly dripping line of rust-red blood which steadily spread along the collar of his gray shirt leaving a dull brown colored line. Kal retained his grip on his tight-lipped nephew's arm guiding the enraged youth along behind his father. Yue may have been heir apparent to Clan Orlak however, his uncle's demeanor left him in no doubt that any further indiscretion would result in a more physical act than simple restraint.

The group came to a halt beside a simple, unadorned door, which retracted into the wall as the Guardian touched his gloved hand to a sensor pad concealed below the wall's surface. "Your quarters, Clan Lord Vek. I shall return in one hour and escort you to the Hall of Equals."

Vek nodded his thanks to the Guardian who remained unmoving by the door until the three members of Clan Orlak entered their quarters upon which the door slid closed behind them sealing them inside. Only as Kal heard the locking mechanism give a small click did he release Yue and take the two steps to his brother's side. Gently pushing Vek's head to one side and inspecting the wound. The Guardian's strike had been as precise as a laser scalpel. The cut halted within a hairsbreadth of the artery and, though superficial, it continued to bleed. Hurriedly Kal pressed the flat of his hand firmly against the wound temporarily halting the flow of blood.

"Quickly, boy." Kal ordered Yue. "Find something to staunch the bleeding."

Yue head spun as he desperately searched the room for something, anything which he may be of use. Eyes flicked across simple, utilitarian beds. An ablutions area separated from the main room by an opaque panel. A single desk and straight-backed seat until, at last, his search lit upon a medical kit hanging on the wall. Covering the short distance in a half dozen long strides he recovered the kit and returned to his uncle.

"Well, don't stand there like some gormless oaf. Open it!"

Fumbling with the seal Yue nearly dropped the kit. Balancing it in one hand he managed to pop the seal and the lid obediently rose to reveal a compact, though comprehensive, array of medical equipment. Yue located a blood clot dispenser and offered it to his uncle. With a deftness of one who had treated uncounted numbers of wounds received in both combat and training, Kal removed the hand applying pressure to Vek's wound while immediately replacing it with the dispenser which he ran along the length of the cut. The bright blue foam filled the incision preventing any further loss of blood. Releasing the dispenser, Kal allowed it to drop to the floor holding his now empty hand out to Yue.

"Is there a bonder in there?"

Yue passed the skin bonder to his uncle who ran the small device over the wound twice. The bonder's rows of small claws reached out, pinched Vek's skin either side of the wound and forced the skin together before applying a thin layer of strong sealant which glued the edges and sealed the wound shut. The bonder joined the dispenser on the floor as Kal moved Vek's head and neck this way and that to inspect his handy work. With a grunt Kal stepped back, satisfied.

"It'll do until we get home and a we can get you to a med tech."

Vek raised his hand to the site of the wound running one finger along the raised surface where Kal had sealed the wound before letting out a short chuckle.

"I fear you have missed your calling, brother. Perhaps, you should've been a healer rather than a warrior."

"Ah!" Cried Kal dismissively. "I would have spent all my time patching you back together instead of sharing in the fun."

The brothers shared a hearty laugh which slowly tapered off before Vek turned to look at Yue. The young man refused to meet his father's eyes instead keeping them fixed resolutely on the well-worn, dull plastic covered floor.

Vek's reached out and placed a hand on his son's shoulder giving it a gentle squeeze. Yue's head came up and for the first time in what seemed an age Vek saw embarrassment, no something more. Genuine fear in those eyes.

"Yue-" Began Vek only for the younger man to interrupt him.

"Father... Father, I thought..." Words seemed to fail him.

"What did you think?" Asked Vek softly.

Yue swallowed deeply before answering. "I thought the Guardian was going to kill you and ..."

Vek waited patiently as his son struggled to finish the sentence.

"I thought the Guardian was going to kill you and it was my fault. My outburst. My lack of respect. My failure to abide by the rules of Home which you and Uncle Kal have instructed me on, even before the Guardian's agreed to your audience."

Vek felt a shudder run through the body of his eldest son and heir but still he held his tongue. Of every attribute that made a great clan lord the ability to learn from one's own mistakes was of the utmost importance. The small room lapsed into silence for a moment, until Yue gave himself a mental and physical shake. The youth's spine straightened, and his red eyes were hard as they met and held those of his father.

"I promise on the honor of my clan. It shall never happen again." His voice said firmly.

Vek released his son's shoulder and gave his arm a firm slap as a large grin spread across his face. "Then we shall say nothing more of it eh, Kal?"

"Say nothing more about what, my lord?" Replied Kal turning away from the father and son to retrieve one of three small cases deposited in their quarters by an unseen mechanism. Placing the case on a low bed Kal opened it and began rummaging through it.

"Perhaps, a fresh shirt before we meet the other clan lords? It appears the one you wear has become somewhat stained."

✳ ✳ ✳

The Hall of Equals, thought Yue as he sat shoulder to shoulder with his uncle Kal in the cramped, unlit recess behind his father's plain metal chair, was a very grand name for a ten meter diameter circular room constructed from the same drab gray concrete as the rest of bunker like structure that was the Turak's last foothold on the planet of their birth. Everything the heir to Clan Orlak had seen in the short time since his arrival on Home had emphasized the austerity by which the Guardians lived their lives as if they were going to great lengths to show how they had rejected the affluence normally associated in Turak society with power and influence. Yue's own father, Vek, had spared no expense outfitting his living chambers with the most luxurious of dressings.

Handmade silks draped the audience chamber. Carvings of stone, quarried from the hard-to-reach worlds of their territory lined the walls, while jewels and rare minerals embedded Vek's sumptuous chair.

Guarding it all, were the ranks of Clan Lord Vek's personal guard.

Each warrior having proved themselves in combat a hundred times over and equipped with the most sophisticated weaponry and latest battle armor found anywhere in the hundreds of stars controlled by the Turak. However, here, on Home, the amassed riches of Clan Orlak meant nothing.

"I call this assembly of the Clan Lords of the Turak to order." Rumbled a deep authoritative voice silencing the few whispered conversations that reached Yue's ears. The confining walls of the recess and the bulky figure of his father's seated figure blocked his view of the speaker. Straining his neck forward as far as he could without leaving his seat which, according to Kal would bring forth the wrath of the gray armored Guardians who stood like concrete statues lining the halls outer wall in the spaces between the sixteen assembled clan lords representing every surviving clan, big or small, who claimed their ancestral roots were buried deep on this scarred and barren world.

Yue's head managed to just clear the corner of the recess, his eyes were drawn to a figure standing before a plain, metal chair placed upon a raised dais; so he stood a single step higher than the gathered clan lords, to get a better look of the figure dressed in matching gray long-sleeved top and pants. In contrast the sash worn around his waist assaulted the eyes, sixteen colors intricately woven together and not one color more prominent than another. Each strand represented a clan.

The sash proclaimed the wearer's alignment to no single clan but rather to all Turak. However, the clothing failed to disguise the frailness of the body beneath. Yue's breath caught in his throat and his pupils went wide as he realized he was likely witnessing the oldest Turak he was ever to see.

Yue caught movement out of the corner of his eye and his warrior's gaze homed in on its source, only for his eyes to lock on those of another who stared directly back at him. His right hand moved of its own accord; palm outwards to show the empty hand, fingers spread toward the greeted person proved they did not conceal even the smallest of weapons between them.

A reciprocating gesture came from across the narrow expanse of the hall, though the hand was slightly smaller, for it was a female hand. As if emerging from behind a cloud on a moonlit night a face appeared from the darkness of the alcove above the raised hand. The sight caused Yue's twin hearts to skip a beat for the face belonged to Waynal, only daughter and heir of Clan Lord Mynut, leader of Clan Hurak.

Clan Hurak and Yue's Clan Orlak had long been rivals. Indeed, there had been several skirmishes along the bordering star systems, which separated the two clan's territory, over the years. And it was one such skirmish which had seen the two opposing clans settle into their current uneasy peace. When Yue had been but a youngling, a force of Orlak warships had been dispatched under the command of his mother to investigate reports of raiders operating along the border with Clan Hurak.

When Yue's mother arrived in the area her ships were ambushed, not by the small group of raiders she had expected to find, but by a far larger force of Hurak warships.

The Hurak had the upper hand from the beginning and in a last desperate measure to save her embattled ships, Yue's mother had rammed the Hurak command ship. The cataclysmic explosion which followed caused a momentary disruption to the Hurak command and control structure allowing the remaining Orlak ships to escape.

In his grief-driven rage, Lord Vek had assembled the mightiest fleet of warships ever seen in Orlak space. The legend said there were so many ships they could have used them as steppingstones to walk from one side of the system to the other. Lord Vek was intent on retribution for the loss of his wife, and mother of his infant son. Only the complete annihilation of Clan Hurak would sate his blood lust.

Clan Orlak had speared into Hurak space leaving only burning cities and airless, floating hulks of spaceships in their wake. Not in generations of skirmishes had such destruction been wrought on one clan by another. As if possessed, even Vek's closest advisors failed to make him recognize that his rage blinded him to the moral repercussions of his actions.

It had taken the intervention of the Guardians to bring an end to the slaughter, which left Clan Hurak a shell of its former self, and Clan Orlak without half of its warships and their brave crews. In the two decades that had passed since an uneasy peace had reigned along the two clans border regions, though, Yue suspected that it would take a single spark to give his father the excuse he needed to reignite a war still raging deep within him.

"Lord Vek of Clan Orlak-" On hearing his father's name Yue dragged his eyes away from Waynal and centered his attention once more on the ancient Guardian. "You petitioned for this gathering; I will hear you speak as to your reasons." The Guardian waved a frail hand towards Vek as he returned his slight frame to his seat.

Proceedings paused while Vek rose to his feet in response to the Guardian's invitation, however, several clan lords took the opportunity to show their hostility toward Vek and Clan Orlak by hissing beneath their breath.

As if spurred on by their dislike Vek took a solid step forward and raised himself to his full height, chin jutting forward in defiance. "I have requested the attendance the Clan Lords today, because I have news. An ancient enemy, one that many of us, myself included, thought their barren stench removed from this galaxy forever-"

"I see you're still here, though!" Interjected Mynut with a chuckle that some around the room echoed.

Yue saw his father's hand drop to where he would normally carry his ceremonial dagger only to find fresh air, for the Guardians tolerated no weapons in Home. Before Vek responded the elderly Guardian's stern voice cut across the chamber.

"I would remind Lord Mynut that common courtesy is expected here-" The elderly Turak leaned forward and pointed a wrinkled finger at Mynut. "And if a lesson in etiquette is required then it shall be done, most... expeditiously." On cue the gray-armored Guardian nearest Mynut spun on their heel to face him, with their hand resting suggestively on the guard of their Boka. The Guardian's meaning obvious to all.

Tipping his head so his eyes looked at the floor Mynut spoke. "My apologies, Guardian. There shall be no further interruption while Lord Vek continues with his... tale." Yue felt the familiar stirrings of anger rise within him as Mynut finished his sentence and his cheek muscles contracted in a smirk. The elderly Guardian chose to pay no head to the implied slight and, instead, returned to his original seated position.

"My tale, as Lord Mynut chooses to call it, is backed by solid proof which I will share freely with all Turak." This caught several of the clan lords off-guard, for Turak shared only when sure to gain an advantage.

"The Saiph have returned..."

Shouts of derision and clan lord's calling. "Liar!" drowned Vek out.

Through this hostile barrage Vek held his ground. Head held high, balled fists resting on hips. The Guardian allowed the uproar to go on for a few moments longer.

"Enough!" The amplified voice boomed off the stark walls bringing all other discussions to an abrupt halt. The elderly Guardian pulled himself to his feet and the assembled clan lords retook theirs out of respect. "I have seen the evidence Lord Vek speaks of with my own eyes and the Guardians chose to accept it as genuine." There were grumbles but none chose to dispute the words of the Guardian. "The data is now being distributed to your rooms. I call a recess to give each of you the opportunity to study the data. We will reconvene here at sunrise." The Guardian turned to leave, and the clan lords stood respectfully.

Yue took the opportunity to glance across to where Waynal was standing, his hand already half raised in greeting only to find her father, Mynut, regarding him with eyes ablaze with anger. Yue quickly returned his hand to his side, fixed his most stoic face and kept it that way until the room emptied and their armored Guardian escorted them back to their quarters.

On entering Uncle Kal gave him a strange look before switching his attention to Vek. "Well?" He demanded.

A worried frown creased Vek's brow. "The Guardian is convinced. Now we wait and see what those other cretins think."

✳ ✳ ✳

Sunrise on Home was more of a time than an actual event. The brooding storm clouds never dissipated, the rain seemed continuous and the wind blew constantly. Yue had slept a broken sleep. On the occasions that he had awoken it had been to the sound of muffled voices and at one point he half opened his eyes to see his father and uncle hunched together and holding a conversation in whispered tones. The confines of the spartan room prevented Yue from eavesdropping without his father noticing so he decided to try and get what precious sleep that he could in preparation for the day ahead and perhaps another chance to see Waynal.

When Uncle Kal called his name bringing him to full consciousness it came as a relief for his mind had been replaying the angry face of Mynut over and over and each time Waynal's father's stare had become more intense. The problem of how to tell their warring parents about their feelings for each other was one Yue was not looking forward to facing.

The incessant chatter of Uncle Kal made the short walk, trailing behind the ever-present, somber Guardian which ended in the equally somber Hall of Equals, more bearable, for today's session the Guardians had directed that all representatives be present.

His uncle's presence only made the recess behind his father's chair all that much tighter as both uncle and nephew did their best not to elbow each other in the ribs. As Mynut entered the hall followed by Waynal and a hulking Turak that Yue recognized as Opel, Mynut's personal aide, Yue could not help but follow her with his head. A movement which did not escape his uncle's attention.

"I would avert your gaze, young Yue, before you find your eyes on the end of Mynut's blade." Kal whispered harshly.

"Truth." Said Vek out of the side of his mouth without turning his head from its position facing the empty chair on the raised dais.

Yue opened his mouth to speak but no words would pass the lump in his throat. He had thought that Waynal and he had been so discreet, so careful in their furtive meetings and coded correspondence. Now, it seemed that not only was his father aware of his covert actions, but his uncle also. With his indiscretion out in the open Yue was in no doubt that his father would be speaking to him later about the matter. For now, there was nothing more to say.

Vek stood as did the other Clan Lord's as the elderly form of the Guardian shuffled into the room and made his way to his place on the dais. The clan lords resumed their own seats and waited for the Guardian to speak.

"Have you had sufficient time to examine the evidence presented by Vek of Clan, Orlak?" Nods of consent answered the Guardian's question.

"Does anyone dispute the evidence?" Again silence was the Guardians answer.

"Then we are in agreement." The Guardian said solemnly. "Our ancient enemy have returned. Those who laid waste to Home and scattered the Turak to the stars now deign to show their faces among us again." The Guardian's voice dropped an octave and forcing Yue to concentrate to hear his next words. "The Turak have not forgotten. Our ancestors swore an oath to have their vengeance on the Saiph and now that time is upon us." From around the hall came grunts of agreement. "The ancient laws have foreseen this day. A day when all Turak must set aside their petty squabbles and honor the oath of our fathers. As Guardian of Home and Keeper of the Laws -" Yue noted with confusion his father stiffened in his seat and Kal bend forward to place a steadying hand on his elder brother's bicep. Yue's eyes darted around the room and he could see that every Clan Lord had reacted to the Guardian's words as his father had. What was happening?

"I declare Vek no longer Clan Lord of Clan Orlak -" Yue felt the breath catch in his throat; his eyes widened in disbelief. Had the Guardian just removed his father as Clan Lord? For what reason? What infringement of law had he broken by bring this news to the Guardians? Anger filled his belly and he moved to stand, to denounce this travesty only to find the strong arm of his uncle pinning him to his seat.

"Sit, boy, or I will knock you to the ground!" Came Kal's harsh voice.

Anger mixed with confusion in Yue's head as he tried to comprehend what was happening. The Guardian spoke once more.

"Vek is now War Chief of all Turak! Step forward, Vek." Commanded the Guardian.

Unhesitatingly Vek rose to his feet and purposely walked to stand before the Guardian who rose to meet him. "Vek of the Orlak. Do you accept the challenge I place on your shoulders?"

"I do." Vek declared loud enough for all to hear.

From within his gray robes a blade, no longer than a finger, appeared in the Guardian's hand. In one deft stroke the distinctive scarlet sash representing Clan Orlak fell to the ground. The Guardian held out his hand and a Guardian who had been standing statue like behind the dais stepped forward and handed the elder Turak a new sash. This one identical to the one worn by the elder. A fine weave of sixteen independent colors which came together to form one sash. "Be forever of all Turak, Vek." Yue looked aghast as his father tied the sash around his waist, unable to fully comprehend what he was witnessing. However, the Guardian had not finished.

"War Chief Vek, I ask you to choose your First. The one among us, here, who will stand in your stead if you fall and honor our ancestor's oath."

Around the room, Yue saw each clan lord go rigid with anticipation and now, seeing their reaction to his father's selection, it dawned on Yue that what was happening to his father was not a disparagement. It was, in fact, a great honor.

Vek's strong voice carried through the hall. "I choose Clan Lord Mynut of Clan Hurak to be my First." The stifled gasps of surprise which filled the room where silenced as Mynut rose to his feet and joined Vek before the Guardian. His face impassive, shoulders back and spine straight.

"Mynut of the Hurak. Do you accept the challenge I place on your shoulders?" Asked the Guardian once more.

"I do." Replied Mynut.

Once more the Guardian's blade flashed. The same multicolored sash adorning Vek replaced the now fallen, forest green sash of Clan Hurak.

"Be forever of all Turak, Mynut." The Guardian intoned deeply.

Yue never thought to see what happened next.

Mynut stepped around the Guardian and positioned himself slightly behind and to the right of Vek. A position Yue recognized as one every unarmed combat instructor taught never to allow your opponent to attain.

"I stand behind my war chief." Said Mynut loudly enough for all to hear. "I follow his commands and his alone, forsaking my allegiance to any clan. I stand ready to take his place in the fray against all enemies of the Turak and I call upon all those gathered here to show fealty to their war chief."

A painful dig in the ribs reminded Yue that his uncle still sat beside him. "Stand and show fealty, my lord." Kal's use of *my lord-* used only to address a clan lord, confused Yue who looked at him questioningly.

Momentarily, the Uncle Kal persona returned. "My Lord Vek is no longer of Clan Orlak, his assumption of the position as War Chief means you, my nephew, are Clan Lord of the Orlak and it is for you to decide our clans' intentions."

Yue's jaw dropped and his wide eyes flitted between his uncle and his father's impassive face, who stood tall before the clan lords congregating before Yue, heads bowed, eyes downcast in their show of submission to his will.

"Well, my lord. Is Clan Orlak to stand with your father against the Saiph?" Queried Kal.

Yue tried to control the rising of his stomach contents to his throat, which threatened to erupt from his mouth. "But, I'm not ready to lead! My father has many years ahead of him and I shall learn all I need to know by his side." Yue did not care that his voice carried more than a hint of desperation, for he spoke the truth.

Kal placed a reassuring hand firmly on the young man's shoulders. "Do you think your father was born with all his knowledge. He was not more than your age when his father passed into the great beyond and thrust him into the position of Clan Lord. Now that mantle has been thrust upon you my boy and you must embrace it."

Desperately Yue searched the hall for help. His father remained still as a rock as if refusing to meet his son's gaze and then, from across the hall the figure of Waynal stepped forth from the recess which had hidden her. It suddenly occurred to Yue that she too had been elevated to the position of leading her clan. Of all the people in this room she would most understand what he was going through at this moment and, by the way she carried herself with the supreme elegance of the high born that she was, Waynal had no intention of allowing anyone present to see the turmoil that must be raging within her. In that moment Yue knew what he had to do. Taking a deep breath he summoned up all his courage and stepped out of the shadows. Striding purposefully across the hall, not towards his father, but to the side of Waynal. As Yue neared Waynal her head turned at the sound of his approaching steps and, just for a moment her mask slipped, and Yue saw in her own eyes the fear and doubt he felt in his heart.

"Clan Lady Waynal." Yue said in his most formal voice. "May I have the honor of standing by your side, as we show fealty in this most desperate time of Turak need."

"Clan Lord Yue. The honor is mine." Replied Waynal.

Together they made the short walk to stand before War Chief Vek and his First, Mynut. Before Yue made the formal movement of submission, he caught his father's eyes, and, in the briefest of instants, swore he saw a smile in them. Bowing his head Yue realized that by naming Mynut as his First, his father had secured the accession of Waynal to Clan Lady removing any objection Mynut may have had to a relationship between his daughter and the son of his sworn enemy. Yue stifled a chortle, even faced with the return of the ancient enemy his father had seen an opportunity to aid his son and seized it. *I have a lot to learn* thought Yue.

"Fealty has been shown!" Declared the Guardian allowing the various clan lords to once more look upon their new War Chief. Vek took a moment to scan the assembled heads of each clan before speaking.

"Not since ancient times have the Turak come together as one to fight a common foe. At one time each of you here where either my friend or my enemy. Now though, our fleets are forged into one mighty Boka, which I will drive into the heart of our enemy and tear him asunder!"

The feral war cry that burst from their throats threatened to shake the hall to its foundations as the entire Turak race set itself on a course to wipe the scourge of the Saiph from the entire galaxy.

CHAPTER SEVEN

THE EMPIRE'S DECEIT

COMMONWEALTH UNION OF PLANETS EMBASSY | ALONA | 50,000 LIGHT-YEARS FROM EARTH

"You see? There it is again, ma'am." The Benii major indicated, with one long silver finger, a section of the message. Colonel Nathalie Fantozzi's pale blue eyes focused on the same area that her second in command had identified.

The Human colonel and the Benii major looked at odd couple, a short and a little overweight Colonel and the atypical tall and lanky Benii figure of Major Tolan.

At the obligatory embassy affairs that they never failed to attend it was hard to miss either of the CUOP embassy's military public affairs' officers and both Fantozzi and Tolan were renowned as articulate on *any* subject.

In no time at all, both Alonan and CUOP personnel had dismissed the pair as a mild irritation that they put up with occasionally. That was fine with Fantozzi and Tolan for it allowed them to go about their real job while hiding in plain sight.

For the women were highly skilled intelligence operatives, tasked to uncover every little thing they could about the Alonan military and, Fantozzi had to agree, Tolan had stumbled across something *odd*, and anything classified as odd in the intelligence world was worthy of investigation.

"That's pretty damned unusual wouldn't you say, Major?" Said Fantozzi as she scanned the message a second time.

The Benii gave a strange jerky nod doing her best to imitate the Human sign of agreement. "Yes, Colonel. I went over the night intercepts and it jumped right out at me." Tapping a control, she highlighted a single sentence of text: Immediate transfer to Foram.

Fantozzi slid into her chair and lifted her legs up before propping them on the desk and letting out a gentle, "Hmmm."

Although, the Empire and the CUOP were not at war with each other, it did not, in any way, mean peace reigned. In fact, a different type of war raged in the shadows and each side regularly intercepted the communications of the other, doing their best to decode them and glean the smallest piece of useful information.

The nightly flurry of messages from the Alonan navy's communication hub, which floated serenely in geostationary orbit 120 kilometers directly above the capital, was a particularly fruitful source of intelligence. For the past six weeks a highly advanced computer had been analyzing the Alonan's encrypted messages and had identified a single repetitive phrase which it had then used to crack the current Alonan encryption key. As long as the Alonans continued to use it the Commonwealth intelligence services were able to read virtually every message the naval high command was sending to their fleet. A major coup for Fantozzi and her small staff but one that she knew could not last forever. As soon as the Alonans changed the encryption key Fantozzi would be right back at square one again. But, as her father used to say, make hay while the sun shines, and that was exactly what Bliek had been doing. The intercepts had allowed Commonwealth intelligence to build up a virtually complete picture of the Alonan order of battle. They knew the current and projected position of every ship in the Alonan fleet; their state of readiness, their maintenance cycle, in fact their knowledge reached the unprecedented level of which personnel received which assignment.

It was this final piece of information that had Fantozzi and her second in command locked away in her office this morning.

Tolan had, with practice, began to recognize the signs of her boss slipping into thinking mode so decided to stand silently while her boss considered the possibilities. After a few minutes of furrowed brow concentration Fantozzi leaned back in her chair, pursing her lips while closing her eyes and massaging the bridge of her nose between a thumb and index finger. Without opening her eyes, she spoke.

"How many is that now?"

Tolan quickly consulted her PAD ensuring she gave the colonel the latest number. "As of this morning that's seventeen officers of senior captain grade, twenty-three commander or lieutenant commanders and 131 other ranks."

"And there is no mention of what this *Foram* is? A ship? A place? A secret project? For all we know it could be a waste management plant on a tramp steamer in the outer system" Fantozzi said failing to hide her exasperation. Opening her eyes to read the message again as if by re-reading the text she could fathom the true meaning of Foram. "And we have no mention of Foram in any other intercept?" Fantozzi asked her subordinate.

Tolan shook her head mimicking the negative response of her human boss. "No, ma'am. Whatever it is, the Alonans are keeping it off the grid. I think, whoever is signing-off on these movement orders has no idea that they shouldn't be mentioning Foram."

The human colonel grunted her agreement with her Benii second in command's statement. These intercepts were the Commonwealth's first sniff of anything to do with Foram. "Anything from the Observers?" Asked Bliek referring to the military observers that, since the direct intervention of Admiral Jing months before, following the *misunderstanding* at Balat.

The destruction of the Alonan colony by the Black Ships had led to that misunderstanding, damn nearly escalating into open war between the Commonwealth and the Alonan Empire. Admiral Jing's solution was simple; Alonan military observers aboard the largest of the Commonwealth's installations, by permission of course, with that permission stretching to include observation of the movement and exercising of major fleet elements.

A reciprocal agreement placed Commonwealth observers on equivalent Empire units.

Jing's hoped the observers would reassure their respective governments that neither side was planning a sneak attack on its neighbor. So far as Fantozzi was aware no observer from either side had had their movements restricted. As long as the observers know what to look for mused Fantozzi.

"The only thing of note-" Tolan began again referring to her PAD to ensure she gave accurate information. "Is a report from the embedded Garundan observer at the Empire's Naval War College. He's spent the last few months cultivating a relationship with an Alonan senior grade captain who's on fast track to flag rank."

Fantozzi searched her memory for a name. "Ah, yes. Captain Rikel. He scored pretty highly on the Advanced Tactics Course, if memory serves."

"Rikel came top of his class. The observer attended the graduation dinner two nights ago and a tipsy Rikel let slip he's been nominated for command of brand-new warship. The warship would put the Empire on par with anything the Commonwealth has in space."

"That was a bit silly of him." Smirked Fantozzi.

"Indeed, ma'am." Agreed Tolan. "I cross referenced the observer's report with our intercepts and found a movement order sending the good captain to..."

"Foram." Interjected Fantozzi. A small smile played on Fantozzi's lips as she considered the fate of the faceless administration officer when their superiors found out that they had been flinging the name of what, perhaps, was the Alonan Empires closest guarded secret around in poorly encrypted movement orders.

"OK, Major, lets cross-reference the names of Alonans who've been assigned to Foram. I want everything we have; especially performance ratings and any recent combat experience." The Benii tapped furiously on her PAD and entered the commands needed to achieve Fantozzi's order.

"I've got a bad feeling that our sneaky little Alonan friends are up to something and whatever it is I don't think it's good for us."

***

FORAM SYSTEM

Captain Rikel had been a spacer for his entire military career and recognized the significance of the slight shuddering of the deck plates beneath his feet. The transport carrying Rikel and his compatriots had cut its gravity drive and re-entered normal space.

"Well, looks like we've arrived at our destination." Remarked a commander, who's name Rikel could not recall, even though she had sat diagonally across the small table from Rikel since embarking the transport at Emperor Yalu IV station.

"Wherever that is." Mumbled a voice Rikel did recognize.

"Oh, cheer up, Tova." Rikel admonished his fellow naval captain and former classmate on the Advanced Tactics Course at the naval warfare college. "For all we know this is a secret, naval beach-side retreat, reserved for officers who've shown outstanding performance and leadership in the field of... er... drinking."

The comment received a forced grunt from Tova and a few chortles from Rikel's traveling companions, a dozen or so officers of varying ranks.

"I'm sure those goons from Imperial Security who checked, and double checked our identities, before putting us aboard this rust bucket, were not doing so to make sure a junior officer sneaked on board, hoping to get a tan." Tova's reply caused the room to drop into silence. "Besides, I recognized at least another half dozen or so spacers that I have served with over the years hovering around the personnel lock we boarded through." Tova pointed a fat finger at Rikel. "I'm willing to bet they are aboard this ship, sitting in a cabin like and wondering where the gods have landed us and why."

Tova's remarks only served to reawaken the questions that Rikel himself had put to the back of his mind ever since he had received his orders to report to a specific docking bay on the Emperor Yalu IV space station at a specific time and date. After graduating at the top of his class Rikel had expected to receive orders giving him command of a shiny new cruiser instead, his orders only fueled the conspiracy theory that ran rife through his classmates at the naval warfare college. Gossip had it that the High Command had plucked large numbers of officers and ratings from their current assignments throughout the fleet and simply vanished them.

Their disappearance had left gaps in ship's personnel that remained unfilled and lead to major performance issues among the fleet, at a time when the threat to the Empire appeared larger than ever. The rumors led to many a late-night discussion in the Officer's Mess. Now, it seemed, Rikel and those with him, where about to add to those issues.

From his earliest days as a junior ensign aboard a bulk freighter shuttling back and forth between Alona and the ore processing plants spread throughout the Alonan systems thick asteroid belt. His superiors quickly identified Rikel as a fast learner and he rapidly found himself on the promotion fast track. Short, sharp tours of duty, on ever larger and powerful Imperial Navy units, broken up by promotion and spells as a staff and logistics' officer, ensured that Rikel received a rounded, thorough knowledge of the intricacies of the modern Imperial Navy.

Officers like Rikel were in even higher demand after first contact with an alien race. Humans.

The appearance of the TDF James Cook and its subsequent rescue of an Alonan vessel in distress had sent shock waves through Alonan society. Now, cried the scientists who had for generations been telling anyone who would listen that somewhere out among the countless stars there must be another civilization at least equal if not more advanced than their own, the Empire had proof that they were not alone.

A growing sense of dread quickly followed the initial shock of discovering that life existed elsewhere. The Humans claimed to be peaceful explorers with the ability to travel between the stars using a gravity drive, a technology the Humans refused to share.

The Emperor and his subjects could not tolerate this situation.

Who were these Humans, to deny the Empire? The Empire's dread morphed into resentment. Resentment of all things Human. So, began a covert operation to secure the gravity drive for the Empire. Vast sums of money changed hands in shady deals which, in the fullness of time, saw the Empire procure what it sought; working examples of the Human's gravity drive. With uncommon haste, the Empire set to work their engineers, technicians, and theoretical scientists and within months, the Emperor launched the INS *Emperor Katcha*; with Lieutenant Rikel as its fresh-faced Weapons' Officer.

A year later Lieutenant Commander Rikel found himself in a hardened command center as the Others threatened to snuff the Empire from existence. An enemy which the Humans had known about and had, in their blatant disregard for the Empire, failed to warn the Alonans about. Despite the best efforts of the brave souls staffing the ships of the Imperial Navy who, with courage that would hail them as heroes, flung themselves upon the Others' relentlessly advancing behemoths. Those brave souls died in their tens of thousands as it nothing stopped the enemy closing on the very heart of the Empire Alona.

At the last moment, it had taken a Human fleet commanded by Admiral Ai Jing to save the day. The alien shapes of battleships and heavy cruisers of the Terran Defense Force filled the space around Alona and formed a wall of speeding missiles and blinking coherent light which at first slowed, and then halted the enemy's advance.

Under Jing, the Human Battle Fleet advanced and took the fight to the Others. Pushing forward repeatedly and leaving a trail of wrecked, atmosphere-spewing starships in their wake, Jing's forces ripped the heart from the Others' attack.

With victory assured, the Human Fleet had not paused to take breath and receive the heartfelt thanks of the Empire, before vanishing as quickly as they had arrived, leaving the surviving units of the once proud Imperial Navy to pick up the pieces of the titanic clash and to relegation to a tertiary role, in the defense of its own home.

It was not the Human's victory that would be Rikel's abiding memory of that day, it was the look on the face of Grand Admiral Raga as he left the bunker on the conclusion of the battle. The admiral's face reflected the shame of the entire Imperial Navy, they had failed in their one responsibility; the safety of the Empire.

On that day Lieutenant Commander Rikel, along with every other officer and rating of the fleet, had sworn that never again would the fate of the Empire rest with outsiders.

A deep, double tone sounded from the speakers concealed in the ceiling warning of an impending announcement. After a pause, the transport captain's voice addressed the ship's crew and passengers.

"All hands, this is the captain. We have arrived at our destination." A smile tugged at the edges of Rikel's lips as, even now, the announcement conspicuously left out the name of the secret base.

"We'll remain under power for approximately two hours, as we make our approach to space dock, where all passengers will disembark. At this time, I would remind all passengers and crew that all data devices, no matter how secure, must remain powered down until they have been inspected and passed by space dock security." Absently Rikel reached for the personal comp which was a permanent fixture on his belt. During his time on the Advanced Tactics Course he had found himself growingly intrigued by how rapidly the naval forces of the Commonwealth had adapted its weaponry and tactics as it faced the ever changing and various threats of first the Others, then the Turak and now the Black Ships. Rikel had been actively encouraged by the course instructors to research and produce a thesis which, and Rikel took great pride informing anyone who would listen, would become part of the courses curriculum once he had completed it.

The captain's thumb brushed the power down icon; however, his thumb only partially covered the icon, the other part of his thumb came to rest on the power up icon. The circuitry controlling the small device registered the conflicting commands and, as there was more pressure on power up, decided to remain operational. As per its programming when it failed to detect any further inputs after thirty seconds the small display screen went dark. Anyone giving the device a cursory glance, including its owner, assumed that it was powered down.

Rikel's attention returned to his discussion with Tova, oblivious to the state of his personal comp.

✳ ✳ ✳

ABOARD THE *SAVIOR*

If an artificial intelligence had the ability to physically display emotion, then Chera would have been the epitome of frustration. Despite her best efforts over the past five months she had failed to penetrate the veil of security that the Alonans had draped around their computer cores. As she had explained to Commander Okal at length it was not that the Alonans had superior firewalls or computing power to block her efforts to invade their systems. Rather they had gone for a far simpler solution. They had either powered down every non-essential computer core going as far as physically disconnecting every cable and interface or, where computer assistance was essential, it had been scrubbed clean of all data not required to perform its immediate task.

The growing number of completed warships that were being moved to holding areas around the system for trials prior to being commissioned into service were doing so minus all but the most limited of navigational data. Barely enough for them to navigate around Foram without plunging themselves into some local planetary body or rocky asteroid. With Okal's permission Chera had gone a step further in her efforts to secure more information on the Alonans. The AI had developed piggyback programs that she had covertly inserted into Captain Calan's personal comp. The Alonan officer had been assigned to Okal as his personal liaison and had become the Saiph ship commanders constant shadow. However, Okal and Chera's plans had been thwarted by the good captains end of day routine. Before Calan returned for his nightly briefings with General Lura and Chief Scientist Kilor in the command center the Alonan stripped out of all the clothing he had been wearing while in Okal's presence and put on a fresh uniform while Calan's personal comp remained secure in a locker ready for him the following day. The discarded clothing was then vaporized. It may have struck some as an extreme measure however, it was effective in preventing Okal or any of his crew from attaching a listening device to the Alonan.

During Okal's initial meeting with General Lura and Kilor the Alonans had gone to great lengths to lay out the danger facing their empire. Okal sat through a well-orchestrated and rehearsed presentation where he was subjected to image after image of ravaged worlds laid waste by the unwitting, fanatical Others and, once revealed, the puppet masters themselves. The Black Ships of The Leader. The general gave Okal a detailed briefing on the defeat of an alliance of worlds called the Commonwealth Union of Planets. This alliance had been made up of the remains of what Okal had identified as the remaining Seed Worlds and, to Okal's horror, even their combined strength had not been enough to overcome the single minded purpose of the Others to rid the galaxy of any threat to The Leaders plan of Saiph domination of the galaxy.

Okal recognized that as the last remaining Seed World the carefully constructed plans of the Elders were within a hairs width of being destroyed. The current perilous situation that the Empire found itself in was only compounded in Okal's opinion as Kilor detailed how the Empire had been able to match and, in some areas, supersede the technology employed by the Others. However, matching the technology of the Black Ships was simply beyond the Empires capability.

Okal was forced to agree with General Lura's analysis of the Empires current predicament. Facing the numerically superior, though technologically inferior, forces of the Others, in the balance of probabilities, the Empire had every reason to assume that they would be victorious. The Black Ships were another matter entirely. Lura's explanation for The Leaders decision to reveal himself and his forces was that he could see the Empire was gaining the upper hand in their war with the Others so he had therefore decided to strengthen the Others hand by employing the Black Ships and their technological edge to secure victory at crucial points in the ongoing war.

The Saiph commander had found this piece meal tactical employment of the Black Ships puzzling. As Kilor had gone to great lengths to explain the Black Ships were generations beyond anything the Empire had the ability to build. The Black Ships energy shielding made them virtually impervious to any weaponry the Empire could bring to bear while the Black Ships antimatter warheads could lay waste to any target of their choosing. Why had The Leader not seized his obvious advantages and sought a swift and decisive battle to end the war? Why, if he had already defeated this Commonwealth and scoured their home worlds clean of life, had The Leader not done the same to Alona? The version of the truth that General Lura and Chief Scientist Kilor were spinning was too full of holes for Okal to swallow. The final straw had been the look in Captain Calan's eyes as he had stood silently throughout his superior's brief. The junior officers face may have remained stoically impassive however, the man's eyes showed the turmoil behind the mask. Then and there Okal resolved to re double his efforts to get to the real truth behind what was happening beyond the limits of the Foram system. For the time being though, he and his crew would play along. Whatever else was behind the Alonan's attempt to deceive him Okal was in no doubt that the long dead Saiph Elders would have wanted him to extort every muscle and sinew to salvage what he could from their grand plan to ensure that some trace of their legacy survived. A legacy which The Leader and his followers with their warped idea of Saiph genetic superiority appeared dead set on destroying.

Okal's thoughts filled with images of the *Savior*'s storage banks. Safe and secure within those rows upon rows of glass vials was the Elders last gasp gamble at ensuring a future for the Saiph as a race. Seeds of every description. Fertilized embryos of every living creature on the planet at the time of *Savior* and her sister ships launch. At the time it had seemed to many, even some of the Elders, that they were being overly cautious. The Leader and those misguided souls that followed him had fled and vanished among the stars. Okal and his crew had not even been born until two generations after The Leaders escape from prison. However, the Saiph were a patient and thoughtful race. No decision was ever rushed. Every move was carefully planned, its ramifications considered to the Nth degree. History weighed heavy on the Elders.

Long ago, when the Saiph aspired to be a benevolent guiding hand among the less developed worlds, a misguided intervention on a primitive, warring planet had ended in cataclysmic failure. This failure had seen the Saiph physically withdraw from space in all but the most basic of ways. The plans for vast fleets of ships which would spread out from Saiph and carry multitudes of eager colonists was scrapped with only a small number having ever been completed. The events on that distant, primitive world had been burned so deep into the Saiph physic that never again would the Saiph physically set foot on another world or intervene in an established civilizations growth. Instead, the Elders would select worlds in the early stages of development. With a genetic tweak there, and a helping hand there, the Saiph would ensure the success of a single evolutionary line. And embedded within that species DNA would be traces of Saiph. When, inevitably, the star around which the world of the Saiph orbited, died, taking the Saiph with it this plan would ensure that something of them would remain.

Now, however, it fell upon Okal to intervene once more in the affairs of the galaxy. The Alonans had taken Commander Okal at his word when the Saiph had offered technological aid in their struggle against The Leader. Members of the *Savior*'s crew worked shoulder to shoulder with Alonan engineers adapting ship and weaponry design. Overnight the Imperial Navy made advances that otherwise would have taken generations. All that was required was the crews that would man these new ships. And it was the transports carrying these crews that Chera had identified as the new target of her attempts to secure the information Okal had commanded of her.

With subtle ethereal tendrils Chera infiltrated every Alonan computer and communications system she could. Searching for the answers that Okal needed without success. A tight beam transmission between Foram port control and an arriving transport had carried an extra few lines of computer code. The highly sophisticated program had given Chera unrestricted access to the transports on board systems. The lack of data held in the ships navigational systems had come as no surprise to Chera. Two sets of coordinates. A point of origin and a destination. The encrypted communications logs were similarly free of anything useful. The transports manifest held only the barest of details on the ship's crew and passengers. Names and ranks with no indication of previous duty stations. Chera had to grudgingly admit that the Alonans took their security measures seriously.

Spreading out through the transports internal systems Chera tried in vain to access any electronic systems which were being carried as cargo. The simple expedient of air gapping the cargo and removing their power sources denied any potential information source to her. Onward through the transports systems she swept. Remorseless in her hunt. Then, a brief flare in a spectrum that no eye conceived by nature would ever spot but which stood out to Chera like a star going supernova. A single, steady signal source attached to the transports power conduits. A device sipping minuscule amounts of energy as it kept itself fully charged. Chera barreled toward it like a subway train down a tunnel. Chera flung herself across the radio link between the power transfer node and the devices receiver. Impatiently the AI crashed through the inadequate encryption protocols into the mass of data beyond.

The low beep at his waist caused Captain Rikel to look down where his eyes fell upon the steady green light illuminated on the control panel of his personal comp. "What!"

"Security are going to give you hell, Rikel." Chided a softly chortling Tova.

Rikel mumbled a string of expletives as he pulled the comp off his belt and forcefully thumbed the power down icon before flicking the small device over and slipping out the power source tapping a finger against his nose.

"What security don't know can't hurt them." He said to the older man.

Both Alonan captains chuckled at their shared contempt for the officers of Imperial Security returning their attention to the conversation going on around them expounding theories of their eventual destination.

✳ ✳ ✳

The tingling of Okal's subcutaneous implant connected by wires finer than the thinnest strand of hair directly into the speech and hearing centers of his brain alerted the Saiph commander that the ships AI had an urgent message for him which she did not want to share with another's ears. That other was currently sharing a lunch time meal with the commander and the *Savior*'s chief engineer.

Okal discreetly glanced across at Captain Calan smothering an amused smile as the poor Alonan's eyes glazed over with incomprehension as the *Savior*'s chief engineer began a highly technical explanation of the intricacies of the energy shielding employed by the Black Ships and how to overcome it. Okal guessed that he had at least a few minutes to communicate with Chera before Captain Calan managed to maneuver the conversation around to something he at least had a chance of understanding.

"Go ahead, Chera."

"Commander, your suspicions are correct. The Alonans have been lying to us."

A grimace formed on Okal's face before he quickly blanked his features hoping the ever observant Calan had not noticed his momentary slip of composure. The sound of the ongoing conversation between the engineer and the Alonan gave no hint that Calan was aware of anything unusual.

"How badly?" Asked Okal already feeling a growing sense of foreboding before Chera answered.

"Let's say that the Alonan's version of the war with the Supreme Leader is more fantasy than truth."

"Very well. Compile a full report for senior staff and we shall convene this evening after the majority of our Alonan friends have left for the night."

"Understood, Commander." Replied Chera terminating her link leaving Okal with his thoughts. The Saiph commander raised his head from his food eying the Alonan captain who, despite himself, Okal had come to regard as a friend which only made the sense of betrayal hurt even more. The chief engineer shared a joke with Captain Calan catching with a mouth full of food which turned his laugh into a spluttering cough, eyes filling with water he reached for the glass of water on the table before him. Calan's reaction to the bad joke only made the engineer laugh harder. Distracted, Calan failed to notice the sad look which cast a shadow over Okal's features. By the time the Alonan recovered and his eyes cleared the Saiph commander had a wide smile fixed on his face as he too pretended to enjoy Calan's discomfort.

✳✳✳

The small gathering in Okal's private quarters had sat in growing disbelief as Chera had relayed to them the salient points of the Alonan Rikel's diligent research for his academy paper. For his part, Okal had spent the time watching his officer's reactions having already gone over this new intelligence with the *Savior*'s AI. Throughout Chera's presentation there had been the occasional gasp of horror, followed by shakes of the head and the odd muffled curse. Okal understood his subordinates' reactions completely for Rikel's paper did not pull any punches. The Alonan captain had succinctly and without prejudice covered everything from the Alonan's first encounter with the pre-Commonwealth humans, the conflict which had spawned the Commonwealth's formation and the Alonan's refusal to join it, through to the ultimate defeat of the Others by this multiracial Commonwealth and the discovery of the true extent of their holy Ehita as they scoured the galaxy of all sentient life in the name of the Creator.

It was this final revelation that had led to the sullen silence that had descended on Okal's quarters. It appeared that although the version of events that General Lura had shared with Okal where peppered with lies, the core truth had remained. The Saiph were responsible for a genocide which had spanned the stars killing countless billions. The weight of history lay heavy on every shoulder in the room.

"Friends." Okal's voice was low and soft. "As we suspected, the Alonans have lied to us." There came grunts of agreement and nodding heads. "However," Said Okal his voice firming. "If we'd been in their position would we not have done the same?" Okal scanned the room for a disagreeing voice but there was none. "As I thought, so, my decision to aid the Alonans has not changed..." Okal paused as heads came up sharply, mouths opening ready to voice objections. Okal raised a hand halting any disagreement. "For the moment." All eyes in the room locked onto their commander as the officers focused their attention awaiting Okal's plan.

"Chera, display the star chart." Instantly a mass of stars appeared. Hovering in the center of the room and rotating slowly. "From our unwitting Alonan source Chera has plotted the star systems under Alonan control." The display expanded to show Alona, seat of the Empire, and Geta, the second life-bearing planet of the system. Similarly, Chera had highlighted the Alonan colony worlds of Balat, Kathan and Opero.

"Now this." Okal paused dramatically as the Alonan Empire worlds receded into the mass of stars and dozens upon dozens of new worlds replaced them. "My friends, are the worlds controlled by the Commonwealth." The gasps from the officers were not of horror but of disbelief.

"The scrupulously laid plans of the Elders have borne fruit." Okal said finding it hard to keep the pride out of his voice. "The Seed Worlds have prospered more than we could ever have hoped for. And-" Again Okal paused as a single world flashed. "This is Edasich, despite the Others' attacking this planet and murdering its population as part of their Ehita, the Commonwealth located survivors hiding underground on the planet's moon. Survivors who are not descended from any of the original Seed Worlds." The room was so still, you could have heard a pin drop. Okal scanned his officers and allowed them a moment to take in what he had said.

"Yes, my friends. Even though millennium ago, the Elders searched for basic civilizations and found none, which triggered their decision to expend massive resources on the Seed World program, all along," Okal extended one brown furred digit and pointed at the small world, "On Edasich, without outside interference, a life form had grown, became intelligent, built an industrial civilization, and reached for the stars."

"Commander, what does this line represent?" Asked *Savior*'s chief engineer.

The worlds of the Commonwealth receded as the worlds of the Alonan Empire had done before them. Instead a wavy, wandering line, colored the deepest red cut across the montage of stars. "That." Said Okal as he walked into the mist of the display to stand before the line. "Is the border with the race the Commonwealth known as the Turak. The extent of their space is unknown as the Turak allow no one to cross beyond this line. What we do know is that, like the Edasich, the Turak are not a product of our Seed World program."

"And what of this Supreme Leader?" Asked the engineer through clenched teeth.

"Chera." Okal said and the spread of stars disappeared to be replaced with the image of a sleek, space black warship. Weapons pylons jutting out from flattened, broad hulls like some nightmarish sea monster. "As the Alonans have told us, warships armed with antimatter missiles, high output lasers and grasers and protected by energy shields are appearing in ever larger numbers. Chera has extracted from this intelligence that neither the Alonans, the Commonwealth nor, the secretive Turak are a match for them."

"We have no choice, then, but to continue aiding the Alonans." Stated the chief engineer frankly.

Okal's head bobbed in agreement.

"But surely we can't restrict the aid to the Alonans." Interjected a voice from the back of the room.

Okal's eyes searched out and found the source. Salo. The *Savior*'s medical officer. Her large, round, pleading eyes demanded an answer. Okal favored her with a small smile.

"You are, as usual, correct Salo. However," He said addressing everyone in the room. "We must ensure the Alonans have the ability to defend themselves against the threat they face from the Supreme Leader and his renegades. Chera has assured me that with the technology we've shared with the Alonans, and our instruction in its use, it is a matter of months before they become self-sufficient and, at that time, we shall make our move."

"And what is our move, Commander?" Asked the chief engineer.

Alongside the Black Ship a large, sprawling space station sprung into existence. "This is the nearest Commonwealth base. Waypoint 4. It is here that we will reveal ourselves to the races of the Commonwealth and offer the same aid to them as we have to the Alonans."

Okal gave the gathering a moment, then clapped his hands loudly and snapped the room out of a growing melancholic mood.

"Now." He said in a voice with forced levity. "Does anybody have any ideas on how we are going to manage our departure from Alonan space?"

Okal's question and tone had the desired effect. A chorus of laughter filled the room. *Enjoy this moment*, thought Okal. For there are dangerous times ahead. Mentally shaking himself, Okal resolved to get down to serious planning with his officers.

CHAPTER EIGHT

NEW BOSS SAME AS THE OLD BOSS

FORTRESS COMMAND | EARTH ORBIT | SOL SYSTEM

Kris Madkin reached up and released the constricting collar of his expensive business suit, made all the more expensive by the tissue thin polymorphic armor that the Presidential Office of Security agents insisted he wear whenever he was in public. Kris' eyes fell on the behemoth which rested like a second moon beyond the armored glass of the Shuttle One's round portholes. Fortress Command, six million tonnes of armored steel and lethal directed energy weapons, missiles and Mosquito space-fighters ready to discourage anyone foolish enough to come close enough to Earth with the thought of harming humanities home world.

Today however, a visit to Fortress Command had not been the primary reason for a visit from the President of the Terran Republic. No, today, that massive construct had been playing host to the commissioning ceremonies of the Terran Defense Forces latest warships. The second and third ships of the Itus Carrier Class, TDF *Montu* and TDF *Bastet*. These two vessels would soon become the hub of their own Carrier Strike Groups and follow the lead ship in the class, TDF *Itus*, as Admiral Ai Jing's answer to the need to provide protection and security to the seemingly unstoppable expansion of the colonization program. A low groan escaped Kris, his thoughts had turned to the impending round of budget and legislator battles that would see him fight to secure the promises he had made on the campaign trail. Battles he had to fight while trying to get key appointments filled within his own presidency. Rebecca had been so right when she had said that his first hundred days in office would be the hardest, but she had failed to mention that the second hundred would show no signs of easing up the pace.

The sound of gentle clinking against glass brought Kris out of the melancholy spiral that he was rapidly descending into. Turning his head away from the imposing sight of Fortress Command and the two carriers that resembled toys beside the space stations imposing bulk Kris felt a smile tug at his lips as he refocused on the crystal glass filled with a liquid that had the deepest, grainy aroma of the finest highland whiskey cooled with two ice cubes.

"You, Clement Bradshaw, are a life saver." Kris said as he took the glass from the outstretched hand of his Chief of Staff. For a fleeting moment something sad passed over Clement's eyes before he quickly shook it off and gave Kris a gentle smile. Internally Kris kicked himself for his turn of phrase for he had indeed saved Clement's life on a cold winter's day outside a restaurant in Geneva when an assassin had tried and failed to kill both men. Three POS agents had been killed that night before a badly injured Kris was able to use one of the dead agents' weapons to get a couple of shots off before falling into unconsciousness as his own wounds poured his life giving blood onto the sidewalk. Luckily his faltering vision had kept the weapon straight and true killing the would-be assassin. Hence his POS details code name for him. 'Deadshot'.

By Clement's quick recovery Kris guessed that the older man had no intention of reliving that moment, so Kris moved on to more pressing concerns. "I'm not liking what I'm hearing from our friends at naval intelligence."

Clement lowered himself into the seat opposite allowing himself thinking time by taking a sip of his own drink. An amber colored beer that Clement swore had once been foisted on him by a barman during a visit to a craft brewery in Munich and one he had never been able to shake the taste of. Much to the disdain of the navy crew of Shuttle One who had had to track down the craft brewery and ensure that there was always a constant supply aboard in case the Chief of Staff fancied a light refreshment.

"Yes, it appears the Alonans are up to something and want to keep us in the dark."

"It's bad enough that our allies run operations without giving us a heads up. But, this latest incident with the Alonans has caused an atmosphere of suspicion and is in flagrant breach of the Joint Observer Protocol." Kris swigged his drink as he tried to control his exasperation.

Clement eyed the younger man over the rim of his glass. Kris sat there with his head back, eyes half closed and Clement had come to recognize the signs that Kris was wondering why he had ever agreed to run for president. Well, thought Clement, this is why Rebecca had insisted that if she was going to give her backing to a senator whom hardly anyone had ever heard against the Earth First people led by Mathias Grant III with the deep coffers of Seaton Anderson either buying off or straight out blackmailing anyone in the Grant's run for the presidency then Kris would be in desperate need of he an older, perhaps wiser, hand to help guide him. And that was exactly what Clement intended to do.

"Chairman Volak is indeed a wily one, Mr. President." Said Clement referring to the Persai who had risen to lead the Council of Twelve following the death of Tarrov who had been a close personal friend and steadfast ally of Rebecca Coston. "We consider him a Hawk in our own nomenclature. Perhaps, at the next quarterly meeting of the heads of the Commonwealth you should get to know him better, strike up a friendship."

With eyes closed, Kris grunted and signaled his acquiescence to Clement's suggestion. Satisfied with the president's tacit agreement, Clement pushed onto the next, more difficult, subject. The Alonans.

"The Alonan Empire on the other hand is a more -" Clement looked for the right word, "Prickly subject."

Kris chuckled. "I should ask Admiral Jing to send his shiny new ships on a visit to Alona, so the Emperor can look up from his palace and see what I think about him obstructing one of our observers from doing their job." The hand holding Kris' glass gestured toward Clement while a playful smile spread across the president's lips. "I've always wondered what Gun Boat Diplomacy looked like with starships."

The frown that formed on Clement's face reminded Kris of one his mother gave him when his boyhood self-suggested something that would get him into trouble. Kris laughed out loud at the similarity, which caused Clement's frown to deepen.

"When you are quite finished, Mr. President." Scolded Clement.

"Please continue." Kris managed between laughs.

"The Alonans have always been jealous of their military's activities and, since their whole society is based on a quasi-military format, that means they don't like us having our military observers on their ships; looking over shoulders and gleaning intelligence. Until now the Alonans have put up with this de facto spying for the simple reason that they are doing the exact same thing to us."

"Alonan observers are found on virtually every one of our major bases and capital ships. The fact that they were willing to stretch to extent of injuring one of our observers- to stop him boarding a naval ship we believe is bound for this..." Clement searched his memory for the name that naval intelligence was so keen to get its eyes on.

"Foram." Kris said helpfully. "And Admiral Vadis over at the Naval Intelligence Service is unwilling to call it a place, operation, or even a person."

"Whatever," said Clement, "that does not change the fact that our observer was nearly killed when the airlock door leading onto the transport linked to Foram had an unexpected malfunction and closed without warning. The observer was damned lucky it only crushed his leg, a fraction longer and the door would have closed on his chest."

Kris placed his now half empty glass on the table before him as he mulled over his next move. Clement allowed him the time to think, after all he may have been Chief of

Staff however, this sort of decision had to come from the top and you did not get any further up the chain of command than the President.

"OK, Clement, let's draft a diplomatic note of protest and have the Ambassador deliver it to the hands of the Emperor personally. That should signal gravity of the situation."

Clement was nodding his agreement while making a note on his PAD only for Kris to interrupt him. "Oh, and Clement –"

"Yes, Mr. President?" Clement said as he lifted his head from the PAD.

"Let's light a fire under Admiral Vadis and his people. If the Alonans are willing to go this far to protect their dirty little secret, then it's pretty important we find out what it is. Don't you agree?"

"Agreed." Replied Clement as a naval steward entered the small lounge and cleared his throat.

"Twenty minutes till we touch down at Geneva, Mr. President. Do you require anything else?"

"No, thank you." Kris answered. The steward left as silently as he had entered while Kris shifted his gaze, once more, to the porthole and the view beyond.

Holding steady off Shuttle One's port side was a naval Katana assault shuttle. In the distance Kris caught brief flashes of light reflected off the fuselage of a pair of Mosquito space-fighters, providing a constant Combat Space Patrol while the president's shuttle lay beyond the reach of the high-altitude aero fighters. Undoubtedly, at this moment the aero fighters tore through the atmosphere to rendezvous with Shuttle One ready to escort him safely to Geneva. The Presidential Office of Security took their job very seriously, thought Kris, as he closed his eyes for a cat nap before to landing.

✳ ✳ ✳

NAVAL INTELLIGENCE SERVICE | CARSON CITY | EARTH | SOL SYSTEM

"The President's Office would like the Naval Intelligence Service to expedite any and all collection of intelligence in relation to the Empire of Alona's ongoing project known only at this time as Foram." Aleksandr Vadis said through gritted teeth as he stared at the message displayed on his Top-Secret terminal. A stare that, in the opinion of Brigadier General Earl Statham, was about to morph into the swinging of solid objects at the screen.

"I should have followed Olaf into retirement." Grumbled Vadis.

Statham let out a deep chuckle at Vadis' statement. "Yeah, I can see you and Olaf sitting outside that shack of his he has the temerity to call a house on an island no bigger than the landing pad on the roof of this building surrounded by nothing but water for hundreds of kilometers on a planet located at the ass end of nowhere. You would kill each other within a week."

Vadis let out a deep sigh as he cleared the message from the screen and walked around his desk to join his friend who was relaxing leisurely on a sofa helping himself to coffee.

"If Elizabeth Wilson was in my employ, I would set her on the Alonans, and God help them." Vadis growled.

Statham raised his coffee mug in mock salute. "Now that, Aleksandr, would have been a sight worth waiting for. Unfortunately, I believe that she may be otherwise busy being your opposite number at the Janus Office of Naval Intelligence and all."

Vadis subconsciously grimaced. The First Earth movement had driven a hell of a lot of damn fine officers and ratings into the waiting arms of a Janus eager to expand its own capabilities as it strove to prove beyond anyone's doubt that it could not only stand on its own two feet it could rank up there with the two core powers of the Commonwealth. Earth and Pars. Maybe he should have retired when Rebecca Coston stepped down? Olaf Helsett, Coston's Secretary of Defense, had taken the opportunity so why hadn't he? Because the job's not done yet, Aleksandr that's why, Vadis admonished himself.

"Earth calling Aleksandr. Come in Aleksandr." Called Statham forcing Vadis to break off his chain of thought.

"Yes, yes, I'm here." Vadis said as he popped himself down on the couch. "For the moment let's see what this diplomatic note shakes free. Maybe Colonel Fantozzi will pick up another lead. In the meantime, lets employ some of your Department of Special Projects' little toys and see if we can find out where those transports are headed."

Statham thought for a moment before speaking. "One of our lot have been playing with the idea of being able to place a tracking device onto a gravity drive capable ship."

That caused Vadis to lean forward. The implications of being able to follow a gravity drive star ship to its destination could have massive ramifications for how the navy evolved its tactics. As it stood, the moment a ships gravity drive was activated and it fled into fold space all contact was lost with it so you had no idea where it was going to reemerge into normal space that's why even normal multi ship formations took such extraordinary measures to ensure that each and every ship in a formation had precise navigational data before activating its gravity drive. Get it wrong and the ships either emerged all on top of each other which would end badly for all involved or, more likely, your ships ended up spread all over space and having to make a number of smaller folds to regroup.

"Now don't get too excited, Aleksandr." Statham cautioned his boss. "This is highly experimental. Something about knowing the exact position of the target ship, the direction of travel. Energy supply to the gravity drive as a... coefficient of length of engine... engagement and a myriad of other factors which, I'll be honest with you, left my head hurting. I'm not even sure Admiral Glandinning out at Zarminda fully grasped the concept and he's one of the smartest flag officers I know."

"I know what you mean." Commented Vadis. "I made the mistake once -" Vadis cocked an eyebrow at Statham, "of asking him to explain how his staff worked out the antimatter containment field miniaturization problems which had been the major stumbling block on the development of the High-Velocity Antimatter Missile." Vadis shook his head slowly. "His explanation left my brain hurting for days." The men laughed,

"Moving onto a subject which I have a chance of understanding, what's the progress on Project Bright Star?"

"Bright Star? Right, the issues identified by Doctor Sarkisian with the Deployable Stellar Detection Grid are close to being rectified. New components have been manufactured and are in the final stages of testing."

"Hmm, might have been an idea to do that the first time around." Mumbled Vadis.

"Ensign Burkett has taken it upon himself to test each module personally. Both Admiral Glandinning and the doctor speak highly of him, though he'd deny it. I think the admiral has taken a bit of a shine to our young ensign and would like him assigned to Zarminda following completion of his current tour."

"Yes, I'm sure that can be arranged." Said Vadis waving a hand indicating for Statham to continue. "The Tycho Brahe reports ready to sortie as soon as the testing of the DSDG is complete."

"And what of Wilson?" Inquired Vadis. When Statham did not reply immediately Vadis fixed him with a quizzical look. "Problems?"

"Sir-," Statham had changed his form of address and Vadis became wary, his old friend was about to broach a touchy subject.

"With Lieutenant Wilson's aunt running a foreign intelligence service..." Statham paused as if awaiting permission to continue. Vadis didn't particularly like the direction of the conversation, but he trusted Statham to have considered all the implications before going there.

"Go on."

"There's no doubt that Wilson is doing an extremely capable job within the boundaries of his current project, however..."

Here it comes thought Vadis.

"The Lieutenant's familial connections may, in the future, prove to be a hindrance and, possibly, a security risk."

There he had said it.

Although uncomfortable hearing, it was a fact. Vadis rubbed his chin with one hand as he considered Statham's words. Unfortunately, for Terrance Wilson, Statham had a point and, in the intelligence game, any opportunity to mitigate a potential threat to security had to be dealt with.

"Wilson is married, isn't he?"

"Yes. And they have a young child."

"Very well. On completion of his current assignment Lieutenant Terrance Wilson will receive a promotion and a nice assignment earth-side. Logistics or training. Something which doesn't require him to hold a security clearance above Secret."

And with that the naval intelligence career of Terrance Wilson ended, without him ever knowing it.

CHAPTER NINE

COLONIZATION RUNS AMUCK

CHARON BASE | ORBIT OF PLUTO | SOL SYSTEM

From the screams and cussing coming from the inner office, Ensign Zak decided it prudent to cancel the admiral's 1300 hours appointment. Hastily typing the required apologetic email, the Garundan tapped the send button with one claw while amending the admiral's diary for today with the other hand. Task complete, Zak let out a silent thank you to his ancestors that he was not the point of his admiral's wrath this particular day.

When he had applied for the Commonwealth Union of Planets' Naval Officer's Exchange Program Zak doubted whether he could pass the first hurdle; a comprehensive English language test. But, as a teen he had studied the dialects of his planet's new allies, turns out these studies had stood him in good stead. Zak had become accomplished in English, the chosen language of the Terran Republican, though he was nowhere near as proficient in Mandarin, which was also spoken by a goodly number of humans. Something to do with the lack of flexibility in his non-human lips.

Progressing through the application process, Zak had been subjected to a varied battery of tests; from Terran history to eating etiquette. He still found it strange that humans preferred their food dead and reheated, rather than a Garundan's reptilian preference for *fresh* food, though the necessities of space travel had gradually introduced a diverse catering regime at home.

The shouting from within the admiral's office petered out and was shortly followed by the gentle, feminine tones of Yeoman Rota as she spoke over her desk-mounted comm, meaning only one thing.

The admiral was ready for his next victim.

Having canceled the unfortunate, would-be victim's appointment, it fell upon Zak to take their place.

He stood then paused at the floor to ceiling mirror, Zak was convinced had been installed for potential quarry to look themselves over and wish they hadn't ventured into the heady heights of flag country (the lofty area where admirals deigned to meet the unwary), and ran an eye over his own uniform before straightening his shoulders and moving forward to knock twice on the doors of the inner sanctum.

Zak entered without permission, one of the few perks of being an admiral's aide.

Walking purposefully to the no-nonsense desk, adorned by a single holo frame displaying a middle-aged human female smiling brightly while surrounded by several other, younger, human females, Zak looked the admiral in the eye, for he had learned quickly that Vice Admiral Christos Papadomas measured a man, or a Garundan, by looking into their eyes.

"Ensign Zak." Began Papadomas in his low, steady voice that belied the screaming and cussing he was responsible for only a scant few minutes before. "It appears my appointment with the representatives of Yang and Schmidt Off-Planet Mining has been canceled. Can you shed some light on this change to my diary, by any chance?"

"Admiral, it occurred to me that the initial proposal for a mining license in the Q120 system needed some adjustment. I thought, an extra few days would be a sufficient delay for them to make the required changes before presenting their proposal to you in person."

Papadomas tilted his head to one side and gave the ensign a faint tease of a smile. "And what led you to that conclusion?"

This time, Zak's eyes briefly flicked away from the admiral's unblinking stare. *Probably the new Greek cuss words I've learned in the last five minutes,* Zak stifled the thought and answered. "I am aware of the admiral's penchant for grammar and spelling and I noted a few errors in need of correction."

Papadomas' shoulders shook as his bellowing laughter filled the room. Zak remained impassive while Papadomas struggled to curb his outburst and wagged a thick finger at the Garundan ensign. "You, Ensign Zak, are a skilled liar, so much so that I believe you have selected the wrong path. Perhaps you should have considered a career as a politician?"

"I shall consider that a compliment, sir." Replied Zak poker faced.

"And what have you chosen to fill the sudden hole in my schedule with, Ensign?" Asked Papadomas, a smile now fixed on his face.

"Unfortunately, sir, you have yet to complete the review of the new legislation which Geneva is proposing to bring forward in the new year." Zak winced as Papadomas let out a loud groan.

"The best thing Geneva could do is force the Bureau of Colonization to take a hiatus on the issuing of all licenses across the board!" Exclaimed Papadomas and Zak settled himself in for the usual admiral's rant about politicians.

"I don't know how many times I've told the Joint Chiefs, that Survey Command doesn't have enough ships to carry out our primary task of surveying potential systems, never mind this running around trying to police the odd nut job who thinks he can land on any old planet and claim it for himself, or some corporation, that decides to do a little exploratory mining in some back of beyond system, where they think we will not notice." Papadomas flung his head back in exasperation and rubbed his hand across his brow.

Zak stood silently awaiting the admiral's frustration to ebb. There was no doubt that everything the admiral had said was truth. Garunda was in the first throes of expansion and their government had discovered these same problems.

Seemingly anyone who owned, or could hire, a gravity drive vessel was rushing off into the dark night to claim their own chunk of the pie. Zak had lost count of the times he had overheard Papadomas remind the Bureau of Colonization that the 'Selene Incident' had been a narrow escape. The Turak, who claimed that system, could easily have blown the SS *Charlotte Dundas* and her crew into atoms before Analisa Chavez and First Fleet rode to their rescue.

The more we expand the more likely we are to meet a race even more belligerent than the Turak, argued Papadomas. It seemed no matter the amount of senate hearings, full of politicians nodding in sage agreement, that Zak accompanied the admiral to, nothing was done to halt the flow of granted licenses.

Papadomas' opposite number at Colonial Support Command, Vice Admiral Zhan, was in full agreement with Papadomas and both admirals had pleaded their case for more funding and personnel before the Joint Chiefs. As usual the purse strings were loosened by a fraction of their requirements, still, it was better than nothing.

Now, this new legislation, sent out by President Madkin for consultation, proposed a new body overseen by the Department of Justice rather than the Department of Defense should form and be given federal powers to enforce federal law on any corporation or citizen of the Terran Republic throughout space.

From what Zak read, this police force would be based roughly on the existing Federal Marshal Service who had the power to call on any federal or local police for assistance. The section which got under Papadomas' skin, however, was that the FMS could request assistance from the Department of Defense in the execution of their duties. Papadomas was vociferously against Survey Command becoming a taxi service or removal service for illegal colonies or miners.

Pulling himself upright in his chair, Papadomas rested his eyes on the waiting ensign. "How about we give the paperwork a pass for the moment, eh?"

Papadomas' gaze shifted to the holo frame on his desk. The smiling miniature image of Kayla and the girls beamed back at him. His eldest daughter, Philippa, was now a lieutenant in the Terran Marine Corps. Maia was now at college on Mars, studying pre-med with plans to be a doctor like Kayla, while Odysseia, his youngest, was a precocious teen who thought she was indestructible and every rule was there to be broken. The picture had been taken by Papadomas while the family had been on vacation in Crete. Those happier times seemed so far away now.

Pushing himself to his feet Papadomas walked around his desk and patted Zak on the shoulder as he strolled past, over his shoulder he called back. "Odysseia has a practice music recital this afternoon. How about we skip out of the office and go catch it?"

Zak knew the admiral's *suggestion* was an order not a polite invitation and the Garundan grimaced as he reflected on the image of the youngest Papadomas girl dragging the bow across the strings of her violin. He could think of nothing worse.

Zak followed the admiral out of the office. Furiously tapping on his PAD, he alerted Mrs. Brown, the Papadomas' nanny come housekeeper, that the admiral was en route to the school and would most likely head home afterward. Zak knew Mrs. Brown would insist that he stay for dinner, that a late evening of work would follow, as the admiral caught up on the tasks he had skipped out on and the day would conclude in the early hours when Zak crashed onto his bed before rising a scant few hours later to prepare the day's briefing papers at 0600 hours.

Perhaps it was not too late for Zak to request a transfer back to Garunda?

✳ ✳ ✳

ZARMINDA | 20.3 LIGHT-YEARS FROM EARTH

"Papadomas huh?" Grunted the slightly balding colonel with a hint of a German accent as he eyed the woman standing to unyielding attention one pace in front of his desk, upon which were neat stacks of data chips and a row of PADs set in a perfect line like troops on a parade square.

"Sir, yes, sir! First Lieutenant Philippa Papadomas, Terran Marine Corps, reporting as ordered."

Colonel Andreas Kendale continued his visual inspection of the officer before him; a spotless dark green uniform with impeccable creases down the arms and legs and pinned to her chest a mix of ribbons, unusual for a junior officer.

Andreas' raised an eyebrow when his eyes fell on the single ribbon with a silver rosette pinned to its center; a Marine Commandant's Commendation upon combat award and above the band of color sat a pair of gold wings indicating the wearer's completion of the Master Drop Course. The ability to deploy covertly via exothermic insertion was a basic requirement of most special force's capable units of the Terran Defense Forces.

Below the golden wings hung the Combat Infantryman and Sniper designators. Then something caught Andreas eye. He raised his hand with index finger extended and pointed at a second set of wings, thinner and silvery than the first.

"Care to explain the pilot wings, Lieutenant?"

Philippa kept her eyes front, locked on the office wall exactly one foot above the colonel's head. "Sir, it seemed prudent to the Lieutenant that the ability to fly herself and those under her command out of a shit storm might be useful."

A choked half laugh caused Andreas to lean sideways at the waist and give the man lounging in the shadows against the wall behind Papadomas a withering look. In response the man raised both hands, palm out wards, before drawing his fingers across his lips in a zipping motion before flipping away an imaginary key. His actions did nothing to placate Andreas.

"Luckily, Lieutenant, we have the best pilots that the TDF have to offer here so hopefully we will not have to test your own piloting skills."

Philippa decided the colonel's statement required no response and remained silent, while the man called up some information which was now projected into the holo display above his desk. Andreas read the floating words slowly, the three occupants in the room remaining silent as he did. When he finished reading, Andreas once more met Philippa's eye.

"You come to us highly recommended, Lieutenant. In fact, the only reason that you are being given this opportunity is because Brigadier General Mills is a personal friend of mine and -" Andreas eyes hardened so Philippa did not mistake his meaning, "the general is not a woman to make these recommendations on a whim. We set the bar high here, Lieutenant, let's hope you reach it. Dismissed."

Philippa's hand came up sharply as she saluted the colonel. Holding the position until Andreas returned the salute with a lazy motion. Spinning in place, Philippa marched out of the office passing the room's other occupant whose face remained obscured in shadow.

With the office door closed once more, Brigadier General Vladimir Egnorov pushed himself off the wall he had been leaning against and flopped into the only other chair in the room. "Well?"

Andreas pushed his chair back from his desk, stretched out his long legs and intertwined his fingers behind his head, his counter persona was complete. "She looks good on paper, however..."

"However, paper is one thing." Agreed Egnorov. "Her saving grace is that she was a Mustang. Those ribbons on her chest are earned, not granted after a tick box course in training. She has paid her due as a grunt, down in the mud along with the rest of us. And you don't get a Commandant's Commendation for having shiny boots." Egnorov pointed out.

"Scuttlebutt has it her platoon commander called her father personally, pleading with him to get her to apply for a commission when he couldn't get her to do it herself." Said Andreas.

Egnorov let out a low whistle. "Now that's ballsy. Admiral Papadomas is not a man to suffer fools lightly."

"So... we give her a team and see how she handles it?" Asked Andreas.

Egnorov gave a confirmatory nod. "Make sure she has a decent Senior Non Com to point her in the right direction."

"Already assigned."

"Who did you give her?" Asked Egnorov.

The wide grin that spread over Andreas' face only served to pique the general's interest. Gradually a name dawned on him.

"No, tell me you didn't!" Exclaimed Egnorov.

Andreas allowed the grin to become a wide, cheesy smile.

Egnorov let out a short, barking laugh.

∗∗∗

As the door closed behind her, Philippa Papadomas let out the breath she had been holding.

That Colonel Kendale sure was a tight-ass, she thought before a cheerfully smiling man blocked her progress and held out his hand to her. Reacting by instinct Philippa shook it feeling the rough calluses on his hand.

This guy is no paper pusher.

"Welcome to Special Operations Unit Thunder, Boss." The man with the smile affixed to his face said.

About to berate him for his lack of salute, Philippa remembered in Thunder the only officer saluted was General Egnorov.

The general firmly believed this practice peculiar to special forces, had grown into a way of making them different from their regular spit and polish comrades-in-arms; despite the convention being born from the necessity to hide an officer's identity from the enemy, and avoid their demise on the battlefield. The same went for the designation 'Boss'. Only the general was called 'Sir' while every other officer in Thunder was known simply as 'Boss'.

Philippa swiftly hunted the man's uniform for a name or rank tag and came up empty. "Uh..." Noting the officer's consternation at not knowing how to address him, the trooper put Philippa out of her misery.

"Staff Sergeant Semple, Boss. I'll be your Team Number Two." Semple glanced down at the two kit bags resting off to one side. "Why don't we get your kit squared away and give you a chance -" Semple gestured to her green uniform, "to get changed into something more suitable before you meet the rest of the team."

Without another word, he set off in the direction of the Officers' Quarters leaving Philippa to hurriedly grab her bags and catch up with him.

"The team's designation is Team Nine." Semple said as soon as Philippa drew level with him. "We have seven troopers, apart from you and I." Semple produced a data chip from his breast pocket and held it out to Philippa.

Shifting one of the heavy bags to join the already considerable load on her other hand, Philippa took the data chip and slipped it into her own pocket before, mercifully, evenly distributing her load again.

"The troopers names are Tai, Browne, Leslie, Bishop, Gavin, Quinn and Rintoul. There service jackets and spec quals are on the data chip. For reasons unbeknown to me, Browne goes by the name Dunkerdink and Rintoul, God love us all, is better known as Sven the Magnificent."

"I think we'll stick to surnames, Staff Sergeant." Philippa said in a way she hoped Semple would take as the end of that particular conversation.

Semple gave a short chuckle. "Works for me, Boss." Rounding a corner, they were confronted by a utilitarian building indistinct from most of the buildings Philippa had seen so far on Thunder's base.

"Ah, here we are." Said Semple as he stopped and made a show of checking his wristwatch. "How about we say half an hour and I'll meet you back here?"

Resentment stirred in Philippa's gut at the way Semple set all the goal posts. *She was the officer here* and perhaps it was time she reminded the Staff Sergeant of that fact.

"No, I don't think so. Have the team muster here in an hour. I've not been for my daily run yet and I could do with stretching my muscles. I'm sure you and the team wouldn't mind joining me?" If Philippa thought her decision would wipe the smile off Semple's face she had miscalculated.

"Outstanding idea, Boss. An hour it is." And with that Semple walked off, a tuneless whistle emanating from his pursed lips.

Philippa watched his retreating back for a few moments before grabbing her bags and heading for the door leading into Officers' Quarters.

An hour to get booked in. Find a room. Get something to eat and then dig out my PT kit. Damn, I might have cut this a bit fine but Semple needs put back in his box before he thinks he can run roughshod over me, thought Philippa picking up her pace.

Semple continued strolling nonchalantly, until he rounded a drab gray building taking him out of his new officers' line of sight and he broke into a brisk jog.

Team Nine's bunk room was on the far side of the base, almost a kilometer and a half from his present location. By the time he got there, rounded up the team, made his way to his own quarters, got changed, and got back here ready for Boss' PT session he would be cutting it close.

Still, he had to smile to himself. Semple had been around the block. In fact, he had been a member of Thunder since its inception and was well aware how unusual it was for a mere lieutenant, let alone one straight out of officer training, to make it into this unit. Most officers never got the experience or combat skills needed to join Thunder until they had reached the rank of captain. The ribbons on Papadomas' chest went part way to explaining her presence within this elite unit. Semple knew her Marine Commandant's Commendation was not awarded lightly, he had two and both had earned him a stay in hospital.

She may have been a low-down grunt like him in the past but now she was an officer, and his new boss had passed a simple but important test in Semple's eyes. Did she have the bottle to remind someone who once outranked her but was now her junior that she was his boss? Semple felt another chuckle growing in his throat.

A PT session.

A great way to assess your team and, also, straight out of the Officer's Training Manual. Still, Papadomas had made the call.

That would do for a start. *This is going to be interesting,* thought Semple as he checked his watch again and increased his pace to give him another couple of minutes to get changed.

CHAPTER TEN

THE SEARCH CONTINUES

TDF *TYCHO BRAHE* | GATEWAY STATION | EDGE OF THE ASTEROID BELT | SOL SYSTEM

Terrance Wilson stepped into the corridor outside the bunk on the scientific research vessel TDF Tycho Brahe that was going to be his home for the foreseeable future. The ever enthusiastic Ensign Burkett was waiting to greet him and immediately began a meandering conversation about how he had spent the past two months either elbow deep in state of the art circuitry or perched in front of a computer terminal going over and over simulations to ensure that the problems which had plagued the first unsuccessful outing of the Deployable Stellar Detection Grid.

The brain child of Doctor Sylvia Sarkisian and designed to detect the earliest fluctuations in stars as far back as the Big Bang itself the project had been effectively hijacked by the navy's Department of Special Projects for the DSDG could very well be the key to locating the home of the Creator, the being responsible for sending the Others on their failed Ehita or religious mission to scour the stars clean of anything the Creator had deemed impure which, basically, meant every life form that was not one of their own. And carry out that mission they had. Untold billions had perished as the Others scoured planet after planet, system after system, clean of all intelligent life. Only by the thinnest of threads had humanity survived, and even then, that survival had come at great cost. It was only after the Others had been defeated that the truth behind the Creator myth came out.

The Others believed that at some time in their past the Creator had taken them from their home world and transported them to Assena where he had selected them among all other life in the galaxy to be his Chosen People and his instrument of destruction. Once the Ehita was complete the Creator had promised to once again reunite with his devout followers and take them to the promised world of Assena where the Chosen People would live forever in harmony with the Creator under the red star that bathed Assena in its warm glow. The Creator then transported them once more to the planet which they named Durav which would be their home until the Ehita was complete. However, the myth that the Others had once visited Assena persisted and it was that myth that had got a young Lieutenant Terrance Wilson who at the time was ensconced in an office at naval intelligence headquarters in Carson City to thinking.

The key to locating this Creator was the red star. Terrance had a rough date as to when the Others in their myth must have visited Assena because the planet where they had originated had been discovered. The fourth planet circling the star that humans called 9 Ceti some 66.5 light-years from Earth. The inhabitants of that planet had been wiped out by an artificially constructed biological plague specifically designed to kill anything that contained the merest trace of Saiph DNA. What had struck the medical team at the time though was that the degree of medical and technical skill to manufacture such a weapon was well beyond that attained by the natural inhabitants. A fact which pointed to outside interference. Again, this matched up with the Creator myth. Blood tests taken from captured Others showed that they were immune to the biological weapon. Another piece of the puzzle fell into place for had the Creator not specifically selected the Chosen People. Taking the destruction of the Others original home world as a basis for his time line, around A.D. 1000 by Earth standard, Terrance had proposed that if the Creator myth was to be believed then the Creator had, in the presence of the Others, made a red star disappear. All they had to do was locate a red star which without explanation suddenly disappeared in or around A.D. 1000. To Terrance that had appeared a simple thing to do, take a gravity drive equipped ship, fold out to a base line of 500 light-years from Durav, deploy the DSDG and hunt for red stars. Once you have located the requisite class of stars pack everything away and fold out fifty light-years. Repeat the same search parameters until one star disappears. Viola, the star that disappears is Assena. Simple.

Only it had proved not to be so simple. Repeated malfunctions of the DSDG had extended a planned fourteen-week mission into six months with nothing to show but a load of broken, expensive equipment at the end of it.

If Terrance was truthful, he was mentally and physically exhausted by the time Tycho Brahe returned to Gateway Station and the opportunity to see his wife Maggie and his bouncing baby son Richard, named after Maggie's father.

"So, how was the holiday on Janus, sir?" Asked Burkett.

It was the first thing that had actually managed to penetrate Terrance's thoughts as he dragged himself back to the present, surprised to find himself and Burkett standing outside the XO's quarters.

"Good. Good, thank you for asking." He replied hurriedly.

Burkett appeared totally oblivious to the fact that Terrance had no idea what he had said in the preceding five minutes during the walk from Terrance's quarters on Deck Four to the XO's quarters on Deck Two.

"I'll leave you here then sir. Meet up in Deployment Control afterward?" Burkett said cheerfully.

"Eh... yeah sure. Deployment Control."

Burkett head off while Terrance took a minute to shake himself mentally before tapping the entry request key on the pad beside the door. With the soft whoosh of hydraulics, the door slipped to one side to reveal the seated form of Lieutenant Commander Darel Apter waving for Terrance to take a seat.

"Good to see you back in one-piece Terrance. What say we get this show on the road?"

Any thoughts of Maggie and Joshua disappeared as Terrance and Apter began going over the new specs of the improved DSDG both determined this time to locate their furtive quarry.

CHAPTER ELEVEN

ASHES TO ASHES AN EMPIRE IN FLAMES

EMPEROR YALO IV SPACEPORT | ALONA SYSTEM | 50,000 LIGHT-YEARS FROM EARTH

Whoever said that the early hours of the morning were the worst time to be on duty had been the wisest Alonan to have ever lived, thought Colonel Salak, Duty Watch Officer aboard Emperor Yalo IV Spaceport. The spaceport hung at the fringes of the Alonan systems' defense grid and was the only authorized gateway into the home system of the Alonan Empire. Beyond the spaceport's thick armor and heavy directed energy weapons, lay vast clouds of floating minefields, the pathways between them changed on a regular basis so no enemy could predict a clear route to the spaceport.

Further in-system lay the numerous buoys containing the oversized gravity drive nulling fields which would wreck any vessel's attempt to circumvent the spaceport and approach Alona or its populated neighbor Geta.

"Excuse me, sir." The voice of the young lieutenant overseeing the radar section sounded in his earphone. A voice that was full of apology for disturbing anyone who held the lofty rank of colonel.

Slowly Salak raised his arms above his head and stretched trying though failing miserably to shake the tiredness from them. "Go ahead, Lieutenant." Salak said as he reached across for his container of steaming kepta tea.

When the younger officer hesitated Salak turned to face the sensor section located less than a dozen meters from Salak's own seat. "Spit it out, Lieutenant." Salak commanded with disdain.

"Could you come over and look at this, sir. I think we have a better fix on those sensor ghosts that the late shift warned us about. And..."

Salak let out an irritated sigh and forced himself to count to five before speaking. "And what, Lieutenant?"

The lieutenant got the distinct feeling he was about to be the target of the colonel's wrath, however, he stuck to his guns, steadied his breathing and tried to speak with confidence that his mildly trembling legs belied. "Sir, I'm tracking multiple inbounds that appear to be attempting to hide their course with a very subtle ECM."

May the emperors passed save us from inexperienced officers that see a threat in every passing meteor cloud thought Salak as he unplugged his headset and casually wandered over to the sensor section. The junior officer subserviently moved aside as the colonel approached. To ensure the Lieutenant understood his superior's annoyance at having to walk a whole fifteen steps Salak made sure to give him a hard stare before switching his attention to the display and the trace which was in all likelihood a few hundred tonnes of rock tumbling through space at the edges of the sensor system's detection range before once more disappearing into the depths of space.

What Salak saw caused his Kepta to halt halfway to his lips. After a moment he pushed the steaming container into the lieutenant's hands while he moved the rating seated directly in front of the display out of the way so he could get an unobstructed view of the screen.

"Emperors protect us!" Salak whispered as he ran back to his console and brought his hand down on the battle station's alarm praying, he was not too late, but in his heart, he knew the truth.

At the equivalent to knife fighting range in space warfare, just three hundred kilometers, the tiny electronic brains of a dozen missiles judged they were within range of their designated targets; electrical pulses cascaded through a series of cables and the complex magnetic fields clutching the warheads collapsed.

Each missile contained just 250 grams of antimatter; enough to annihilate its equivalent weight in matter and release an explosion of ten megatonnes.

In less than a second, the shock wave evaporated the outer armored skin of the spaceport like a butterfly's wings under a high-powered laser.

Onward the shock wave rushed, crushing, pulverizing and super-heating anything it touched.

In less time than it took to blink, Emperor Yalo IV Spaceport and the thousands of Imperial Navy personnel who called it home ceased to exist.

Barely slowed by the bulk of the spaceport, the shock wave plunged in-system, into the mass of the floating mine fields and defensive weapon's platforms, that had already proven ineffective, and rendered all things within a million kilometers utterly useless due to physical damage or from the massive electromagnetic pulse.

The shock wave began to dissipate and revealed asteroids, in existence from the beginning of the Alonan solar system, pulverized to dust.

If any Alonan sensor system had survived the attack it would have noted a series of brief, eerie green flashes beyond the reach of eyes. As the shock wave passed beyond these ghosts, they flickered out of existence and the space around what had once been the gateway to the Alonan system returned to peace.

***

COMMAND DECK | LEAD CRUISER | FIRST WING | SAIPH FLEET
The floor beneath the Supreme Leader's feet vibrated and a satisfied smile spread across his features. The cruiser's engines had switched to full power, taking up the extra load to supplement the energy fields protecting the ship from the fury of the shock wave. The vibration subsided as the shock wave of the weapons he had unleashed against the Alonans passed and raced onward.

"All ships report ready to proceed, Supreme Leader." Reported Star Leader Foral from his seat at the center of the Command Deck. Foral had insisted that the Supreme leader sit in the center seat, however, the Supreme leader was adamant that Foral retain his place of command during the assault on the half-breed's system.

"The fleet is yours, Star Leader Foral. Let us be about our business."

Foral bowed his head in acknowledgment; the Saiph Command Deck personnel had just witnessed the Supreme leader pass the honor of leading the attack against the half-breeds, and bestow that honor on the man who had trained the fleet that now hung like angry beasts, ready to be released and fall upon their prey.

"Communications, signal Second Wing and Third Wing that we are proceeding as planned. The null gravity generators in this sector are destroyed and we will engage our gravity drive to place us closer to the target. We will repeat the process of destroying the generators and enemy vessels by employing antimatter warheads. Inform them I expect this to take no longer than one hour from now. Second Fleet is to assume position at system north to interdict any fleeing enemy vessels or communications drones. Third Wing is to assume reciprocal positions at system south with the same task."

Foral tried not to grip the arms of his seat too tightly as Communications relayed his orders to Second Wing commanded by Wing Leader Nokal and Third Wing commanded by Caretaker Geoll.

Foral had had his doubts about entrusting an entire wing to Geoll, however, the Supreme leader had pointed out that the people needed to see that the Originals, as those who had entered suspended animation with the Supreme Leader had become known, had the utmost faith in their progeny and first among that progeny was the Geoll. By allowing him to command a crucial element of the attack on Alona, it showed the masses awaiting his orders back on the Dyson Sphere that he considered them equals. As much a pure blood Saiph as those who forced from their home world so long ago.

"Orders acknowledged, sir." Came the call from Communications.

The Supreme Leader rested a hand lightly on the shoulder of his oldest friend. "Our destiny awaits, my friend."

"Then let us not keep it waiting, shall we." Foral replied in a voice low enough that only the Supreme Leader heard. "Helm, take us in." Foral said loud enough for the entire Command Deck to hear.

Three hundred Saiph cruisers, the color of the darkest night, blinked out of existence.

The Empire was oblivious to the fact they were already under attack.

* * *

THE IMPERIAL PALACE | ALONA

"Madam Ambassador," began Minister Hozal in that whining tone that grated on \Court of Emperor Paxt, the Ninth of the Alonan Empire and she did her damnedest to keep her face neutral, "the Empire must protest at the overtly aggressive wording used by your joint governments in this communique."

"I believe the language used expresses our concerns of a violation of this magnitude." Unnati replied in her firmest, no nonsense tone.

Too aggressive my behind, she thought, *you crushed a man's leg in a door so badly it had to be amputated!* Unnati knew a prosthetic limb would give the man his full mobility back, but she appreciated the difficulties he and his family faced with months of rehab. *So, screw you and your niceties!*

"There was no violation." Came a strong voice, unused to being questioned.

Unnati moved her gaze away from the Alonan Foreign Minister and steadied it on Grand Admiral Raga, Commander of the Imperial Navy, and the man whose ship the observer had been attempting to board.

Tag teaming me, eh? Obviously, you've not read my file- University's female wrestling champion three years running!

"How is an assault on a serving officer of the Terran Defense Forces not a violation of the Joint Observer Treaty, as signed by the respective heads of my governments and -" Unnati allowed her eyes to linger momentarily on the personage sat upon the raised dais, before which she stood, then returned them to Grand Admiral Raga, "the emperor himself?" Her last comment elicited the expected response

"How dare you cast aspersions upon the honor of the emperor." Raged Hozal. "This is a matter of imperial security..." The minister's voice trailed off as he realized what he had just said, his face reddening even more as he caught the flicker of a smile play across Unnati's lips.

"Imperial security you say-" *Got you!* Thought Unnati as she continued in a deadpan voice, "perhaps if you were to explain why this particular vessel was involved in such a highly sensitive matter, one which precluded the presence of a Commonwealth observer, we could put this matter to bed and move on to the subject of suitable compensation for the officer involved."

"Compensation!" Hozal blustered only for the doors leading to the emperor's private office to abruptly open. Four Alonan soldiers sprinted in, weapons drawn and looking like they would broker no interference.

Three of the soldiers spaced themselves equally around the dais the fourth, the commander, took the steps two at a time and with no hesitation leaned in close to the emperor and whispered a short, curt sentence. The emperor turned white as a sheet for a moment, before recovering and speaking directly to Unnati.

"I am sorry, Madam Ambassador, this audience is at an end. The Palace Guard will be here shortly to escort you safely back to your embassy."

Unnati's head spun with the sudden turn of events.

Only once, in her years of diplomatic service had she witnessed such an action play out in view of a foreign diplomat. That had been when the Black Ships attacked and destroyed Dagger Station in the Garundan System. Unnati had been second in command of the CUOP's liaison office and was in the middle of negotiating a new trade treaty when a similar group of heavily armed Garundan soldiers had burst into the room and hustled the entire Garundan delegation from the room. It was only after the all clear was given that Unnati came to realize that she and the remaining open-mouthed in disbelief diplomats, had been left to fend for themselves.

By the looks of things, she would be abandoned again, unless she did something about it.

"We know about Foram!" She blurted out.

Even at the height of this emergency the name Foram caused a reaction. Grand Admiral Raga flung a look her way before grabbing the arm of the nearest soldier. "Bring her."

Without a care for her modesty the soldier wrapped a meaty hand around the human woman's arm, so hard, Unnati was sure it would leave a bruise. Nearly lifting her off her feet she was half carried, half dragged through the doors into the emperor's private office where one section of ornately decorated wall had slid aside to reveal a hidden elevator.

Seven Garundans and one human squeezed into a space designed for half that number, Unnati guessed. The doors closed and the elevator dropped like an earth-sick stone. The contents of Unnati's stomach did its best to climb back up her throat as the elevator continued to plummet.

After an eternity or more likely, less than a minute, the doors slid open and Unnati was once more a mere puppet in the arms of the soldier. The elevator opened onto a short tunnel with a curved roof and rough walls. After a short distance, the corridor reached a door, the like of which Unnati had never seen outside the bridge of a battleship. It stretched from floor to ceiling and, in its open position, Unnati saw it was at least two meters thick. With little pause the group moved through the entrance and, belying its size, the door closed as quietly as a mouse behind them. A faint popping in her ears eluded to the fact that they were now in a pressurized environment.

"Stand in the corner and be quiet." Ordered Raga roughly. The hard look in the eyes of her escort assured her that, ambassador or not, she would follow the grand admiral's orders.

"Report!" Ordered Raga to a harried looking captain who madly dashed between multiple terminals to extract and assess the flood of information. His delayed response did not bode well for his career prospects. "I said report!" Roared Raga as his head swiveled from left to right and took in the picture of confusion. "Where is the duty officer?" Raga asked in low, threatening tones.

The agitated captain threw a glance at the heavy, armored doors, implying to those in the room that the officer in charge of the bunker had found himself on the wrong side of the door, on the most crucial day of his military life.

Aware that the captain was about to lose his mind, the emperor himself stepped around Raga, gently placed his hands on the man's shoulders and looked into his pale face.

"Captain, take a deep breath and tell us what you know."

The captain, in return, took several shuddering breaths while his mouth continued to work without sound. After a few moments, the officer closed his eyes, took one final, calming breath then opened his eyes and began to speak.

"Ten minutes ago, all contact with Emperor Yalo IV Spaceport was lost. We've also lost communication with all vessels, both military and civilian, which were reported in the vicinity of the spaceport."

"Probably just a solar flare interfering with communications." Proposed Minister Hozal. His comment earned him a derisory look from Raga. "A solar flare would have hit us first, Minister, not a space station millions of kilometers further out than we are from the sun." Dismissing the politician Raga returned his attention to the captain. "Continue."

"Central Command have detected massive detonations in the area of the spaceport and a second series of detonations, further in-system minutes later. At this time Central Command theorize that the Alonan System is under attack and are responding accordingly."

Raga scanned the information appearing at an alarming rate on the terminal behind the captain. "I need to get to Central Command and take charge. This is an attack, and from the energy profiles of these weapons I would bet my life that somebody out there is flinging around antimatter warheads."

Despite her previous warning to be silent, Unnati could not help herself. "Antimatter? There is only one group who have that tech and are willing to use it..."

"The Saiph." Said the emperor finishing Unnati's sentence for her.

"Your Majesty, time is of the essence I must reach Central Command and coordinate our defense."

The emperor nodded and the captain tapped a series of commands into his computer. With a gentle whoosh the armored door swung open, when the opening became just wide enough, Raga raced through and headed to the elevator at a dead run.

"Good luck, my friend." Unnati heard the emperor say in a low whisper as the captain re sealed the bunker. Turning to face Unnati he gave her a wry smile. "It looks like we are in the hands of the emperor's past ambassador." As though the last few minutes had drained the energy from him the emperor reached for a chair only for one of his bodyguards to rush forward and fetch it for him.

"Thank you. Perhaps one for Minister Hozal, and the ambassador, also?"

The clatter of casters rolling across the rough flooring broke the comparative peace of the bunker as the bodyguard hurried to obey. Unnati gratefully sat, suddenly feeling exhausted; logic dictated that the adrenalin ebbing from her system was the culprit, but logic couldn't stop her letting out a soft satisfied sigh as she sat on the soft seat.

That moment of relaxation disappeared when the captain's animated voice filled the bunker. "The fleet is engaging, Your Majesty!"

* * *

INS *RAKO* | 200 MILLION KILOMETERS FROM ALONA

Lieutenant Commander Wail Bitar grunted as his restraints cut into his shoulder blades as the Alonan heavy cruiser INS *Rako* completed its radical maneuver to avoid a barrage of directed energy weapons slicing through the space where the cruiser had just been.

"Comms, order *Yavalo* and *Juslak* to continue their attack. *Rako*, *Tuval* and *Posak* will retire and regroup at -" Brigadier General Wavak punched a series of queries into the nav computer mounted on his seat's armrest, "One-eight-nine-five-six, mark two eight."

"Bow magazine is running critically low, sir!" Called someone from Bitar's right.

Abruptly, the *Rako* heaved upwards and lifted Bitar clear from his seat only for the restraints to react and lock him in place once more. His head bounced off the padding of the neck rest and caused stars to form in front of his eyes.

Bitar shook his head to clear his vision and tried to focus on the large holo display that sat at the center of the *Rako's* bridge. When Wail Bitar had come aboard the *Rako* as part of the Observer Program he had familiarized himself with as much Alonan equipment as possible, that was his job as an intelligence officer, after all. As such, he was able to interpret the current tactical situation as competently as Wavak and the other members of the bridge crew. The Alonans were taking a beating and no matter the firepower they flung at the oncoming Black Ships of the Saiph they appeared unstoppable.

The Alonans had been caught flat footed.

The Empire relied completely on their gravity drive nulling generators to prevent vessels encroaching on the inner system. They had not counted on an enemy that was willing to expend hundreds of antimatter missiles to blow holes in their defenses then fold into the gap and repeat the process.

Instead of the aggressors taking hours, if not days, battling through DEW platforms, minefields and the Imperial Navy, the Saiph had taken less than forty-five minutes to reach the final Alonan defensive line, before the Black Ships could fold directly into orbit around the heart of the Empire.

The gravity drive nulling generators were supposed to make it impossible for an enemy to use their gravity drive engines and fold within the Alonan System, instead, they had hindered the Imperial Navy's response.

With the generators active the Imperial Navy found its units scattered throughout the system and unable to present a cohesive counterattack with enough force to block or stall the Saiph. Unfortunately, Bitar fully understood their predicament. Deactivate the generators and the Saiph would simply fold into Alonan orbit and attack the planet directly. Leave the generators online and the Imperial Navy would have to rely on their standard drive systems to maneuver them into a position and engage the enemy.

The holo display made it plain to Bitar, the Imperial Navy could not win this race.

Rako bucked again, this time an ear-piercing whistle accompanied the wrenching. *Shit! We're losing atmosphere,* Bitar thought as he grabbed for the helmet stowed in the rack beside his seat.

With a loud screech, like the death throes of a giant animal, the entire front end of the *Rako* tore away and exposed the bridge to the cold of space. Bright pinpoints of stars, slowly rotating, replaced the holo display and Bitar, still strapped into his seat, tumbled away.

"How beautiful." Bitar commented on the brilliant flashes of light filling the sky, before the absence of oxygen caused him to slip into unconsciousness and into the icy grasp of death.

∗ ∗ ∗

THE BUNKER | 750 METERS BELOW THE IMPERIAL PALACE | ALONA

"We are no longer the masters of our own destiny." Said Emperor Paxt softly.

"Excuse me, Your Majesty?" Asked Unnati thinking she had misheard him.

The emperor graced her with a slow smile gesturing upwards at the gray, rough cast ceiling with one finger. "Somewhere up there, brave soldiers are fighting and dying while I sit safe and secure here, in this armored hole in the ground."

"I wouldn't put it like that…" Unnati began to say before Minister Hozal spoke over her.

"Continuity of government and the safety of the emperor are the highest priorities of the state, Your Majesty."

"Yes, yes, Hozal, I am fully aware of our policy." The emperor let out a soft sigh. "Still –"

"Our forces will be victorious, Your Majesty. Of that I am certain." Gushed Hozal enthusiastically.

Emperor Paxt patted the minister's leg gently and gave him a wry smile. "Of that, I am not so sure."

Unnati cleared her throat to gain the emperor's attention. "I request that I be allowed to contact my embassy, Your Majesty."

Before the emperor replied the ground beneath them shook and the air filled with fine, powdery dust. Two of the bodyguards moved in and shielded the emperor's body with their own.

"Enough!" Shouted the emperor as he pushed them away. "Do you think your flesh and blood will be enough to protect me, if the roof and the mountain above decide to fall on top of us?" The bodyguards retreated sheepishly and resumed their positions at the periphery of the room.

Ignoring them, the emperor turned his attention to the captain still fixated on his displays despite, what could only have been, a near miss from a nuclear detonation.

Thoughts of the death and destruction, which must have been raging through his beloved capital city of Bozra, dominated his mind. He pictured the Imperial Palace, built by the very first emperor, to be nothing but tangled and twisted lumps of steel and concrete. To collect his thoughts, the emperor closed his eyes for a moment, before speaking. "Captain. Connect the ambassador with her embassy please."

After five attempts and more than one phrase which should not be said within earshot of the emperor, the captain turned to the emperor and Unnati with a troubled look in his eyes. "I'm sorry, Your Majesty, all communications beyond this room are out. We are completely isolated."

Unnati pushed back in her chair and ran a frustrated hand through her hair. She realized the embassy and everyone in it was gone; taken by the initial nuclear blast or the shock wave or the intense fireball which followed close behind. Unnati closed her eyes to block out the images of friends and colleagues that were no longer here.

A surprisingly warm hand cupped her own and she opened her eyes to see the emperor leaning in close to her. "I am sorry."

Unnati wiped at the tears which began to blur her vision, slowly nodding her head in thanks at the emperor's empathy, while above ground his capital city lay in ruins. Shaking off her morbidity she asked the question responsible for her presence there in the first place.

"Am I ever going to find out what Foram is?"

Hozal opened his mouth to say something, however, the upraised hand of the emperor stopped him dead in his tracks.

"Foram, Madam Ambassador, is the Empire's last hope."

Unnati was looking at him with wide, questioning eyes as a fifty megatonnes warhead detonated on the surface directly above the bunker.

The shock wave travelled through the ground and pulverized the bunker and its occupants in the blink of an eye.

✳✳✳

LEAD CRUISER | FIRST WING | SAIPH FLEET

The Supreme Leader watched impassively as flashes lit up the dense clouds rapidly obscuring the surface of the planet below.

The deaths of billions of innocents did not faze him, for those dying at his hand were half-breeds; the spawn of the misjudged and poorly executed plans of the Elders who had died at his command, if not at his own hand, so long ago.

Star Leader Foral walked toward him and stopped at his side. Once they had entered orbit, the Supreme Leader had left the Command Deck and made his way to one of the few places on the cruiser where there was a window with an outside view. They stood in silence as flickers of light penetrated the debris-filled atmosphere for brief moments.

"Is it not a wondrous sight, my friend?" Said the Supreme Leader breaking the silence.

"Strangely hypnotic." Replied Foral.

Silence again filled the small room until the cloud cover became too dense to detect any further detonations.

"Have you come to report the successful conclusion of our objectives?"

"I have." Said Foral formally. "I can report that the two populated worlds in this system have been cleansed of the half-breed infestation. All Alonan orbital facilities are obliterated. Their fleet, for what it was worth, is now nothing more than pieces of floating debris and clouds of gas."

"And what of ships fleeing the system or attempts to launch communications drones?"

"Second and Third Wing have successfully intercepted every vessel making such an attempt. As per your orders, they dispatched each ship when it came into range. We have no indication that any communications drones escaped, to warn either the Alonan colony worlds or the Commonwealth. Second Wing is now carrying out a purge of the half-breed's mining facilities in the asteroid belt, while Third Wing is hunting any small, low-lying ships which may be avoiding us."

The Supreme Leader clapped Foral on the back happily. "Excellent work. Are you confident now in Geoll and his crew mates?"

"They have carried out their orders without hesitation Supreme Leader. Caretaker Geoll has earned my full confidence and trust. He is a true Saiph and dedicated to our goal."

"Then please inform Second and Third Wings to complete their tasks forthwith, join up with us and we shall head for home. We have much to celebrate after our victory today."

"And the many victories to come." Said Foral before leaving the Supreme Leader alone gazing out the window that gave such a breathtaking view of the dying gasps of the Alonan Empire.

✳ ✳ ✳

COMMAND DECK | LEAD CRUISER | SECOND WING | SAIPH FLEET

"Unknown warship! Unknown warship! We are an unarmed mining station. We have no offensive or defensive weaponry. We surrender! We surrender! Please acknowledge. For pity's sake we have women and children aboard!"

Geoll tapped a control and cut the pleading voice in his ear bud.

Swiveling his head so he saw the weapons officer clearly. "Confirm weapons lock and fire at will."

"Lock confirmed... Missile away!"

Geoll averted his eyes from the holo display tracking the progress of the single missile.

"Time to impact fifteen seconds... ten seconds... five seconds... target destroyed." Reported the weapons officer.

"Very well." Said Geoll struggling to keep the unfamiliar emotions tugging at his soul from presenting in his voice. "Navigation. Set course for the flag ship."

As Geoll bent to read the departmental situation reports gradually compiling on his command display, he caught the eye of Trakl, his second in command, and noticed something odd. Trakl's features seemed to reflect the troubling thoughts entering his own mind, no matter how hard he tried to suppress them. Each Saiph held the other's eyes for a split second longer before returning to their duties.

There was a war to be won, Geoll reminded himself, and in war actions must be taken for the greater good. No matter how unpleasant.

Don't they?

CHAPTER TWELVE

THE EMPEROR IS DEAD, LONG LIVE THE EMPEROR

WAYPOINT 4. | 5,000 LIGHT-YEARS FROM ALONA | INTERSTELLAR SPACE
A flashing red light in the top right corner of the small holo display accompanied the demanding buzzing of an incoming comms call that held a currently never-ending list of quarterly performance reviews that, the Executive Officer said, required his sign-off. Kenichi Sutou was unconvinced and suggested, half in jest and half in seriousness, that the XO learn to forge the Commanding Officer of TDF *Sorcerer*'s signature. Thankful for a respite in the tedious paperwork Kenichi accepted the incoming call. The face of a Persai Sub Leader replaced the mind-numbing list of files. The title bar along the bottom of the display indicated that he was the Communication Officer aboard Waypoint 4., the final Commonwealth outpost before entering Alonan Imperial space.

"Commander Sutou." Said the Persai in the deep growl of an officer who wanted to see the end of his shift, before the sheer boredom of his job caused him to fling himself out of the nearest airlock.

"The daily diplomatic communications drone from Alona has not arrived. Two subsequent requests by drone for updates to the embassies status have also failed to return." Kenichi could feel whatever relief had had at the thought of a break from paperwork drain out of him as he realized what was coming next.

"Standard Operating Procedure requires that the duty courier ship of the day –" the Persai officers eyes shifted momentarily as he checked something on a different display, "I'm showing that to be your ship TDF *Sorcerer*. Is to make its way without delay to Emperor Yalo IV Spaceport and ascertain the current situation at the embassy." The Persai's face softened as much as an eight-foot werewolf like face could. "If it's any consolation Commander the last ship through here reported that the Alonans were having some equipment issues. Something about sensor ghosts and interference on their comms' channels so, you might discover that it's simply an equipment fault at their end and your trip is a waste of time."

"Let's all hope so." Kenichi replied through gritted teeth. As the link terminated Kenichi's chin dropped to his chest and a loud sigh passed his lips. Hey, look on the bright side Kenichi he thought at least you get out of doing the paperwork for a while. An evil smile spread across his face as he eyed the large red button protected by the clear plastic cover that lay easily within arm's reach. Well, we may as well get some training value out of this milk run and with a flourish, he flipped up the cover and depressed the red button below. The hooting sound of the battle stations alarm blared out in every section of the ship and Kenichi hummed quietly to himself as he sealed the collar of his uniform. The sound of shouts and running feet came from the corridor beyond his cabin as the crew of the *Sorcerer* raced to their stations.

✳ ✳ ✳

TDF *SORCERER* | WAYPOINT 4.

"Ready to fold on your order, Sir."

Kenichi paused for a second before answering allowing his eyes one final inspection of the *Sorcerer*'s bridge noting with a small smile the freshly pressed uniform that adorned the XO. It was in stark contrast to the one he had been wearing when Kenichi had sauntered onto the bridge after sounding the battle stations alarm and giving the crew a small, unscheduled drill. That particular uniform had had a very large brown coffee stain which had covered the entire upper chest and lap of the normally pristine XO. To rub salt into the wound Kenichi had allowed the drill to progress until each and every department had reported sealed and ready for action before he had stood the ship down allowing the XO to quickly nip off to his quarters and get changed into a fresh uniform.

Now however, *Sorcerer* was at Condition 3. with fully one-third of the crew on watch and all strategic stations, including weapons, manned. After *Sorcerer*'s last foray into Alonan space everyone appreciated Kenichi's wariness. If it had not been for the lighting reactions of the ships helmsman when the destroyer had been facing a squadron of Imperial Cruisers who were out for the blood of whoever was responsible for laying waste to the colony world of Balat then there was a very good chance that they would not have been here today.

"Fold!" Ordered Kenichi as he felt that now all too familiar mild disorientation as his body and the ship briefly entered null space before reemerging once more into normal space. Kenichi was about to order a complete sensor suite when the hull of the *Sorcerer* wrung like some giant had struck it with a hammer.

"What the hell..." Began Kenichi only to be drowned out by the collision alarm. There shouldn't be a debris field here thought Kenichi this is the major approach lane to the biggest space station in Imperial space.

"Get us into some clear space and then find out where the hell we are because it sure ain't Alona."

Sorcerer continued to bang like a gong for longer than Kenichi would have liked as the ship maneuvered clear of the debris field. Eventually peace and quiet returned with the exception of Navigation where the XO was leaning over the shoulder of the Nav Officer and his chief as they worked furiously to figure out where they had gone awry in their computations and where that error had dumped *Sorcerer*. After a few minutes where Kenichi witnessed a number of intense discussions between the XO, the Nav Officer and the chief, Kenichi decided to intervene.

"If you ladies have come to a conclusion would you choose to enlighten the rest of us?"

"Sir," said the XO, "we have arrived at our intended destination. This is indeed the Alonan System and Emperor Yalo IV Spaceport should be directly ahead of us."

Kenichi regarded the XO for less than a heartbeat before he sprang into action. "Sound battle stations! Sensors full, I don't give a damn if the Alonans don't like us using our sensors so close to their space. Comms, all frequencies broadcast. Identify us and warn any vessel not to approach or they may be fired upon without warning. XO, once we have a full sensor picture, I want it and our logs downloaded to the ready comms probe and get it away soonest."

If anyone on the bridge thought that Kenichi was overreacting, then they held their tongues instead choosing to follow Kenichi's orders. It took only a few minutes for his prudent behavior to be proved correct.

"All indications point to one hell of a fight happening here, and not too long-ago sir." The XO reported. "My best guess is that the debris field we emerged in was actually the remains of the spaceport. I'm also getting massive readings from further in-system. I would confidently say that a massive fleet action took place here, and sir..."

Kenichi tore his eyes away from the data which the XO based his findings on scrolling across his repeater screen. "Spit it out XO."

"Somebody has been flinging antimatter around this system like confetti. To the best of my knowledge the only people who have access to those sorts of weapons in the quantity required to give these readings are the Saiph."

The XO's final statement made Kenichi's mind up for him. "Navigation. Plot us a course back to Waypoint 4. I've seen enough for one day."

Minutes later *Sorcerer* entered fold space leaving the ghosts of the Alonan Empire the only residents of the dead system... Well not quite.

From behind an asteroid over a hundred kilometers across, crept a small personnel shuttle, almost dwarfed by its own gravity drive. The crew of the shuttle had been en route to Foram. However, a ridiculous rule, so thought the shuttle crew, denied any vessel, folding out to Foram, from entering fold space directly from the Alonan System

The crew decided the protocol was devised by a security weasel who had never been into space for everyone knew it was impossible to track a ship through fold space.

Now, though. That same rule had saved the life of the four Alonans aboard the shuttle. The pilot had decided to have a bit of fun with the rule and had shaped her course to take him through an extremely thick part of the systems asteroid belt thinking that she may as well get some practice in while carrying out her orders to the letter. When the Saiph had appeared without warning the shuttle was already well into a boulder strewn field which, more by chance than planning, provided excellent cover from the Saiph sensors. For hours the crew and passengers had forced themselves to listen to the ongoing battle. Then had come the declarations of surrender swiftly followed by the calls for mercy. When the comms frequencies had fallen silent the small shuttle had stayed put until the air had started to thicken and the cold had begun to penetrate the thin hull. The female pilot had been about to emerge from cover when the Human destroyer had arrived. Once more, they went into hiding not knowing whether the Humans were friend or foe. Now they had left, the pilot edged the shuttle clear of the asteroid and set course for Foram, praying to the ancestors that the base still existed and had not fallen to the Saiph.

✳ ✳ ✳

FORAM SYSTEM | THIRTY-SIX LIGHT-YEARS FROM ALONA

"This is certainly a most impressive facility you have here General Lura." Stated Governor Posta. The Governor of the Alonan colony world of Kathan sentiments were reinforced by those of her fellow governor. Governor Dala of Opero.

"Yes, indeed General. And the Empire managed to keep this beyond the prying eyes of the Commonwealth. Indeed, remarkable."

"Believe me Governors it was not an easy thing to do and we had our suspicions that the Commonwealth had at least an inkling that something was being kept from them. However, all that we have done to keep this facility and its secrets has been for naught." Lura gestured for the governors to sit.

Lura's frankness was, in a way, refreshing thought Chief Scientist Kilor who continued to sit quietly as the necessary pleasantries were completed. Both the governors were political appointments and as such conversed in the vain of their profession. The situation at hand though, called for more direct speaking.

"The situation as we understand it at the moment is this." Lura began with the minimum of preamble. "The entire Alonan System has been destroyed. Population centers, big and small, on both Alona itself and Geta were target by high order nuclear detonations. My initial estimate is that casualties among the civilian population will be near total."

Whatever the governors had expected to hear it was worse than they had feared. Governor Dala clasped his hands together to cover a mild shake while Governor Posta said nothing though her body posture allied with her slow steady breathing spoke volumes of the struggle she was having internally to control herself. Lura appeared oblivious to it all as he continued speaking

"Our industrial and manufacturing base has ceased to exist. Both your colonies can no longer rely on the home system providing you with essentials."

"But. But..." Stammered Dala. "We are nowhere near self-sufficient for even the basics such as food and raw materials for construction. Never mind that the Saiph could turn up in our space any second. I demand that you dispatch warships immediately to protect us!" Dala flicked a look across to Posta obviously expecting her to support him. If he did then he had miscalculated for when she spoke, she ignored Dala and addressed Lura directly.

"You are the expert here General. What are our options?"

Lura regarded her steadily for a moment before speaking. "In plain language Governors, we lost."

Both politician's jaws dropped open in unison and, if this had not been so serious, Kilor was sure he would have burst out in uncontrollable laughter.

"The Emperor is most certainly dead. As is the Cabinet. The Legislator. The heads of all the armed forces. All the elected governors," Lura managed to crack a small smile which did not reach his eyes, "with the exception of present company of course. Kathan is nowhere near self-sufficient. Opero barely so." Lura spread his arms to indicate the room around him. "Here at Foram we have barely enough food and water to survive a couple of months, possibly three if we introduce rationing."

Governor Dala had managed to recover his wits somewhat and was now thinking with his brain again and not his fear. "A military man like you always has a plan General. So, tell us. What do you think we should do?"

Lura stood and paced around the small room with his hands clasped behind his back attempting to give himself time to figure out how to explain his plan. Kilor did it for him.

"We propose to go to the Commonwealth and request aid." Said the chief scientist sitting back and preparing for the onslaught of derision that he knew must follow. The Empire hated the Commonwealth. A hatred born of humiliation and that sort of hatred went all the way through you to the bones.

Dala opened his mouth to protest however, Posta laid a restraining hand on his forearm.

"Think about it logically for a moment Dala." She said. "How are you going to feed and clothe your people? How are you going to keep them warm in winter? And, past Emperors bless us, how are you going to protect them if the Saiph return?"

"We will fight them!" Dala said resolutely.

Kilor could not contain himself and a small chuckle escaped him. "With what Governor? Sticks and stones."

Enraged Dala sprung to his feet leaning his face close enough into the scientist that Kilor could smell his fetid breath. "With the warships that are floating so serenely beyond these walls! What are you? Are you a coward Kilor?"

The scientist began to rise to his own feet only for a strong hand to press him back down into his seat.

"No Dala. Kilor has a better grasp of the practicalities of the situation than you. Yes, I could send my warships against the Saiph and I can tell you right now what would happen -" Lura paused to ensure Dala was paying full, undivided attention. "Every person aboard those ships would die a glorious, futile death and achieve nothing!"

"And why would the Commonwealth come to our aid?" Asked Dala derisively. "Out of the goodness of their hearts. Out of some sense of higher moral purpose?"

"Possibly." Countered Lura. "They have done it before. When the Others attacked had it not been for the Human Admiral Jing the Empire could very well have fallen that day."

That brought a loud harrumph from Dala who pushed back from the table and folded his arms signaling he had finished being a part of this conversation. Posta, on the other hand, sensed that the General had something more up his sleeve and was determined to sniff it out.

"Those warships we seen as we arrived General -" For the first time a genuine smile flickered on the face of Lura. "I'm no expert but they seem awfully advanced. No disrespect to Chief Scientist Kilor here -" she said nodding in Kilor's direction, "per chance have you had some outside assistance the identity of which you would be willing to share with us?"

Lura gave Kilor a curt nod and the scientist tapped a control which activated a holo cube. Within the holo cube hung a ship. A ship so different in appearance to any in the Alonan inventory that it literally screamed out 'Alien'!

"This is the *Savior*. Designed and built by the Saiph generations ago to store in stasis everything required to build a new Saiph home world from the ground up."

By the state of the eyeballs bulging out of Dala and Posta's heads Kilor was sure he had their full and undivided attention.

"For the past year or so we have been taking the best of Saiph technology and incorporating it into our own designs resulting in the warships you, Governor Dala, alluded to. We believe these ships to be the equal of any Black Ship the Saiph can currently field. Our problem is numbers. We simply did not have the resources to build enough ships quickly enough to counter the Saiph threat."

Posta pointedly looked at Lura. "But the Commonwealth do."

Lura shrugged his shoulders. "They are, by far, the largest and most efficient producers of high tech in the known galaxy."

Dala continued to stare at the Savior for a few moments longer before speaking. "Even with full access to a ship like that it would have taken you years, possibly decades to reverse engineer what I saw floating outside. You must have had help."

Kilor looked to Lura for permission before tapping another control. In the holo cube the image of the Savior disappeared to be replaced by that of a Saiph dressed in a one-piece dark blue uniform.

"Meet Okal. Commander of the Savior. He and his crew have been instrumental in helping us understand and adapt their technology for incorporation in our own ships. Without him, what you have seen outside would not exist."

For the second time in as many minutes jaws dropped open in disbelief though both Governors recovered more quickly this time.

"And why would a Saiph willingly help us? Build weapons that he knows will be used to kill other Saiph?" Demanded Dala.

"Quite simple really." Answered Lura. "The Saiph that crew the Black Ships are under the command of a man Okal calls the Supreme Leader. Apparently in the dim and distant past he had a bit of a falling out with the Elders who ran Saiph society. They imprisoned him and he promptly escaped fleeing the Saiph home world with a number of ships and followers. They established themselves somewhere among the stars before returning and destroying the Saiph home world."

Posta regarded Lura quizzically. "Your telling me that it was the Saiph who were responsible for wiping out the Saiph."

Lura nodded. "More or less."

Dala pointed a finger at the image of Okal. "And the Commander?"

"He –" Answered Kilor, "firmly believes that if the Elders were around today then they would want him to help us defeat the Supreme Leader. Simple really." Added Kilor with a wry smile.

"You are going to offer the Commonwealth Saiph tech and a real live crew of Saiph to help them make it work." Said Posta.

Lura shrugged in acknowledgment. "In exchange we get everything we need to turn Kathan and Opero into viable colonies. The Empire rises from the ashes."

Dala screwed up his face. "I see one major flaw in your plan General."

"There may be many flaws in my plan Governor. To which one do you refer?"

"For there to be an Empire it needs an Emperor and, as we have all accepted, Emperor Paxt perished with Alona."

All conversation in the room died as thoughts turned to the billions no longer with them. It fell to Posta to break the silence as she stood and straightened her spine taking a deep breath before speaking.

"General, Governor Dala and I may be political appointees however, we were also originally elected to the Legislator. I believe that fulfills the necessary requirements by law for us to select a new Emperor."

Kilor was struggling to believe what he was hearing. Was this woman vying to have herself crowned Empress in the midst of the near extinction of Alona not only as an Empire but as a race.

"You, however, are a military man and, in normal times would not be eligible to be considered for elevation to Emperor." Posta's voice grew firm and it seemed that Dala drew strength from her words. "These are not normal times General. The Alonan people need. No, demand a warrior to lead us. Our empire was born out of war, Emperor Paxt The First was a soldier with no mandate from the people. Today, here and now I wish to give you that mandate. The Empire needs an Emperor General Lura, are you willing to serve?"

Surprisingly Dala rose and stood shoulder to shoulder with Posta. "As elected Governor of Opero I second the proposal made by the Governor of Kathan."

Kilor was glad that he was sitting down as the conversation played out. He and Lura had discussed prior to the arrival of the Governors how they would effectively ambush them to get them to agree to the generals plan but *this*, this was completely unexpected. However, Lura had described him as a practical man and he could see the requirement for the few remaining Alonans to need a figure head. And what better figurehead could you have than an Emperor who was going to lead what was left of the Imperial Navy into battle. Under the table Kilor flicked his foot out, kicking Lura in the shin. The action broke the general out of the spell he had been in since Posta began speaking.

Tugging at the base of his uniform jacket the general brought himself to attention. "It would be my honor."

In unison Governor's Dala and Posta spoke the words heard so many times in the Imperial Palace. "The Emperor is dead, long live the Emperor!"

CHAPTER THIRTEEN

STRIKING A DEAL

WAYPOINT 4 | 5,000 LIGHT-YEARS FROM ALONA | INTERSTELLAR SPACE
Half a million kilometers from Waypoint 4. what a moment before had been an empty piece of space was now filled with a warship. A warship that the computers of the Commonwealth station were telling the duty personnel staring at their screens was definitely not of any design among the thousands logged in the main frame's prodigious memory. Hence, the blaring sound of alarms which echoed not only on the station but among the mass of Commonwealth firepower that was designated BatFor 2.3.

As the mighty warships slowly rumbled toward the intruder a single whisper laser reached out from the unidentified ship and locked onto a receiver on the BatFor 2.3's flagship. TDF *Gauntlet*, a Bismarck Class battleship commanded by Vice Admiral Atu Sy.

"Incoming message from Bogey One, Admiral." Called the Flag Bridges Comms Officer.

Well at least they want to talk thought Atu. "Patch it through."

One entire wall of the Flag Bridge was a vast holographic cube so when the communications link went live every member of the bridge crew was able to see with crystal clear clarity the red winged beast, the talons of its four extended legs picked out in gold and piercing the beast from head through to breast a bright silver sword with an intricately designed pommel. There was no mistaking the symbol of the Imperial Alonan Navy. Sat in front of the emblem of imperial power was an Alonan who sat straight backed, hands resting lightly on the arms of his chair. His light brown uniform adorned only by a single broach identical to the emblem mounted on the wall behind him.

Atu searched for anything which would designate his rank however, his search was in vain for he found none. It was obvious that the Alonan had no intention of starting the conversation so Atu decided to jump straight in the same way any military man would have. With a warning.

"Unidentified warship, this is Admiral Atu Sy, Commanding Officer of the Terran Defense Force Battle Force 2.3. You have entered Commonwealth space declare your intentions immediately or you will be fired upon."

In response the Alonan raised a single digit as if signaling to someone out of range of the camera. The reaction on the Flag Bridge was nearly instantaneous.

"Admiral," cried the Tactical Officer, "Bogey One has activated some form of energy shielding. Sir, its virtually identical to that employed by the Black Ships!"

"Unidentified warship..." Atu began again only for the Alonan to raise a second digit.

This time the Tactical Officer dispensed with the pleasantries of rank. "Vampire! Vampire! Vampire! Single missile launch from Bogey One. Tracking shows it running on a course that will take above and behind Bogey One."

"Weapons tight across all units unless you receive an explicit order from me contradicting that!" Atu worked his jaw furiously not caring who saw him. What the hell was going on?

"Missile detonation." Reported the Tactical Officer. "My god! It was an antimatter warhead. Brace for shock wave impact."

Across the Flag Bridge restraints were double checked and the odd hand dropped to feel for the vacuum helmet stowed in its seat rack. Atu gritted his teeth and stared back at the impassive Alonan who had yet to speak.

Seconds later one of the largest ships ever built by humanity was shaken to its keel as the rapidly dissipating shock wave crashed into battle armor designed to take the impact of nuclear detonation. Damage alarms sounded balefully, and the lights of the Flag Bridge blinked on and off for a few moments before coming back on at full intensity.

"Damage report." Demanded Atu.

"Minimal damage. Blown circuits and the odd failed computer run. All weapons' systems, both offensive and defensive are fully operational."

Returning his attention to the holo cube Atu was struggling to hold his legendary temper in check. "Now you listen here mister..."

"I am Emperor Lura of the Empire of Alona. I sit aboard my flagship, the INS *Vengeance*. One of many of this class of warship in my fleet. As you see the Empire has perfected the Saiph shielding technology and their antimatter weapons. I require an immediate meeting with the heads of state of the Commonwealth."

"And what is the purpose of this meeting, Emperor." Asked Atu incredulously.

"The Empire is willing to share its Saiph technology for a guarantee from the Commonwealth that it will provide whatever aid is required to ensure the survival of our colonies on Kathan and Opero. Time is short Admiral Atu for the Black Ships could return at any moment and their next target may very well be you."

As the transmission ended, a feather could have knocked Atu over. *Where the hell had the Alonans hidden those ships?*

They had them this whole time?

Why the hell had they not used them to defend Alona, now nothing but a burnt cinder circling its star?

And, Who the hell is Emperor Lura? The Emperor was dead the last he'd heard.

"Comms. Get a flash signal off to the Joint Chiefs, I think this's well above my pay grade."

* * *

TDF *CUTLASS* | ON APPROACH TO WAYPOINT 4. | INTERSTELLAR SPACE

"This is becoming a bit of a habit Captain." Stage whispered Nicholas Schamu from his seat behind and to the right of Captain Denise Parks. The commander of SurvFlot Ones flagship TDF *Cutlass* took a breath and counted to ten before fixing her best ass kissing smile onto her face and allowing her seat to spin to face Schamu. The Ambassador looked as well-groomed as the last time she had been forced to spend any time with him.

"If you must know Ambassador, it was a sheer coincidence that the President was on a planned inspection tour of Charon when his ship developed an engine fault and Cutlass was re tasked to bring him to this meeting."

Nicholas glanced around before leaning forward and whispering, "Admit it Captain, secretly you like the designation *Space Force One*."

The temptation to shove Schamu's china teacup down his throat was one that Denise nearly gave in to. If it had not been for the sliding open of the bridge hatch and the instantly recognizable figure of President Madkin striding onto her bridge, there was a very good chance Denise would have taken her chances with a court martial.

"President on deck!" Called the armed marine stationed by the hatch causing all present excluding essential personnel to rise to their feet. Denise noted that even the insufferable Schamu showed deference when the President was around.

"At ease people." Called President Madkin releasing the bridge crew to return to their stations. Denise and Schamu remained standing as the President halted beside them.

"Are we on time, Captain?" Madkin asked.

"Yes, Mr. President. We are on final approach now. Waypoint 4. reports the other heads of state have already arrived and are assembling in the Flag Mess" Answered Denise.

"Then let's be getting on with it shall we. Wouldn't do to be tardy for our first meeting with the new Emperor would it." Madkin said with an infectious smile that Denise found herself subconsciously returning. Madkin sat himself in the free chair to Denise's left-hand side and a yeoman stepped forward to help the President with his shock harness. Madkin waved the man away and deftly secured himself into place. Once a marine, always a marine noted Denise as she touched a stud on her arm rest activating a comms link to the station.

"Waypoint 4. Control, this is Cut... correction. This is *Space Force One* on finals requesting permission to dock." Out of the corner of her eye Denise caught Schamu beginning to lean forward mouth half open. Without turning she raised her hand halting him in his tracks.

"Permission granted *Space Force One* and welcome to Waypoint 4."

Damn it thought Denise, *that peacock Schamu might be right she could get used to this red-carpet treatment after all.*

✳ ✳ ✳

FLAG MESS | WAYPOINT 4. | INTERSTELLAR SPACE
In all his years as a career diplomat, Nicholas Schamu could not recall the last time he had been present at such a high-powered meeting as this.

The opulent surrounding of the Flag Mess barely coped with the numbers of leaders from every Commonwealth state and their aides. A brief flurry of diplomatic exchanges ensured that representatives from the Edasich, though not a full member, managed to attend.

As far as Nicholas saw the only race not represented were the Turak. *No surprise there*, he thought, then noted the Deres and the Nilmerg were also missing. Though, if the information from the latest Diplomatic Corps briefing pack was reliable, then the Deres and Nilmerg were in the process of protracted peace negotiations which, surprisingly, could bring a cessation to generations of warfare in that corner of the galaxy.

Nicholas glanced across to where President Madkin was in deep conversation with Chancellor Volak of Pars. The Persai's midnight black fur and impressive eight feet in height dwarfed the human president, even though Nicholas knew Madkin was a hair below six feet four inches. Today, Nicholas reflected, was going to be a trial by fire for the new president.

By unanimous decision they agreed that the race supplying the current Chairman of the Commonwealth Council would lead the discussions with the Alonans. That meant that President Madkin would chair the meeting.

A white liveried steward caught Nicholas' eye. That was the sign that the Alonans had arrived. Nicholas deftly maneuvered himself across the crowded room until he was able to catch the Presidents attention. Having forewarned his charge Nicholas retrieved the PAD from his inside jacket pocket and tapped a single key. The sound of a single bell chime carried across the mix of conversations going on in the room and the heads of state extricated themselves accompanied by a single aide and made their way into the adjoining conference room. Nicholas ensured he was the last person to enter and closed the large double doors behind him before taking his seat directly behind President Madkin.

Some enterprising soul had found a horseshoe shaped table from within the no doubt limited supply within Waypoint 4. and the Commonwealth leaders were arranged equidistantly around it. President Madkin sat centrally for the simple expedient that he was the elected chair for the meeting. Chancellor Volak sat to his right with the equally tall, though ridiculously thinner, form of Representative Hoolas of the Benii sat on the Persai's right.

To Madkin's left was the squat, reptile skinned figure of Prime Minster Bezled. A longtime friend and ally of President Coston, Nicholas hoped that the Garundans political loyalty had transferred to President Madkin. Beside him sat Thomas Crothers, President of the Janus. Completing the lineup was the only race present who was forced to wear a breathing apparatus, the Edasich. Though not formally a member of the Commonwealth Union of Planets their application was being fast tracked through the various governing bodies of each member state and was, if the rumor mill was to be believed, a simple rubber stamping exercise only delayed because many a politician wanted his or her five minutes in the media spot light before casting their final vote. The Edasich who had traveled from their subterranean base to be present today was the partner of the Edasich leader, Felan. To add a little confusion, it was Edasich tradition that partners used the same family name making no distinction between genders. Therefore, the Edasich representative would be addressed as Felan also. Nicholas was glad he had managed to sidestep that particular assignment though he was sure Ambassador Jelav was having the time of his life. That was one odd Garundan.

Nicholas' PAD vibrated noiselessly in his pocket and he leaned forward and whispered into the Presidents ear.

The President cleared his throat softly and stood. "Ladies and gentlemen. Emperor Lura."

The doors at the opposite side of the room opened and an Alonan unusually tall for his race entered followed closely by an older Alonan who struck Nicholas as more the scholarly type than political.

"Greetings Emperor Lura, it is a pleasure..."

"May we dispense with the niceties President Madkin?" Said Lura cutting Madkin off in mid flow catching the career politicos by surprise. To Madkin's credit he recovered well. Dropping himself back into his seat without waiting for his guest to be seated first it was his turn to catch the Alonans out.

"Certainly. How can we help you?"

Nicholas thought he caught the beginnings of a grin on the Emperor's face before his features once more returned to their stoic appearance.

"The Alonan Empire as was is gone. From a population of billions we are now reduced to the tens of thousands and we will struggle to feed even those that remain."

"We appreciate your honesty Emperor Lura however, in the past you have blocked us at every turn. You have employed espionage, trickery and anything else you could think of to further your own ends. That does not bode well for future good relations between the Commonwealth and the Empire." Madkin pointed out.

"You speak the truth Mr. President but that was yesterday, and this is today. We need you and we are willing to pay."

Boy, this guy is not hanging about thought Schamu. Usually these types of negotiations take weeks if not months to even get both sides to agree the color of the toilet paper.

"What we are proposing is a simple exchange." Said Lura. "We will supply you every piece of Saiph technology that we have on the condition that you in return meet the needs of the populations of Kathan and Opero until such time as both colony worlds are capable of being self-sustaining."

"It could take us years to reverse engineer that sort of technology and you know it." Pointed out Madkin.

Lura nodded in agreement. "Indeed, I do which is why we are willing to supply technicians and engineers to assist you. My Chief Scientist, Kilor, sits beside me today and in his possession is the design schematics for every piece of Saiph technology in our inventory."

With a flourish Kilor deposited a stack of data chips on the tabletop.

Each of the Commonwealth leaders eyed the stack with envious eyes. Contained in that fragile tower of plastic was the answer to overcoming every advantage the Supreme Leader and his Black Ships had over the Commonwealth fleets. Even so it was obvious to Lura that Madkin was hesitating. Time to sweeten the deal.

"As a sign of our good faith we are also able to offer the assistance of, let's call them *specialists* who have a unique knowledge of this technology and are highly motivated to ensure the demise of the Supreme Leader and his ilk."

Lura noted the skepticism on the commonwealth leaders' faces and he decided now was the time to play his ace in the hole. With a nod to Kilor, the scientist stood and walked to the doors through which the Alonans had entered. Opening them he took a step to one side to allow the entity waiting patiently beyond the doors to enter. Walking with unfaltering steps until he stood in plain view within a few meters of Madkin and the gathered leaders, Commander Okal of the Saiph said one word and caused the room to erupt.

"Hello."

✳ ✳ ✳

TDF *CUTLASS* | FORAM SYSTEM | THIRTY-SIX LIGHT-YEARS FROM ALONA

"Excuse my directness Ambassador Schamu, but I am beginning to regret ever meeting you." Said Denise Parks as TDF *Cutlass* threaded its way between floating construction yards big enough to swallow her ship whole and leave room to spare.

Nicholas Schamu was in his usual seat slightly behind her and to the right though his china teacup was nowhere in sight. Instead he was doing his best to interpret all the sensor data that was running along the side bar of the holo cube that was projecting a view from the ships bow cameras. It struck him as nearly beyond belief that the Alonans had managed to conceal this massive construction project from the probing eyes of the various Commonwealth intelligence agencies. Never mind the fact that they had a working Saiph vessel complete with crew. Nicholas was willing to bet that there were a few selected words being had with the heads of intelligence behind closed doors.

"There she is." Half whispered Denise. Nicholas searched the holo cube until his eyes came to rest on the silvery bulk of the *Savior* for the first time. Nicholas had traveled the length and breadth of the Commonwealth and beyond in his time as a topflight diplomat. Up until this moment the most impressive thing he had seen was the home port of Clan Orlak in System 90159 with its huge space station that dwarfed Earths own Fortress Command. The *Savior* was a mere minnow in comparison however, it was not the size of the ship that was so impressive, nor was it the promised technology that made Nicholas stare in wonder at the Saiph ship. No, it was the faith that the Elders had in their own capabilities to bring forth not only a new world but a fresh start for the entire Saiph race from a single ship. Not since the days of the now defunct generation ships which had been proposed as the only viable method of getting humanity to the stars prior to the discovery of the gravity drive had Nicholas been witness to a more audacious plan. Nicholas felt his eagerness to see the wonders contained within the *Savior* tempered by a feeling of sadness that Commander Okal and his crew had traveled so far, slept for so long only to emerge in a universe at war with the Elders ancient enemy once more.

"Status of the Boxer?" Denise question had not been meant for Nicholas however, it did have the effect of bringing him back to the present.

Cutlass' Executive Officer checked his read out before answering. "The transport is directly astern at a distance of 1,000 kilometers, Captain." That innocuous transport thought Denise was crammed to the gunnels with some of the best engineers and scientists the Commonwealth had to offer all desperate to get their hands-on whatever goodies the Saiph and the Alonans had on offer. Dependent, of course, on the Ambassador and his party ironing out the finer details of what was already being called the Waypoint Agreement. I wonder if the Supreme Leader realized that his destruction of Alona had driven implacable enemies into each other's arms and may have sealed his own downfall in the process?

"We are receiving mooring instructions from the Alonans, Captain." Called out the Comms Officer.

"Very well." Turning her chair to face Nicholas, Denise was surprised to see the look of wonder on his face instead of his normal mischievous features that she was sure he reserved for when he was plotting his next childlike act that he knew would get under her skin. "Ambassador?" Denise said gently.

Nicholas' head jerked around so quickly Denise expected to see his eyes spin in their sockets and the mental image that generated caused her to laugh softly. A laugh which threatened to become more raucous as the expression on Nicholas' face resembled that of a child caught with its hand in the cookie jar. Regaining her self-control and clearing her throat to stifle her burgeoning laughter Denise paused while Nicholas once more became the professional politician.

"Yes, Captain."

"It looks like we will not be docking so your party will have to use the shuttles. A bit of an inconvenience though not insurmountable."

Nicholas leisurely released his seat harness and stood, stretching like a cat as he did so. "Time to get to work." Turning on his heel he headed for the bridge doors tapping away on his PAD as he did so.

"Good luck." Denise said to his retreating back.

CHAPTER FOURTEEN

THE ENEMY OF MY ENEMY IS MY FRIEND

SYSTEM 90159 | TURAK SPACE

In the months that had passed since his father was declared War Chief and he himself had been elevated to the position as Clan Lord of Clan Orlak, it seemed to Yue that he had not had a single night that he had had a full night's sleep. The constant beeping which penetrated his drowsy brain signaled that this night would be no different from any other of late. Wearily reaching out from beneath the silk covers, Yue tapped the accept key and the voice of his Uncle Kal burst from the concealed speaker.

"My Lord. I beg your forgiveness for disturbing you at such a late hour however, I have urgent news."

Everything these days seemed to urgent news thought Yue. "And what is this news, uncle." Asked Yue without lifting his head from the soft pillow or opening his eyes for to do so would mean that he had accepted that he would have to acknowledge that he was awake and this was nothing but a bad dream designed to ruin his much needed rest.

"A courier ship has arrived from Home." Kal said, the excitement in his voice barely contained.

Yue's sleep deprived brain was struggling to understand why Kal was so excited about a single courier ship. "Could this not wait until the morning?"

"The courier brings a passenger who requests an immediate audience with you My Lord." Explained Kal.

Yue let out a muffled grunt. "And who is this person who seeks an audience with a Clan Lord in the middle of the night?"

"War Chief Vek."

At the sound of his father's name Yue sat bolt upright in bed, eyes springing open. "Why did you not say so in the first-place uncle?"

From the speaker came the sound of laughter. "I shall remember to do so in the future My Lord."

"Perhaps I should find myself a new adviser and dispense with your services?" Yue joked terminating the call before his uncle could answer while simultaneously flinging off the bed clothes and heading for what he hoped would be a rejuvenating sonic shower.

✳✳✳

Clan Lord Yue sat upon the high backed, jewel encrusted chair raised two steps above the rooms floor level so any person addressing the Clan Lord of Clan Orlak would be forced to crane their necks and look up reminding them that the Clan Lord was a person of the utmost importance and deserving of their respect. As if that image needed to be reinforced Yue was dressed from the neck down in figure hugging armor similarly bejeweled while a Boka sword crafted by the best blacksmiths in all of Turak space rested in its scabbard by Yue's side. Around the outer walls of the opulent room stood his personal guard, imposing in their distinctive scarlet colored body armor, impassive faces hidden behind their helmets which only gave an observer a view of their intense red eyes. Everything in this room was designed to intimidate a visitor. This night however, this visitor was not to be intimidated.

As the doors retreated silently into their concealed recesses Vek, War Chief of the Turak, stepped through and approached the raised seat in the rooms center. In complete contradiction to the lavishness of his surroundings Vek was dressed in simple gray tunic and pants. His only adornment was the multicolored sash worn around his waist. Behind Vek walked a similarly gray clad individual although this time it was powered battle armor that was colored gray and a Boka hung at its waist. The Guardian had become Vek's constant companion since his assumption as the role of War Chief. The Guardians presence a reminder, if any was needed, that Vek now held authority over all Turak and no individual be they a humble farmer through to the mightiest Clan Lord dare disobey him without facing the wrath of the Guardians.

Yue stepped down from his chair to greet his father formally as tradition dictated. "I welcome you in the name of Clan Orlak," Yue dropped his chin to his chest, eyes downcast, "Clan Orlak stand with you War Chief ready to lay down our lives if you so command."

"You do your clan and all Turak proud Clan Lord Yue." Vek responded completing the ancient rite before stepping in close to his son hands reaching out to grasp him strongly. "I see Kal has been teaching you well my son."

"My uncle seems to have made it his life's work to school me in the ways of politics and polite etiquette while I would much rather be practicing my Boka skills."

Vek let out a short chuckle. "Listen to your uncle my son. In all the years he served as my closest adviser his words never steered me wrong."

"I shall father. You have my word."

Vek patted his son's arm before releasing him.

"I am eager to hear what has brought you home father. Do you have news of our enemy?"

"All in good time, all in good time. Perhaps I could impose on you for some breakfast before we get down to business?"

"Ah, Uncle Kal thought you might be hungry and is having breakfast prepared as we speak."

Vek's head fell back as he let out a full belly laugh. "A word of advice my son. Keep that man close and you will never go hungry."

Yue joined in his father's laughter as they made their way to the dining room.

✳ ✳ ✳

Kal regarded his brother over the goblet of steaming grukk. The conversation over breakfast had been lighthearted and Vek had taken great enjoyment ribbing his son about his courting of Clan Lady Waynal. Vek's choice of her father, Clan Lord Mynut of the Hurak, as his First had effectively side lined Mynut and any objections that he may have had to the pair's courtship. The act of selecting Mynut as his First may have seemed like a shrewd political move to the other gathered Clan Lords but deep down Kal knew it Vek had done it to clear the way for his son's happiness.

As the dishes were cleared away the conversation turned to more complex matters. "Brother, I once again need your counsel." Said Vek.

"And you shall have it." Answered Kal.

Vek hesitated before speaking, his eyes narrowing, his brothers body language set off a multitude of alarms in Kal's head.

"We know the Saiph once more leave their fetid stench across the stars."

"That we do." Agreed Kal who glanced across at Yue who chose to keep his own counsel while the two brothers spoke.

"And, although they have attacked us in what the Humans refer to as the Selene System, we have seen no other signs of their activity apart from in the space controlled by the Commonwealth or the Alonan Empire."

"An empire which no longer exists if our reports are to be believed." Pointed out Kal.

"Its demise is yet another example of why we must act at the earliest opportunity to remove this threat to all Turak. It is obvious to me that the Saiph chose to eradicate the Alonans first because they identified them as the weakest of all the alien races."

Kal nodded sagely. "Agreed."

"Their next target is therefore either going to be us or the Commonwealth."

Kal placed his goblet down as he considered his answer for a moment. "Your logic is sound brother and, if I may? I shall take it a step further."

Vek waved his own goblet acquiescing to Kal's request.

"As you indicated our only contact with the Saiph was in the Selene System whereas the Commonwealth has had multiple encounters with the Saiph. In fact, they fought and won a war with the Others who we now know were acting at the behest of the Saiph. Therefore, it seems only logical to expect the next move by the Saiph to be against the Commonwealth."

"My thoughts exactly." Said Vek. "The quandary I find myself in is this: Do I allow the Commonwealth to stand against the Saiph alone allowing them to winnow each other's fleets down to a level where we can step in and defeat the Saiph with minimal losses or, do I seek a temporary alliance with the Commonwealth where our forces fight alongside theirs to defeat our common enemy?"

Kal sipped at his grukk while he composed his thoughts eventually returning the now empty goblet to the table. "I would ask you this brother. We have seen the power of the Saiph ships. A single squadron of their cruisers managed with ease to destroy a much larger force of our own clans' ships. Our reports of the attack on Alona state that there were hundreds of Saiph warships involved in that action. Who is to say that every day we do not fight them they are not growing stronger?" Kal's forehead creased in a frown as his hand played with the empty goblet. "The Commonwealth warships are roughly equivalent to our own. One on one they will lose out to the Saiph every time. Only by massing our forces do we realistically stand a chance of defeating the Saiph. If we wait for the Commonwealth to be defeated, which is a very likely outcome, then we may have missed our opportunity."

Vek sat back to consider his brothers words only to catch sight of Yue's face. The younger Turak look deep in thought. "Do you have a something you wish to add Yue?"

Yue looked surprised by his father's asking of his opinion. For years he has sat quietly listening to his father and Kal discuss everything from strategy and tactics to the vagaries of various flavors of grukk. Steeling himself he spoke. "I was thinking of a phrase that the Humans have which aptly describes the problem at hand and, perhaps, provides a solution."

Both older Turak regarded the younger Yue with skeptical eyes. "I'm listening."

"I have been studying human history to try and get a better grasp of their thought processes."

"A wise thing to do for we will have many interactions with them in the future now our own borders butt up against theirs." Kal intoned.

Yue nodded toward his uncle in thanks. "Human history is littered with conflict. Yet throughout there appears to have been one constant. The ability to form alliances, even with a group or nation that you have recently fought with, to face a stronger foe. The phrase goes something like this 'the enemy of my enemy is my friend'."

Vek and Kal considered this for a moment before both broke into wide smiles. "Perhaps," said Kal, "I should be the pupil and he the teacher."

Vek rolled out of the chair clapping his hands together. "It is decided then," he said as he turned to face his son, "your War Chief has a request of you Clan Lord Yue."

Yue shot to his feet so fast his head went giddy. "If I can fulfill it then it is yours War Chief."

"You shall be my emissary to the Commonwealth. Make my enemy my friend."

Yue held his chin high and there was a gleam in his eye as he answered. "Clan Orlak would be honored War Chief."

CHAPTER FIFTEEN

FOUND YOU

TDF *TYCHO BRAHE* | INTERSTELLAR SPACE | 1136 LIGHT-YEARS FROM EARTH
Terrance Wilson struggled to keep his eyes open as yet another data file was pushed from the main frame across to his own terminal. Beside him Ensign Burkett was happily munching on what had to be his one hundredth bar of candy today. The energy of youth he quietly joked before realizing that Burkett was probably on five or less years younger than he was.

Terrance started at a voice close by his ear. "Terrance, go get some sleep before you leave drool all over the screen." Said Doctor Sylvia Sarkisian like a mother speaking to her overly tired child and right now Terrance felt exactly like that sleepy toddler.

Slipping off the stool he had been perched on Terrance stretched like a cat trying to ease the burgeoning cramps in his shoulders and neck. It had been all hands on deck following the third successful deployment of the DSDG. The improved system had been its own worst enemy as it scoured the quadrant of space around Durav in its search for the red star that Terrance, and the navy's Department of Special Projects, was certain was Assena, fabled home of the Creator aka the Supreme Leader. Before setting off in search of his elusive quarry Terrance had no idea that of the estimated 100 billion stars in the Milky Way some 80 percent, nearly 60 billion, were classified as red dwarfs. If Terrance had actually taken the time to calculate the odds against him finding Assena he would maybe have paused for thought. Unfortunately, as Maggie repeatedly told him, he opened his mouth before thinking and that trait had ended up in him being stood in the forward cargo bay of Tycho Brahe at God knows what hour in the morning, or was it afternoon by now? Manually sifting through the thousands of likely candidates that the state of the art super computer built especially for this mission had spat out as fitting the parameters that Sarkisian had set.

"Yeah, perhaps I will." Terrance managed through a yawn. "A couple of hours rack time will recharge the batteries and I'll be raring to go again."

"By the looks of you, you better make that a couple of days." Joked Sarkisian.

Terrance yawned again and headed for the bay door. He had only made it a couple of steps when a loud, whooping exclamation from Burkett halted him in his tracks.

"Holy crap! I think I've found it." Burkett spun around in on his stool a large idiotic grin spread across his face. "I've really found it!" Without further ado Sarkisian pushed him aside and read the data for herself mumbling as she did. Terrance lent over her shoulder to read the same data, but she pushed him away mumbling something about mass, luminosity and surface temperature. Without lifting her eyes from the data, she waved a hand at a nearby terminal.

"Terrance, bring that other terminal over here." The way she said it the words came out more like an order than a polite request. Terrance jumped to obey placing the requested terminal beside her. Without a word of thanks Sarkisian began typing furiously. After a few corrections she stood back drumming her fingers impatiently on the work top. When the terminal beeped softly to indicate it had finished the task, she had set it Sarkisian pored over the results tapping a few additional queries as she went. Minutes went by as Terrance stood there beside a smiling Burkett. Eventually Sarkisian took a step back her head moving back and forth from each terminal for a few moments longer before she let out a non-committal hmm. "Ensign, drag your terminal over here and display field 1-8-charlie, please."

Positioning herself so she could see all three displays at the same time Sarkisian hopped from one foot to another head in constant motion as she compared individual lines of information against each other from differing displays. Satisfied, Sarkisian went from one terminal to another in turn highlighting the same line of data.

"OK, Terrance be my Devil's Advocate here will you."

Terrance stepped forward so he could read the line of data Sarkisian had highlighted on each terminal. Each line conformed to the one on the corresponding terminal with two exceptions. "The luminosity and the location are different all the other characteristics are identical."

Sarkisian moved around him and tapped a command into each terminal in turn. "And now?"

Terrance flexed his tired neck and let out a breath before repeating his analysis. "Luminosity is decreasing at a steady rate and location is also changing at a fixed rate."

"Exactly!" Burkett said failing to contain his enthusiasm.

"Hold your horses there, Ensign." Said Terrance. "We knew one sure indicator for Assena would be a decreasing luminosity as the construction of the Dyson Sphere gradually masked the star from view. Nobody mentioned a change of location."

"It's a rogue." Said Burkett as he shrugged his shoulders as if that was explanation enough.

Terrance looked at him for a moment before turning to face Sarkisian the look on his face prompting her to explain.

"A rogue star. More correctly termed an intergalactic star is a star that is not gravitationally bound to any galaxy. We think they have been expelled from their original galaxies as a result of either two galaxies colliding or of a multi star system traveling too close to a super massive black hole. The other stars get sucked into the black hole while the surviving star gets ejected at hypervelocity and escapes the gravitational well of the entire galaxy."

"Pretty neat, huh?" Put in Burkett. The look Terrance gave him caused the smile to be wiped from his face as the ensign tried to find some other direction to look in.

"How do we make sure it's actually Assena?" Terrance asked Sarkisian.

"We fold in say, 500 light-years, deploy the DSDG, and take new readings. Then we fold out a thousand light-years and repeat the procedure. The closer we are the dimmer the star should be. The further out the brighter. Firm up the locations and we should be able to predict a direction of travel..."

"And an exact location." Terrance finished the scientist's sentence. The implications of their discovery hit Terrance like a freight train. He took a couple of deep breaths before heading for the bay door while calling over his shoulder. "Outstanding job Ensign. Outstanding!"

✳✳✳

NAVAL INTELLIGENCE SERVICE | CARSON CITY | EARTH | SOL SYSTEM

"Hey Earl, what was so important that it's dragged you out of those windowless offices of Special Projects to visit us mere mortals." Snorted Aleksandr Vadis as the door closed softly behind Brigadier General Earl Statham. The serious look on Earl's face caused Vadis to pause.

"When was the last time your office was swept?" Statham asked without preamble.

Vadis opened his mouth to retort the ridiculousness of the question. He was the head of Naval Intelligence, if his office had a listening device then he deserved to be sacked on the spot. Only the look in his friend's eyes was one of complete seriousness. Vadis walked around his desk, placing his palm down on what appeared to be an innocuous piece of desktop. A soft beep confirmed that the stand-alone computer built into the desk was running its lock down program. Behind Vadis the stunning view of the Sierra Nevada mountains disappeared as the custom manufactured glass obscured and the thin copper filament embedded in the glass made contact with matching elements that ran through the rooms walls, floor and ceiling turning the room into a Faraday's Cage completely blocking out all electromagnetic fields. From the desk came a double beep informing Vadis that it had completed its sweep with negative results.

"We are clean." Said Vadis.

"Half an hour ago I received a signal from Lieutenant Wilson on the Tycho Brahe -"

Vadis felt his heart pound harder in his chest.

"The signal consisted of three words: Red Star Found."

* * *

2287 LIGHT-YEARS FROM EARTH

A midnight black shape coated in the stealthiest material the Commonwealth Union of Planets could manufacture winked into existence traveling at for modern star ships was the snail's pace of eighteen kilometers a second as it crossed the systems predicted heliosphere at an oblique angle. Passive sensors recorded every twitch of the electromagnetic spectrum. From the body of the vessel unfurled four narrow, flexible tubes until reaching out almost five kilometers in length in a cross shape with the vessel at its center. With the interferometric gravitational wave detector fully deployed additional data began pouring into the on-board computers. In the cramped cockpit a human pilot sat beside a Persai engineer while a Garundan technician ran a system's check.

The mixed crew's mission was simple. Confirm this to be the location of Assena. Do not be detected. Get home.

□　□　□

NAVAL INTELLIGENCE SERVICE | CARSON CITY | EARTH | SOL SYSTEM

The sound of ice hitting the base of crystal tumblers was swiftly followed by the finest whiskey sloshing on top of the cooling ice. Aleksandr Vadis passed one tumbler to Earl Statham before raising his own in mock salute.

"Confirmation came a few minutes ago."

Statham ran through a plethora of emotions quicker than he could take a single breath. Relief. Justification. Satisfaction. Elation. In the end his body settled on resignation. Resignation because though they had found the Saiph and the Supreme Leader the discovery as far as he could see only had one outcome. Combat.

Abruptly the taste of the expensive whiskey went sour in his throat.

CHAPTER SIXTEEN

STRIKE BEFORE IT'S TOO LATE

ENTRAL COMMAND | MONT SALEVE | EARTH
John Radford was pretty sure that he had heard somewhere that if you allowed too many admirals to congregate in one place it caused a rip in the space time continuum and everyone and everything within a hundred kilometers was sucked into an alternate dimension. As unobtrusively as he could he glanced around him ensuring that he was not about to step into a wormhole or something of its ilk and be whisked away.

"I see you have heard that rumor too." Analisa Chavez whispered conspiratorially as she wondered up beside him.

John cocked his head over so as not to be overheard. "Have you seen this room? I don't think I've ever seen so many fleet commanders gathered together in one place, have you?"

"Nope."

"What are you pair whispering about?" Asked Kaitlin Rocha as she popped a pig in a blanket into her mouth that she had retrieved from the cold buffet laid out on silver trays along one wall of the conference room.

"Have you got any idea what's going on?" Said John as he considered heading over to grab some food himself as he caught sight of Lela Wilder, Commander of CSG *Montu* and Madix Walters, Commander CSG Bastet, gravitating toward the buffet.

"All I know is that I got direct orders from Jing to hot tail it to Central Command for a face-to-face. I was about to depart when Admiral Lewis hailed me, he suggested we travel together since he was headed to the same briefing."

Analisa did a quick 360-degree turn before pursing her lips and releasing a small sigh. "I don't see him. We've been trying to catch up for month."

Kaitlin shook her head as she tried to speak with a mouthful of pig in a blanket. "Uh, no. Someone whisked him off as soon as we touched down to meet with the Combined Joint Chiefs. See? I've always said rank has its privileges."

"Well, it seems we have nothing to do but wait- and eat of course." John said already edging away determined to beat Kaitlin to the buffet. The gentle hiss of hydraulics opening and closing a door put paid to that plan as Admiral Ai Jing entered accompanied by Robert Lewis, his red uniform blouse and black pants announcing to everyone who saw him that he was no longer a serving officer of the Terran Defense Force but rather the very first commander of the Janus Space Navy.

"Ladies and gentlemen, please be seated. Time is short and we have much to do." Jing pulled out the chair at the head of the table and sat down. Robert Lewis took the seat to his immediate right while the other commanders in the room took the first available seat.

Jing waited for the last person to sit, then promptly began. "The Department of Special Projects confirmed today that they have ascertained the base of operations of the Black Ships." At a command, an unseen yeoman activated the holo cube which flickered to life over the center of the conference table. John squinted to make any sense from the projection. Yellows and purples flowed together to form a large spheroid shape at the center with darker greens and near-black colors formed irregular bands spreading outwards. "The images were taken at extreme range are grainy. We've added false color to get a better look at what we're facing."

The image zoomed in to fix on the spherical object. "Ladies and gents, this is a Dyson Sphere." Collectively the gathering took an intake of breath.

You have got to be kidding me! Thought John.

"Up to this point the collective minds of the Commonwealth thought that such a construct was a theoretical thought experiment. Well, as you can see, there is nothing theoretical about it anymore. The Saiph have built it and it is our job to take it away from them or destroy it trying. Speak freely, no holds barred here. We need to do this, and it will be up to you gathered here to get it done."

John gazed upon the object floating above the table wondering where you would even start the construct was simply so big his brain was struggling to comprehend it. Jing gave his commanders a few moments to contemplate the scale of the Dyson Sphere before he rapped sharply on the tabletop. The noise had the desired effect as six sets of eyes focused on him once more.

"Our best-case scenario is that the Saiph have between two hundred and four hundred cruiser class warships to hand."

Analisa Chavez spoke up. "And what is that figure based on, sir?"

"Eyewitness accounts of the Saiph assault on Alona. Taking those numbers into account the Joint Chiefs are considering it a near maximum effort on the part of the Supreme Leader."

Kaitlin Rocha let out a large harrumph. "And we're trusting the Empire now?"

"We haven't got to the good bit yet Kaitlin." Said Robert out of the side of his mouth. A comment which earned him a hard stare from Jing.

"Only four of their cruisers damn near gutted my entire command." Pointed out John to grunts of agreement from Lela Wilder and Madix Walters. John did some math in his head. "If we take the casualties *Itus* suffered at Guzman as a working example of the damage those Saiph cruisers can inflict then my losses will be increased a hundredfold." John ran a wary eye around the room. "600 destroyers, 3,800 fighters, 500 cruisers, 200 battleships and," John had to swallow before he spoke the final number, "238,400 men and women." The palpable silence descended on the room.

It was left to Robert Lewis to break the silence. "And if we are not willing to accept those sorts of casualties, we are looking at something far worse John..." Robert lent forward on his elbows to emphasize his point. "Extinction. Plain and simple. This isn't some vid game where we can press reset and I hope to god we all know that. It's us or them and I for one would rather it was them than us."

"I think we all get that Robert." Said Analisa momentarily forgetting that as the commander of the Janus Space Navy, Robert Lewis was now two ranks higher than she. If he was bothered by her break in etiquette Robert did not show it. "However, the numbers are against us. The TDF simply does not have those sorts of numbers available. Even at the height of the war against the Others we had nowhere near that amount of tonnage to hand. I wish we did but..."

Jing held up a hand to stop Analisa. "This will be a joint operation Analisa. And by joint, I mean exactly that." Jing shifted his weight in his seat which was a sure sign to anyone who knew him that he was uncomfortable with what he was about to say next. "At an extraordinary meeting of the Commonwealth Union of Planets Council was held late last night. The Council unanimously agreed to activate the Mutual Defense Clause which requires all member and associated star nations to make available to the Commonwealth Combined Joint Chiefs of Staff what resources the Joint Chiefs deem appropriate to meet the current perceived threat. Before joining this meeting, I signed off on a request from the Joint Chiefs that all warships of destroyer class and above immediately rendezvous at a location that I designated where they will come under command of the Combined Fleet Commander."

Jing let the room soak that in for a few seconds before the unseen yeoman again changed the image in the holo cube. This time it was lists of ships indexed by nationality and class. John had to concentrate to stop his mouth gaping open as ship name after ship name raced by in front of him. The entire current front-line warships of the Terran Defense Force including all three Carrier Strike Groups, Home Fleet, Second Fleet and Survey Commands cruiser complement. Garunda was contributing nearly 80 percent of Third Fleet. The Persai had committed an equivalent number from its own navy. When the Janus Space Navy names appeared in the holo cube Robert

Lewis sat a bit straighter in seat. They may only have three Vigilant class battleships and a handful of cruisers in their inventory however, each and every one of them was on the list as well as an additional type that indicated that there was sixty of its type available. The others may have missed it but not Kaitlin Rocha who gave Roberts elbow a nudge.

"What's a 'Hornet'?"

Robert let a smile spread slowly across his face like the cat who had got the milk. "Remember those cargo doors that you were so interested in?"

Robert swore that he could see the light bulb going off behind Kaitlin's eyes. "You sneaky son of a..."

The snort that escaped her once commanding officer led to him receiving a rather painful punch to the bicep. "Fighters! You didn't have the time or money to build your own carriers, so you bastardized your battleships to do two jobs rolled into one."

Robert used his index finger to tap the side of his nose. "Don't tell anyone will you."

The names in the holo cube were nearly completed scrolling through as last, but not least, a list of Benii carriers and heavy cruisers went past. John, for one, was glad to see them. His own Mosquito fighters had probably been one of his main assets in his fight against the Saiph cruisers at Guzman and seeing more than two dozen Benii carriers each with eighty Freiba space-fighters aboard. Add them to the Mosquitos of the three TDF Carrier Strike Groups and the JSN's sixty Hornets and that gave them 2,196 deadly buzzing bees that the Saiph had shown at Guzman not to have an answer to. John rubbed his chin as he considered what options this Combined Fleet Commander might have. The numbers were not great, not by a long chalk. However, they would have a fighting chance all they needed was a bit of luck.

If something to balance the odds a little bit was what John wanted, then Jing was about to deliver it. "To the list you see before you we have a few additions."

"I said you would like this." Robert staged whispered to Kaitlin.

Jing chose to ignore the voice to his right and continued speaking. "The Emperor of Alona are committing seventeen of their most advanced cruisers to the fight. According to the tech team from Zarminda who have been allowed unrestricted access to these vessels each Imperial cruiser is easily the match, if not superior too, its Saiph opposite number."

Madix Walters let out a low whistle. "Where do I get myself a half dozen of those bad puppies."

"Unfortunately, Madix, according to Admiral Glandinning, it would take divine intervention for us to even complete a design never mind build a ship of that type in the next year."

"What about the antimatter missiles we've heard so much about?" Asked Lela Wilder.

"Ah, now there we have some good news." Reported Jing. "The box launchers for the capital ship missiles have been in production for some months and Zarminda are confident that they will be able to supply enough for at least a limited engagement therefore the phrase here is 'use prudently'".

"What about the HVAMM's?" Inquired John. "We are going to have plenty of fighters the question is will we have the missiles to equip them. Those things could be a game changer if we can get our fighters close enough to knock down the Saiph energy shields."

"The Alonans have antimatter to spare, thanks to Commander Okal and the *Savior's* production plants. We're transporting the antimatter to the Janus shipyards and President Crothers has made the High Velocity Antimatter Missiles top priority for the fabrication plants." Jing tipped his head to Robert Lewis. "I don't doubt that Janus will hold up its reputation as equaling our own yards for bulk production."

"We are still outgunned." Noted Madix Walters. A comment that garnered mumbled agreements from around the table.

Jing steepled his fingers before him and tapped the tips of his index fingers against pursed lips; as if contemplating how to formulate the words to impart his vital information. Rolling his shoulders forward in to release the tension growing between them, Jing shared the news he had received the morning before, and led to frantic planning by the Joint Chiefs Strategy Committee, prior to their presentation to the Commonwealth Council, which in turn led them to invoke the Mutual Defense Clause.

"As I said prior, this is a joint operation. Not only will Commonwealth and Alonan forces be involved..." Jing paused and used the time to meet each officers eye trying to gauge their reaction to what he was about to reveal. "Yesterday morning a representative of the Turak approached the Commonwealth with a proposal. He proposed that, if the Saiph could be located, then the Turak would be willing to form a temporary alliance with Commonwealth forces to engage and defeat the Saiph."

It was not often that a group, like this, were so shocked by a briefing that they were speechless. John was the first to recover. "What sort of numbers are we talking?"

Jing activated his PAD and read directly from its compact display. "302 battleships, 543 heavy cruisers, 487 light cruisers and 749 destroyers and frigates." When Jing looked up stunned faces greeted him, except for the face of John Radford who had a stupid grin plastered on his.

"Something amusing, John?"

John abruptly stood up and started pacing up and down all the time that stupid grin of his remained glued to his features.

"Care to share John?" Jing asked with a degree of mild irritation.

John stopped pacing and turned to address the table. "We can do this! I'm confident we can do this. It's going to cost us dearly no mistaking that however, you were right sir." He said leveling a finger at Jing. "If we don't cease this opportunity then the

Saiph will defeat us in detail at least if we take the fight to them, we have a better than even chance of pulling it off."

Jing lent back in his chair and pulled out a small box which he slid in Johns direction. John automatically reached out and stopped the box from sliding over the tables edge.

"You might be needing those." Chortled Jing.

John looked from the box to Jing and back again. Taking a deep breath, he opened the hinged top of the box to reveal five silver stars resting on a bed of black velvet.

"Technically I suppose you outrank me now -" Jing stood raising his right hand until the upper arm was parallel to the ground and the forearm at exactly forty-five degrees. The tip of his forefinger touching the outside edge of his eyebrow. "Congratulations on your promotion, Admiral."

CHAPTER SEVENTEEN

THE GRAND ALLIANCE

INTERSTELLAR SPACE | ONE HUNDRED LIGHT-YEARS FROM THE DYSON SPHERE John Radford had decided that time had been in too desperately short supply for him to break in a new command crew so had elected to remain aboard TDF *Itus* much to the consternation of Captain Cecilia Bose who abruptly found herself responsible not only for fighting her carrier but for keeping the commander of the biggest fleet ever to be assembled safe.

After his last staff meeting John was fairly sure that he had heard Bose mumbling to herself something about she should have listened to her mother and married a dentist instead of joining the navy.

Right now, John stood behind a side party of marines resplendent in their blue dress uniforms. Number One Landing Bay had been cleared pending the arrival of the single largest contributor to the Combined Fleet. The Turak.

Buzzing like the sound of a bee flying past your ear signaled the passage of the small craft through the wavering energy field that kept the cold vacuum of space beyond from causing the entire bay to suffer abrupt and violent decompression ensuring a short, violent death for all who stood here.

The Turak craft hovered less than a meter off the deck and completed a neat 180-degree turn so that its nose was pointed back the way it came. Ready to make a quick exit thought John.

As the craft kissed the deck John noted the thick scarlet colored band that ran completely around the ship. If his briefing notes were to be believed, that identified the craft as belonging to Clan Orlak, though intelligence had identified a further fifteen distinct colors banding the huge armada of Turak ships, which had emerged from fold space in the past two hours. It didn't take a massive leap of reasoning to conclude that this armada represented the combined resources of sixteen clans. A fact which was already causing the sociologists to reconsider their thoughts on Turak society.

Two parallel lines formed on the hull of the craft and expanded vertically before making a ninety degree turn and joining top and bottom. The entire section dropped back a couple of centimeters before slipping to the left and receding into the hull allowing a set of steps to extend until they touched the deck. Almost immediately a pair of Turak in crimson colored battle armor complete with helmets descended the steps and formed up on either side of them. In their gauntleted hands they held energy rifles of some description and at their waist hung a short broad saber. John found it strange that a society that had developed energy weapons and the gravity drive employed something requiring such physical dexterity as a sword.

Movement at the top of the steps caught John's eye and he was surprised to see a Turak similarly armored, with the exception of a helmet, descending the steps. This was John's first opportunity to see a Turak in the flesh. The head was shaped like a human skull, though the skull was completely hairless. The skin was a dark and leathery, but creaseless. This Turak struck John as relatively young however, it was the eyes they drew John's full attention. A fierce ruby red that looked like at any moment lasers would burst from them and skewer you with their intensity.

As if on cue, the marine side party snapped to attention and with a clash of hands striking carbon fiber, brought their rifles to the present arms.

Captain Bose tensed as she prepared to step forward and greet their visitor only for her to pause as this Turak reached the bottom of the steps and moved to one side. John was beginning to wonder how many people this small craft could carry when a single Turak, dressed in a loose gray fitting long sleeved top and matching pants appeared at the top of the steps. John ran an assessing eye quickly over him. This Turak's skin was more creased than the younger one who awaited him at the bottom of the steps. An intricate sash of multiple colors was wrapped around his waist and, unusually for the Turak that John had seen so far, no obvious weapons were on show. As the Turak started down the steps the hulking figure of a gray armored clad Turak, hand resting on the pommel of the saber sheathed at his waist stepped out behind him following close behind as the older Turak descended. John recognized a bodyguard when he saw one and this one had the air of a man you did not want to annoy.

Captain Bose stepped forward, hands clasped behind her back and gave the Turak a curt head bow. "Welcome aboard the *Itus*. I am Captain Bose, commander of this ship."

John's brief had warned him that the Turak were a naturally aggressive race and that intimidation was a part of their psychological make up so the Turak's first words did not come as a surprise to him or Bose who had obviously read the same brief.

"You are not Radford! I came to meet the Human who purports to lead your forces into combat not," the Turak waved at Bose dismissively, "the driver of a broken-down waste hauler fit only to be dropped into the nearest star to burn up!" John inwardly winced as the pride of the Terran Defense Force was described in such a manner. To Bose's credit she failed to react to the Turak's blatant insult instead standing her ground and looking the Turak square in the eye.

"If you wish to speak to Admiral Radford, Commander of the Combined Fleet, then you will do me the courtesy of identifying yourself or you may take yourself and your lackeys back aboard that piece of junk you arrived in and remove it and your stench from my vessel."

For a tense moment, the pair continued to stare at each other like two children having a staring competition in the school yard before the Turak cocked his head to one side to look beyond Bose to where John was standing silently at parade rest.

The Turak's head came vertical and he parroted Bose's earlier move by curtly nodding to her. "I am Vek, War Chief of the Turak and I am honored to be aboard your flagship."

Insults exchanged and repudiated I would call that a draw thought John as he stepped forward to greet his guest.

"John Radford." He said by way of introduction keeping it simple.

Vek decided to follow John's lead. "Vek. May I introduce my son, Clan Lord Yue of Clan Orlak." The younger Turak dipped his head sharply once and John returned the greeting.

"We have much to discuss War Chief." Said John. "Perhaps you would care to join my staff and I and we can get started?"

"My son," Vek indicated Yue, "is keen to learn all he can about your Commonwealth. Would it be possible for him to have a tour of the ship while we talk?"

John struggled to hide his surprise at Vek's request however, Bose came to his rescue. "It would be my pleasure to conduct the tour personally, Admiral."

"You have my thanks, Captain." Replied Vek as one of the armored Turak, his crimson armor reflecting the overhead lights, moved to Yue's side. "Alas, a Clan Lord must be accompanied by at least one member of his personal guard at all times."

"I completely understand." Bose said with a courteous smile while two fingers of her half concealed left hand flicked out. The marine major in charge of the side party interpreted Bose's message correctly as the major's deep voice called out sharply.

"Bennett. Oyer. Front and center." With that the two largest marines in the side party went from present arms to shoulder arms in a series of deft movements, then without a further command, took up position behind Bose.

Vek let out a bellowing laugh that echoed around the Landing Bay. "I see your Captain Bose has a sense of humor, Admiral."

"That she does War Chief Vek, that she does. Now shall we get started?" John indicated the doors to the elevator that would take them to the Flag Bridge.

***

THE DOMINATOR | FLAGSHIP OF THE TURAK

Mynut touched a control that rewound the video taken by the video pick up concealed in the armor of Yue's escort. Letting the video run forward again he paused it as the shape of a sleek, small craft came into shot.

"So, these are the Human space-fighters that I have heard so much about?"

"Yes, First." Answered Yue who relaxed in a comfortable padded seat holding a goblet of grukk. To Vek, who sat in an identical seat, Yue reminded him of a time so long ago when Kal and he would spend long evenings discussing anything that popped into their heads. The resemblance and demeanor were so striking. Even down to that foul-tasting choice of drink.

"And this?" Asked Mynut, intruding on Vek's reminiscing. Vek moved his eyes to the image that had caught Mynut's attention. The display showed a close up of a compact, stubby missile hanging from a pylon that projected out from the space-fighter.

"Intelligence is calling it an antimatter missile." Explained Yue. "I think we caught them off guard as once the fighters ground crew realized we were there they attempted to cover the missile while Captain Bose ushered us out of the area as quickly as she could."

Mynut grunted softly. Vek had been surprised at how quickly Mynut has accepted Yue. The War Chief had expected at least blatant resentment from the bullish Mynut however, his selection as Vek's First and the casting off, of all previous clan loyalties seemed to have a had a sobering effect on the man who had once sworn to destroy Clan Orlak. Perhaps Mynut would even come to accept the upcoming bonding of Yue and Waynal. In a complete break with tradition that was rumored to be causing cross words on both sides the soon to be bonded couple intended on combining their two clans under a new clan name. The first entirely new clan since the Turak were forced to flee Home so many generations ago. Vek shook himself out of his daydreaming as Mynut continued to speak.

"If the Commonwealth have succeeded in incorporating antimatter into a missile that can be delivered by something as small and agile as their space-fighter then that presents us with a threat that our fleet is not equipped to handle."

"Truth." Agreed Vek. "On this occasion though, we are the Commonwealth's allies."

"Truth." Said Mynut.

"Truth." Echoed Yue.

ADMIRAL'S QUARTERS | TDF *ITUS*

"I don't trust that lot as far as I could fling them?" Grumbled Analisa Chavez, John's pick for second-in-command for the upcoming battle.

"Not in a month of Sunday's." Agreed Robert Lewis the only other person physically present in the room. The remaining Commonwealth commanders were all attending via holo conferencing.

"Are we talking about the Turak or the Alonans?" Asked Admiral Dekal, Commander Third Fleet.

Lela Wilder let out a snort which the high definition sound system repeated faithfully. "Both."

For the purposes of command integration John had paired the three battleships of the Janus Space Navy with the seventeen cruisers of the Imperial Navy though it had come as a surprise to everyone that Emperor Lura had taken personal command of the Imperial ships. His arrival had caused a lot of head scratching as John had originally planned for Robert to assume command of the Imperial ships. The problem was solved however, when one of John's enterprising staff officers pointed out that the most effective way of using the Imperial cruisers technical superiority was as a quasi-independent unit. Task Force Vigilant was born with Robert exerting command and control from the JSN battleship while Emperor Lura remained aboard the INS *Vengeance*. As if that was not enough for one day the Alonans had brought along Commander Okal. The Saiph ship commander apparently had made it a condition of his continuing technical assistance that he and his ships doctor be allowed to accompany the Emperor. Robert had suggested that perhaps Okal wanted to ensure that the Supreme Leader paid for his crimes this time around. The Saiph had been waiting a long time to see him brought to justice. Even if that justice was on the business end of a nuclear tipped missile.

"Do we have an update on the Persai?" John aimed the question at Analisa who had the unenviable task of making some kind of sense out of the various ship types to attempt to produce a balanced fighting force.

Analisa checked her PAD before answering. "Force Leader Tolas is due at zero three hundred hours."

"Admiral Dekal, I'm chopping the Persai to you." The Garundan nodded. "Third Fleet is weak after the battering you took at Dagger Station, and those fast attack cruisers of the Persai are worth at least two standard cruisers on a bad day."

"Understood, Admiral Radford." Acknowledged Dekal.

John smiled at the diminutive Garundan who had replaced him as Commander Third Fleet when John had been recalled to Earth to take over Carrier Strike Group *Itus*. The Saiph had wiped out more than half his command when they carried out their sneak attack on Dagger Station and it had shaken the Garundan Navy to the core. Force Leader Tolas was a seasoned commander and the Persai would bolster not only the

Garundan's weakened fleet but their morale also. Something that Dekal was very aware his crews were in need of.

John switched his attention to the final attendee. Admiral Yula of the Benii Federation had sat silently throughout the meeting her blue on blue eyes gazing out from her lithe silvery form.

"Admiral Yula, you and your carriers are a sight for sore eyes."

If the Benii commander understood John's turn of phrase or not she appreciated the sentiment. "The Daughters of the Benii stand ready, Admiral."

"Have you had a chance to read the Operations Order, Admiral?" Asked Analisa.

"I have, and I agree with your decision to disperse our carriers throughout the fleet. It strikes me as an elegant solution to the fleets lack of fighter cover though I am troubled by the lack of available munitions."

Robert intervened in an attempt to soothe Yula's worries. "The fabrication facilities of Janus are working around the clock to produce HVAMM's as rapidly as possible, Admiral Yula, dispersion of the available missiles will be based on need as per the fleets overall strategic plan and not at the tactical level."

By the look on the Benii admirals face she was not overly happy with Robert's answer though she decided to keep any protests to herself.

John clapped his hands together and rose from his seat. "Well, I think we will call it a night there. We all have a lot of work to do over the coming days to ensure the fleet is battle ready. Thank you for your time."

The various holo cubes blinked out and those physically present began to filter out. At the back of the room Captain Bose caught John's eye and he signaled for her to wait as the room emptied. With the doors closed John and Bose were left alone.

"Well?" Asked John.

In response Bose opened her hand revealing more than a dozen tiny black cubes. "We are finding these in every compartment that Clan Lord Yue visited. They record audio and video as well as being able to tap into any nearby computer system. Pretty neat actually." Bose said with a note of admiration in her voice.

"What about the fighter bay?"

"I made sure the maintenance crew chief played it up to the full. He had his guys running around like headless chickens when we walked in trying to hide the HVAMM." Bose said with a grin. "I might have to suggest he joins the ships drama society."

"As long as the Turak got the message that we have not only space-fighters that they don't have but we also have a nice little missile that they can carry that can kill the biggest ship they have in one pass." John said from beneath a furrowed brow.

Bose's features took on a wariness of their own. "Do you really think its that bad, Admiral?"

John shrugged his shoulders. "Let's deal with the Saiph first and worry about the Turak tomorrow, shall we?"

CHAPTER EIGHTEEN

MARCH TO THE SOUND OF THE DRUMS

FLAG BRIDGE | TDF *ITUS* | ONE HUNDRED LIGHT-YEARS FROM THE DYSON SPHERE

John had lost count how many times his eyes had strayed to the red numerals of the clock mounted on the bulkhead above the holo cube that was displaying the current positions of the largest fleet ever assembled.

With aching slowness, the time crept toward zero. As the numbers changed to zero, *Itus* and the massed firepower of six races activated their gravity drives as one. In less time than it took to blink millions of tons of battle armor, missiles, lasers, space-fighters and the flesh and blood manning them disappeared from normal space to reappear in the belly of the beast. A beast that John Radford was here to slay.

John slowly released the breath he had been holding as the ship count went from red to green indicating the successful arrival of the various parts of the fleet.

"Deploy the Blockers." Ordered John and the Tactical Officer who had his finger poised above the transmit key applied the required pressure and the first part of John's plan slipped into gear as over a hundred destroyers and frigates once more activated their gravity drives only to reemerge scattered throughout a wide globe completely encircling the Dyson Sphere. John tapped a finger nervously as the clock restarted. When it reached one minute, he gave his next order.

"Activate!"

The engineers had told him that it would not be possible to fit gravity drive nullifying generators into anything as small as a destroyer never mind a frigate. They had not reckoned with one Bosun's Mate and a plasma torch. Each one of the 'modified' ships would need a significant amount of time in the repair yards when this was all over but the generators had been squeezed into place and now they formed overlapping bubbles of space where it was simply impossible to activate a gravity drive and enter fold space. These would be John's Blockers. Whatever Saiph vessels were in this system where trapped and if the Saiph attempted to destroy the Blockers John was sure the fleet footed vessels would have the legs to outrun their pursuer in normal space while the other Blockers would adjust their formation to cover the hole left by their shipmates. At least that was the theory.

As the clock struck two minutes in-system John spoke once more. "Comms. The fleet will advance."

From four different directions thousands of warships lit off their engines. So began the battle.

✳ ✳ ✳

THE DYSON SPHERE

The high-speed carriage carrying the Supreme Leader and Star Leader Foral raced through the darkness in silence on its magnetic rails. A silence that was reflected in the carriage's interior. Lorai, designer of the Dyson Sphere and director of the breeding program which had populated it, had immediately called Foral when the alarm was raised that there was an enemy fleet approaching.

"How have they found us?" Lorai had demanded to know. "What shall we do?" She had cried.

"We will fight them, and we will be victorious against the half-breeds!" Screamed Foral as he had terminated the connection. Now though, having seen the strength of the not one but four separate fleets homing in on the Dyson Sphere he felt the first stirrings of self-doubt. Glancing across at the Supreme Leader deep in thought as the carriage sped them to the docks where the ships of First Wing lay idle awaiting their arrival Foral steeled himself. They were Saiph and Saiph were destined to rule the stars.

"Foral, what is the latest from Third Wing?"

"Geoll, and a small element of his command were conducting a training cruise for a new batch of crew and are beyond the defensive envelope of our fixed weapons' emplacements. Computer predictions indicate that, even at maximum drive, the half-breeds will intercept them long before they reach safety. Geoll's only hope is that we sally forth with all available ships and come to his aid. The remainder of the fleet could then join us and cover our withdrawal."

The Supreme Leader brought his fist crashing down on the edge of his seat in frustration. "Losing Geoll will be a blow to our standing. The populace looks up to him. Respect him. To them, we are something that they've read about in historical texts. They've had no chance to warm to us. To appreciate that we, the Originals who fled the corruption and misguided ways of the Elders; *we* will lead them to victory over the half-breeds."

Foral remained silent as the Supreme Leader vented his frustration. As commander of the Saiph fleet he had witnessed firsthand how occasionally, furtively an order given by him would led to an exchange of glances between officers and enlisted alike before the order was executed. It was a momentary pause and one that Foral had initially dismissed as simple nervousness among an inexperienced crew. Something that would disappear once they had tasted their first fire of combat. Worryingly, this had not been so. It appeared to Foral that there were some among his officer corps who were experiencing doubts. Perhaps not in the aim of ensuring the Saiph were the pinnacle of civilizations in the galaxy. No, it was more with the Supreme Leaders commitment to achieving that goal by eradicating any race that stood in his way. A thought occurred to Foral as the carriage approached its destination. One he chose to share with the Supreme Leader before they arrived within earshot of another.

"Supreme Leader, what if we turn the loss of Geoll to our advantage?"

The Supreme Leader looked at his subordinate with raised eyebrows then, slowly, he understood what Foral was getting at and a thin smile lifted his lips. "We announce our profound sense of loss at Geoll, a hero of the Saiph who gave his life fighting the half-breeds to his last breath. We express our anger and promise that he shall be avenged."

"The people will have their figurehead and you, Supreme Leader, will have secured their unquestioning loyalty."

Foral could see the Supreme Leader was seriously considering his suggestion.

"How long would we have to delay our departure?" Asked the Supreme Leader as he continued to weigh up his options.

Foral reached across to a small control pad and entered his security code. "How may I be of assistance, Star Leader Foral?" Came the dispassionate voice of the artificial intelligence that controlled every function of the Dyson Sphere from maintaining the orbits of the solar panels that encompassed their star and supplied the industries and homes of the Saiph near limitless power, to ensuring the water pressure of a farms hydroponics bay was set correctly. In short, the AI was central to everything and only a handful were trusted with access to the AI directly. Foral had that access.

"Time to intercept of Caretaker Geoll's vessels by the enemy fleet?"

"Twenty-eight vols at current speed, though that may vary dependent on ship maneuvering."

"Recalculate time parameters taking into account the most efficient evasive tactics."

"Thirty-four vols."

"Calculate time required for First Wing to reach Caretaker Geoll's position if we delay its departure until sufficient personnel have manned Second Wing to allow it to deploy?"

"Thirty-three vols." Replied the AI.

The Supreme Leader shook his head. "Not long enough, Foral."

Foral's brain raced as he tried to think of a way to buy himself more time then an idea flashed into his brain. "Where are the majority of Second Wings crew right now?"

"Crews are currently responding to the emergency recall announcements and are proceeding via the mass transit system on priority carriages."

A wicked toothy grin spread across Foral's features. "Recalculate previous time estimate reducing the carriages carrying Second Wing personnel by -", Foral did the rough math, "25 percent."

"Thirty-five vols." The AI reported dispassionately.

The Supreme Leader strode across the carriage and clasped Foral by the shoulder giving him a sharp nod.

"Reduce speed of those carriages by 25 percent with immediate effect." Foral said as their own carriage reached the docks where First Wing were secured. As the vehicle's doors opened both Saiph were assailed by a barrage of noise as orders were shouted and running crew rushed to complete their final tasks that would allow First Wing to race to the rescue of shipmates.

Five thousand kilometers away the speed of the packed carriage carrying Trakl and naval personnel in various states of dress to the docks were Third Wing was moored slowed perceptibly. Geoll's second-in-command had remained behind at Geoll's insistence as it had been Trakl's daughters second birthday and he had planned a visit to the inland sea. Now though, Trakl was berating himself for putting family before duty. He should be on the bridge with Geoll. Fighting the enemy and protecting not only his own family but the Saiph race from the war like half-breeds. Trakl activated his link to the AI to demand an explanation.

"Explain the reduction of speed of -," Trakl hunted for the carriage designator partially hidden by the heads of his fellow passengers, "Eh, X093L2?"

"Carriage X093L2 speed reduced due to a priority command override."

What! What idiot ordered that? Thought Trakl as he stifled a string of expletives that wanted to erupt from his mouth. Taking a deep breath, he calmed himself for the AI was only following orders after all.

"Countermand that order on my authority. Return to previous acceleration forthwith."

"Unable to comply."

Now Trakl did swear out loud causing a number of heads to turn in his direction until they noted his rank and abruptly found something more interesting to look at through the carriage's windows.

"Explain." Demanded Trakl his grip on the stanchion he was leaning against tightening so that his knuckles went white.

"Unable to comply."

Trakl's nostrils flared as he opened his mouth to interrogate the AI further before he realized the fruitlessness in it. Trakl had grown up having the AI instantly available to answer any question or respond to any command that he had adequate authority to instruct. An authority set by firstly his parents, then his tutors and now, finally, by his command authority as a naval officer. That familiarity with how the AI's complex reasoning software worked had taught him one thing if nothing else. When the AI said it was unable to comply with a command no amount of argument or circumnavigation would change its answer. The question that lurked at the back of Trakl's mind now was who had sufficient authority to countermand him.

✻✻ ☐

THIRD WING TRAINING CRUISE

Geoll was flung against his seats restraints as his vessel was lashed by Directed Energy Weapons and rocked by the explosion of multi kiloton nuclear warheads that battered relentlessly at his energy shields. Another explosion caused the bow of his ship to drop sharply flinging Geoll's head sharply back until it impacted on the padded head rest. A sharp pain caused Geoll to reach up and touch his tongue. The finger came away with blood on it. Pungent smoke filled the air from an electrical fire that had broken out in the Navigational Section and crewmembers were dousing it with chemical fire extinguishers, which added to the diminishing visibility and foul air.

"We've lost forward shield emitters!" Cried a voice Geoll struggled to identify in the haze. Damn, I should have spent more time familiarizing myself with this crew before taking them out Geoll chided himself. Geoll could recognize every member of his own crew in the darkest or noisiest of environments however, this ship was straight from the builders yard and the crew was nearly as new with the majority of them having recently graduated from the various naval colleges. That lack of experience was the very reason for Geoll wanting to accompany the four-ship squadron on this training cruise. Geoll saw it as his personnel responsibility to ensure that their training was up to a sufficient standard for them to join the fleet. Nobody had ever in their wildest dreams expected them to be flung into combat on their first cruise. None of that mattered right now for they were in a fight for their lives and they were losing.

Geoll ignored the blood that was now streaming out of his mouth and wiped debris from his tactical screen with the back of one pressure suited hand. The suit made it more difficult to punch the correct icons on the screen however, better the inconvenience than dying a grisly death if the hull was compromised and the compartment suffered explosive decompression.

The computer obediently returned the answer to Geoll's query and he opened his mouth to shout the course corrections to the Navigator as the entire ship wrenched to starboard bouncing his head so hard of the headrest that spots filled his vision. The blaring alarm that briefly filled his ears before the faceplate of his helmet sealed shut was replaced by the high pressure hiss of his suit filling with atmosphere to keep him alive as the air of the bridge blew out into the depths of space through the massive jagged edge hole where three decks had once stood between the bridge and the ships outer hull.

Geoll closed his eyes for a moment and struggled to control his breathing. Geoll remembered his pressure-suit instructor repeating, Heavy breathing mists up the faceplate and makes it harder to see, as Geoll practiced with the suit as a cadet.

The suit has enough air to keep you alive for two hours, so take your time, gather your thoughts, and come up with a plan before you do anything, the instructor had urged.

Heeding the lessons, of long ago, Geoll steadied his breathing, opened his eyes, and surveyed the damage to the bridge.

Devastation. The word Geoll matched to the image in front of him.

Failing power intermittently lit up the bridge. Geoll saw flashes of wrecked consoles. Floating limbs. Bodies of the deceased trapped by the shock harnesses they had worn while the battle raged around them.

Geoll twisted around to see his tactical screen more clearly. Of his four-ship squadron only one was still under way. In comparison, he counted a dozen or more enemy vessels that were either coasting, powerless and streaming precious atmosphere or losing ground in the chase to catch his fleeing ships, indicating they had suffered considerable damage too.

A flash of pride ran through Geoll. His inexperienced crew had fought like demons as he had guided them toward home and safety.

Keep fighting! He had urged them, *Our comrades are, even now, racing to our rescue.* The rescue never appeared, instead the squadrons' tactical screens had filled with enemy ships. Onward they plunged, home growing ever bigger in the viewers, only for the enemy small craft to swarm them, like blood-sucking insects, flitting in and out of range of his weapons; each time stabbing at him with their high-powered lasers and missiles forcing him to change course until, inevitably, the enemy's larger units had closed with him and began their ferocious bombardment.

First, one of the squadrons' energy shields had failed and the small craft had pounced; ripping into the hull, tearing off chunks of armor until the inevitable happened. The ship exploded with the blinding brightness of a dying star.

The second ship of his squadron suffered a similar fate and, when it looked like the two surviving squadron mates might make a last dash for home, a new type of warship had entered the fray and, before his unbelieving eyes, deployed energy shields of its own, stunning Geoll and his shipmates. The Supreme Leader had pointed to the energy shields of the Saiph cruisers as the single-most important advantage they had, and one that gave them impunity against every enemy vessel, such impunity did not exist.

Switching the display from tactical to damage control, Geoll felt a growing sense of dread as he scanned his damaged ship.

His stomach churned as he realized his ship was finished, all he could do was save as many crewmembers as possible. Entering his individual command code into the computer, he ordered it to override all the cruisers communications channels including those built into each crewman's pressure suit.

"This is Geoll. Abandon ship! I say again. Abandon ship!" Duty done, Geoll released his restraints and immediately began to float from his seat.

Deftly using the armrest, he spun himself in the direction of a row of hatches that now had red lights blinking above them to guide the crew to them. He heard the dispassionate voice of the computer repeating the order to abandon ship.

Projected onto Geoll's face plate in bold red lettering was the same command, on the chance that a crewmember had lost voice communications, there was no mistaking their orders. Reaching the hatch, the inbuilt biometrics recognized him and automatically opened. Grabbing a hold of the handle mounted above the hatch Geoll flipped himself through feet first and slid into the acceleration couch. He reached for the straps to secure him in place, while behind him the hatch closed automatically, and the computer started counting down.

Geoll had just secured his last strap when the acceleration pushed him back into the acceleration couch and the escape pod rocketed down the tube. A command from the on-board computer caused an explosive panel to blow on the cruiser's outer hull, a fraction of a second before the escape pod shot past and out into open space.

Geoll flicked the cover off a switch and flipped the emergency transponder on, the little pod now transmitted its location.

Geoll lay back on the couch, the taste of blood in his mouth. He hoped for rescue.

* * *

INS *VENGEANCE*

"Target destroyed, your Majesty." Reported the Alonan colonel who commanded the Imperial Naval Ship *Vengeance*. If the presence of Emperor Lura sat in a makeshift jump seat bolted against the rear bulkhead of the bridge fazed him at all he showed no sign of it though, the presence of two Saiph and their escort in matching jump seats during a battle where he was responsible for destroying one Saiph cruiser and helping turn another into something resembling Swiss cheese was- odd.

"Thank you, Colonel. Are there any indications that the bulk of the Saiph fleet is preparing to sortie from the Sphere?"

"Not at this time, your Majesty."

Lura made a point of turning to meet the eyes of Commander Okal who met his look with an impassive look of his own. The female Saiph, Salo, who sat by his side however, was staring at the Emperor with pleading eyes. The Saiph's escort, Captain Calan, kept his face studiously facing to the front.

Holding Okal's eyes with his own, Lura addressed the colonel. "Please inform Admiral Lewis that we are initiating search and rescue operations."

"Immediately, your Majesty."

As the colonel passed along his orders Lura received a small nod of gratitude from Okal while Salo fiddled with her unfamiliar acceleration harness causing Okal to break eye contact with the Emperor and focus on her.

"What are you doing Salo?"

"Need I remind you Commander that I am a doctor. There may be injured that require my assistance and I can think on no one more qualified on board this ship to treat a Saiph than myself. Can you?" Salo had a reputation for being a stubborn old woman but she also was a fantastic doctor hence her original assignment to the *Savior*.

Okal looked across to Lura who simply waved a hand toward the bridge doors while saying. "Captain Calan, escort Doctor Salo to the medbay."

Calan undid his own restraints with one hand while reaching across and doing the same for Salo with one hand. "If you will follow me, Doctor."

Furtively Okal glanced around the bridge. Everywhere he looked Alonans busily went about their business even Lura's attention was fixed on the repeater screen which projected out of the side of his chair. Ensuring no one was looking in his direction Okal activated his subcutaneous implant. "Chera?"

"I am here, Commander." Replied the soft feminine voice of the *Savior*'s AI.

When Okal had insisted that he accompany Emperor Lura and the Imperial cruisers to battle the Saiph of the Supreme Leader his own ships AI, Chera, had made a very unusual and, it had seemed impossible, request of him. She wished to accompany him. Okal had laughingly asked Chera how he was expected to sneak an AI that was integrated into every single circuit aboard the *Savior* never mind having a central core that stood over two decks tall onto an Alonan ship without anyone noticing. In response the AI had activated a holo cube and projected into it a small device, no bigger than Okal's thumb.

"There is no requirement for me to accompany you, Commander. The device before you will meet your needs. My essential systems, my consciousness if you will, will remain available to you while you are out of contact with the *Savior*. I will have limited capabilities, but I will be able to conduct many of my core functions"

What Okal had initially dismissed out of hand now made a certain amount of sense. "Will infiltration be available?" Okal asked as the seed of a plan germinated in his mind.

"Affirmative, Commander. I will remain able to access and control any computer system that comes within range of this device. Though limited, the device should have sufficient storage capability for me to retain all the data I'm likely to come across in either the Alonan or the Commonwealth's primitive systems."

Now Okal's brain went into overdrive as the seed of a plan began to bud and expand. After they had learned the truth that the Alonans had not been entirely truthful with them Okal had originally planned to escape from Foram and offer his services to the Commonwealth. The destruction of Alona and Emperor Lura's offer to share his new Saiph based technology with the Commonwealth had forced him to swiftly alter his plan. Lura had had no choice but to reveal the truth to him, a truth that the Alonan Emperor had no idea Okal was already well aware of. Okal once more agreed to work alongside the Lura though he was able to leverage the Alonan for direct access to the mass of Commonwealth scientist and engineers that flocked to Foram to gaze in awe at what the Alonans had achieved with Saiph help. And all the while Chera had been stealthily accessing every Commonwealth system that she could. Building up a vast sum of knowledge on not only the Commonwealth but on the Turak also. Even the Commonwealth's most sensitive data proved easy for the advanced computing power of Chera to reach. One of the first tasks Okal had set Chera was to penetrate the Commonwealth communications systems which the AI did in under an hour as encrypted block after block fell to her artificial intelligence that was generations ahead of anything the Commonwealth had even imagined was possible. In less than a week the AI had access to Commonwealth computer systems and data cores throughout known space. Nothing escaped her electronic tendrils.

"And how will we get this device past Alonan and Commonwealth security? They are bound to thoroughly search us prior to leaving and even if you can fool their electronic scanning equipment a simple physical inspection will turn up the device."

"I have considered that, Commander, and I believe I have a solution." Answered Chera and something in her tone made Okal slightly wary but he decided to indulge her.

"Very well, Chera, I'm willing to listen."

"Surgical implantation." The AI said without hesitation.

Now, sat on the bridge of the *Vengeance* Okal tried not to reach around to his left hip where a fresh scar itched as the pseudo skin Doctor Salo had placed over the fresh scar to conceal it from prying eyes. By sheer force of will Okal refrained from jumping up from his seat and using both hands to scratch the niggling irritation.

"How many life pods are there?"

"The Alonans have detected only five life pods which remain viable, Commander, the others have sustained significant damage and are no longer of sustaining life."

Okal clenched his jaw in worthless frustration for the lives that had been sacrificed once more in the Supreme Leader's futile war.

"Commander, I have detected something which I believe may be of interest to you."

"What is it Chera?"

"A communications link, subtle enough that I do not believe the Alonans have detected yet."

"Analysis?"

Chera paused for the briefest of seconds as she confirmed her analysis of the link before answering. "I believe there is another artificial intelligence at work in this system, Commander."

The revelation stunned Okal, his jaw dropped open before he could stop it. In a panic, he hastily glanced around the bridge. The bridge crew were going about their duties, he relaxed, no one had seen his reaction. He resumed his silent conversation with Chera.

"What is the location of the AI? Was it aboard one of the Saiph cruisers?"

"No, Commander. A data link operating on a very obscure frequency connected the Saiph. However, I have detected the same signal emanating from the Sphere. The source of the signal is there."

"Was the AI controlling the cruisers?" Asked Okal before answering the question himself. "No, of course not. What's the point of a living crew if a ship can be completely controlled remotely?" Think Okal, think, he mentally berated himself. Why have a link to a distant AI? An answer started to reveal itself through the fog of confusion.

"Chera, when the Supreme Leader fled home, how common was the use of systems like you?"

"It was common for artificial intelligences of the time to be integrated into every walk of life. Though not as advanced as I, the AIs of the time could run most tasks autonomously, Commander."

Okal raised his eyes until they centered on the massive sphere hovering in the holo cube which filled the entire front wall of the bridge, wondering if he had discovered a way to halt the bloodshed.

❋ ❋ ❋

MED BAY | INS *VENGEANCE*

Geoll's eyelids fluttered as consciousness returned to him. Bright light caused him to scrunch them closed. A sudden wave of nausea caused his head to spin and the contents of his stomach threatened to violently evacuate through his mouth. A gentle hand touched his shoulder and an unfamiliar, though reassuring voice, spoke to him.

"Lie still for a moment. You have got a nasty bump on your head and you removed a pretty big chunk of your tongue. I've repaired the damage and given you a mild pain blocker which might make you a bit dizzy but the side effects will wear off in a few minutes."

Geoll did as he was told and, as promised, the dizziness dissipated, and he was able to open his eyes without feeling that he was about to throw up. With an effort he managed to prop himself up to discover that he was occupying a bed in what a medical facility. Arrayed along the walls were a number of other beds some of which held other injured Saiph. Looking around he was confused by strange writing above the door and at various points along the walls. His confusion was completed by an elderly Saiph female dressed in a one-piece dark blue uniform. A name tag above her left breast identified her as Doctor Salo while a tag on the right had the word *Savior* emblazoned across it. Geoll struggled to recall ever meeting a Doctor Salo or having seen a ship going by the name *Savior* in the Saiph fleet. Ordinarily all Saiph vessels were known simply by their hull number. Not even the Supreme Leaders ship had a specific name. Geoll turned his head at her approach and his eyes fell again onto the undecipherable writing on the facilities walls.

"Where am I?" Geoll demanded as Salo stopped by his bed.

The woman graced him with a soft smile. "Somewhere safe." She reassured him. "What should I call you?"

Geoll looked at the woman incredulously. "Do you not know me?" He said somewhat taken aback by the doctor's ignorance. Surely his was probably the most recognizable face among all Saiph. "I am Geoll. Caretaker of the Saiph." Salo looked back at him with a blank expression. Ignoring her Geoll swung his legs out of the bed and stood upright.

"What of my crew?"

The smile disappeared from Salo's face to be replaced with a sorrowful expression. "I regret to inform you that we only managed to rescue four other survivors."

Geoll felt unable to breath, as if somebody had physically punched him in the stomach. Only four? Four out of the hundreds who had set sail with him that morning. Anger twisted in Geoll's gut his eyes searched for the door and he took an unsteady pace toward it. Where had his reinforcements been? Where had the Supreme Leader been when he and his crews had needed him most? Why had he not come?

"Where are you going?" Salo demanded making to grab his arm.

Geoll shook her off continuing his unsteady progress toward the door answering her question over his shoulder. "I shall speak with the Supreme Leader and demand to know why he sacrificed us to the half-breeds."

A firmer hand grabbed his arm and spun him around and Salo's face was unrecognizable as the gentle woman from only a moment before. "Half-breeds! You ignorant, brain washed simpleton. If it had not been for those so-called half-breeds, you and what was left of your crew would be dead! Frozen corpses preserved forever traveling through space. A testament to that genocidal maniac's lust for power. No wonder the Elders locked him up."

Geoll backed away from Salo aghast that she could say such words. "Silence! You speak lies! It was the Elders who were crazed. It was they who brought Saiph to its needs. It was they who refused to listen to the Supreme Leaders words of wisdom." Screamed Geoll even as something deep inside him doubted those very words.

A short, sharp laugh came from Salo's mouth as she poked a bony finger into Geoll's chest. "It was your beloved Supreme Leader that destroyed Saiph. His puppets bombs and missiles that burned a civilization that had existed for millennia to the ground. Men, women, children. A world turned to ash."

The pleads of the asteroid miners begging him to spare them raced unbidden into Geoll's mind. "No! Lies! Lies!" Shouted Geoll as he backed away from her. "You have no proof of these things!"

Tears formed in Salo's eyes, her voice barely a whisper as her mind filled with images of death and destruction that she thought long buried. "I have no need of proof Geoll. I was there."

It was too much for Geoll. The man slowly sank to the floor, tears escaping from beneath closed eyelids that did nothing to block out the images of missiles impacting defenseless habitat domes or lasers piercing the skins of unarmed cargo vessels as they fled the wrath of the Supreme Leader.

A pair of Alonan medics entered the room alerted by the shouting, worried looks on their faces. The last thing they had expected to see was a Saiph curled up on the floor softly weeping with Doctor Salo bent over him assuring him everything would be alright they paused until Salo beckoned them to help her lift Geoll back onto the bed where he body continued to be wracked by his sobbing. A man who had come to realize the dark deeds he had committed had been all for a lie.

✳ ✳ ✳

"Is he going to recover?" Okal asked Salo as they both stood a few paces from the bed where Geoll lay staring at the ceiling with empty eyes.

Salo rubbed at her chin while she considered her answer. "Hard to tell. If we were back on *Savior*, I could begin him on a regime of psychological impairment meds that would give his mind time to process the fact that his entire life has been a lie." Salo shrugged her shoulders. "As it is, he needs something to give him a new goal in life. Something that will bring meaning, penance if for want of a better word for the acts he has committed."

Okal indicated the other Saiph that occupied beds in the Med Bay. "What about your other patients?"

"I expect them all to recover well. The Alonans have questioned them and apart from that one over in the corner." Salo jerked her head to where an Alonan with a pistol holstered at his waist stood beside a bed holding a shackled Saiph. "He's a diehard believer. Tried to stab me with my own stylus last time I got too close."

"And the other two?" Asked Okal.

A scowl formed on Salo's face. "Glad to be alive. They are so young. I was playing with toys at their age."

Okal looked back to where Geoll was lying.

"They keep asking about him."

"I'm sorry." Okal said as he turned to face the doctor again.

"I said, they keep asking about Geoll."

"That's not unusual. Crew would be expected to ask after their commander if he were injured."

"If he had been their commander."

Okal gave Salo a questioning look. "What do you mean, if Geoll had been their commander?"

"This was only a training cruise. A final test to see if they were fit enough to join the fleet. Apparently Geoll saw it as his personal mission to ensure that now the Supreme Leader had awoken, succeeded Geoll as leader and the war had begun that only the best serve with the fleet."

Okal looked from Salo to the shell of a man lying motionless on the bed and then back to Salo. "Are you telling me that Geoll was once the ultimate authority within the Sphere."

"That's what they told the Alonan who carried out the interrogation."

Okal bent at the waist, resting his hands on the bar at the end of Geoll's bed. His eyes searched the face of the Saiph immobile figure mulling over what Chera and he had discussed earlier. Could this man hold the key to it all?

"May I speak with him?" Okal asked Salo as he walked past her obviously intending on doing so no matter what the doctor said.

"Of course," she said, "I'll get out of your way, shall I?" Before turning on her heel and walking away to check on her other patients.

Okal sat on the edge of Geoll's bed, oblivious to Salo's departure. The pale, lightly furred face motionless as a corpse. The eyes staring off into the distance.

"Geoll," Okal said loud enough that he hoped it would penetrate the near catatonic state the man had descended into, "I need your help to stop the Supreme Leader. Stop the killing of your people."

Geoll's face showed a flicker of movement. A solitary blink.

"Will you help me?"

Geoll blinked again. His head turned to face Okal. A spark of light in those dead eyes.

"Yes."

***

LEAD CRUISER | FIRST WING | SAIPH FLEET

"My revised order stands, Trakl." Said the Supreme Leader to the clearly angry Saiph officer who had assumed command of Third Wing with the presumed loss of Geoll. "I will not risk the fleet in a forlorn gesture. The half-breeds murdered Caretaker Geoll and the brave crew of his ships. And I, your Supreme Leader, must consider the bigger picture. Instead of rushing headlong into battle, we shall remain secure behind the fortifications of the Sphere until I –" The Supreme Leader looked pointedly at Trakl, "and I alone decide to act. Now, will you obey my orders, or will I relieve you of command?"

For a moment it appeared to the Supreme Leader that Trakl would defy him, then Trakl's shoulders drooped and his downcast gaze signaled his acquiescence before his wavering voice confirmed it. "Your orders shall be obeyed, Supreme Leader."

The Supreme Leader killed the link without further conversation. Foral who had been standing to one side stepped closer to the Supreme Leader so no other member of the bridge crew could overhear their conversation.

"That one is going to be trouble."

"Agreed." Nodded the Supreme Leader. "His loyalty to Geoll, though admirable, may become troublesome in the future. Arrange for him to be reassigned. Have it dressed as a promotion from a grateful leader to a loyal servant of the Saiph."

"And what is our next move to be?" Asked Foral referring to the enemy fleet which now hung in space beyond the effective weapons envelope of the Spheres defenses.

"Our walls are thick my friend and our defenses are formidable. Lorai did her job well. While we sit comfortably increasing our strength daily the half-breeds ships will require constant replenishment and maintenance. Let us leave them beyond our walls to fall into disrepair and then, when the time is right, we will launch ourselves upon them."

CHAPTER NINETEEN

MASKIROVKA

ADMIRAL'S BRIEFING ROOM | TDF *ITUS*
"I don't like it, Admiral. I don't like it one bit." Scowled Analisa Chavez leveling an accusing finger at the Alonan who sat opposite her in complete disregard for etiquette. "And I would have thought that you, Emperor Lura, would have been the last to sign up such an off the wall plan."

If the Alonan took offense, then it failed to register on his impassive face. "I will admit, Admiral Chavez, that when Okal approached me I was initially more annoyed that he had chosen to smuggle a piece of his ships AI aboard the *Vengeance* than he proposed boarding the Sphere on a mission that even he admits has minimal survival odds."

"Thanks for the vote of confidence." Came a low, grumbling voice from the back of the room."

John Radford threw a scowl at the black uniformed man who had made the remark only for Vladimir Egnorov to mouth a silent 'what?' The commander of Thunder had dark circles under his eyes from lack of sleep and John wondered how he was managing to keep going considering the mad rush to get his troopers and their equipment ready at such short notice for an operation that John admitted could have been sketched out on the back of a very small piece of paper. John tuned back into what was being said around the table trusting that Vladimir would refrain from further comment.

"Who's going to tell the Turak that we are planning to save 1.8 billion of their blood enemies?" Asked Robert Lewis. "And that's not me volunteering." He followed up quickly. There was a ripple of nervous laughter from around the table. Everyone had seen the sensor data on the truly massive warships at the heart of the Turak Battle

Groups. The Commonwealth intelligence shops had nicknamed Dominator Class and the name had stuck. At over three kilometers long they massed in at more than four of the Commonwealth's Bismarck Class battleships combined and if the data was reliable, then they had just as much punching power. Nobody in this room was foolish enough to think going up against one of those monsters would be a cake walk.

"I have made the decision that War Chief Vek will not be made aware of this part of the operation for a variety of reasons." John said straight faced his demeanor signaling that as far as he was concerned that particular topic was closed.

"Very well then ladies and gentlemen." Announced John. "Operation Maskirovka begins at zero nine hundred hours precisely. I suggest you return to your commands and complete your final preparations."

The commanders of John's amalgamated fleet departed and as the last of them exited the door slid silently shut behind them leaving John alone with a single black clad figure.

Subconsciously John steepled his fingers in the same manner as Ai Jing and regarded Vladimir with brooding eyes for a moment before speaking. "Do you really think you can pull this off?"

The man who had known John longer than probably any other in his command gave him a tired shrug. "If Geoll's codes are still good. If the air defenses don't blow our asses out of the sky. If you can keep the Saiph ships occupied. If Lura's pet Saiph's little box of tricks works as advertised. I give us a 10 percent chance of success."

If John had not thought Vladimir Egnorov foolhardy before then the Russians answer left him in no doubt of that individual trait.

"I like the name though." Joked Vladimir in an attempt to lighten the mood.

John doffed a fictional cap. "Deception seemed a fitting name for this operation."

"You know my forefathers used it to great effect against the Germans during World War Two. At the Battle of Kursk, they misled the Germans into thinking that the Kursk salient was only weakly defended. Boy did they get a surprise when they ran into a fully manned, layered defense that tore them to pieces. Some say it was one of the key turning points of the war on the eastern front."

"Hopefully our little deception will work out just as effectively." Said John in a low voice.

* * *

MOSQUITO | TAIL CODE AE

"Energy weapon tower at your eleven o'clock. 200 kilometers."

In Louise Bo's head-up-display a red targeting icon began blinking above the fresh target her Wizzo or Weapons' Systems' Officer, Charlie Gregson, had called out to her.

Bo's Mosquito space-fighter zipped across the surface of the Sphere at a stomach-churning rate along with the other eleven fighters of VFA-101, 'The Mailed Fists'.

VFA -101 was only a small element of the swarm of Human and Benii fighters that were scouring the surface of the Sphere destroying every weapons tower, radar emplacement, missile launch facility or damn near anything else that the Benii Electronic Warfare birds hovering high above the surface thought likely to challenge the approaching Combined Fleet.

"Fox One!" Called Bo over the squadron frequency as a semi active radar guided missile dropped from its pylon and streaked away homing in on the electronic energy the of the weapons platforms own fire control radar.

Bo's tracking of her missile was interrupted by the voice of *Itus'* Commander Air Group, the Benii Captain Taw over the command link. "Alpha Strike, this is ITUS CAG. Abort your attack runs and return to the barn. Be prepared for a fast turn around and an anti-ship strike package."

"Looks like the big boys are coming out to play." Charlie said cheerfully.

Ah, to be so young and foolish again thought Bo as she pulled the fighter up into a hard corkscrew climb to throw off any Saiph looking to get a good bead on her as she raced away.

✳✳✳

LEAD CRUISER | FIRST WING | SAIPH FLEET

"I don't understand it, Supreme Leader, how could they half-breeds have guessed so accurately the exit gates of the dockyards?" Foral's rhetorical question was ignored by the man who leaned forward as if he could make the cruiser accelerate all that much faster by sheer force of will.

After an interminable amount of time the cruiser cleared the dockyard gates and the Supreme Leader could see for himself the damage caused by the enemy's small craft obvious to even the naked eye. The Spheres surface was pitted and torn where low yield nuclear weapons had impacted. For a brief moment he wondered if he had left his counterattack too late before shaking off his self-doubt and concentrating on the battle ahead.

"Energy shields active." Called Tactical and, as if on cue, the vessel was rocked by a heavy graser striking the bow shields before being absorbed or redirected.

The Supreme Leader let his eyes linger on the holo display as he noted the latest update. There! Where the Commonwealth ships met the Turak. Two forces who would have preferred to have been at each other's throats than attempting to coordinate a fight against him.' The Turak had not yet displayed possession of antimatter missiles nor of the small craft that had proved so much of an annoyance they firmly believed in 'the bigger the better' and against his cruisers with their energy shielding and antimatter missiles they would be easy pickings. That is where they would be at their weakest and that is where he would slash through their lines and take them from the rear.

"First Wing is to form up on the flagship. Second and Third Wings are to fight a delaying action against the Commonwealth fleet and be prepared to move to the attack when First Wing swings around behind them." Orders given, the Supreme Leader tried his best to look collected and confident as a hundred Saiph cruisers charged Turak ships, more than a thousand times their own number.

✳✳✳

FLAG BRIDGE | TDF ITUS

John Radford allowed himself a small fist punch as the tactical display in the holo cube shifted to show over one-third of the Saiph cruisers that had emerged from the Sphere break away and arrow toward the massed ranks of the Turak who crept ever so slowly forwards gradually closing on a yellow dashed line superimposed on the display with the word 'Marne' displayed beside it.

"Tactical. Time to phase line Marne?"

The Tactical Officer checked his terminal before half turning to answer John. "Forty-five minutes on the clock, Admiral. The Turak have opened fire with their Directed Energy Weapons. It's hard to tell at this distance but all indications are that their fire is inflicting minimal damage on the Saiph cruisers designated Force Alpha."

"Status of Force Bravo and Force Charlie?"

"Force Bravo is advancing on the destroyer screen of First Fleet and will be in weapons range in twenty-eight minutes. Force Charlie is advancing on Third Fleet and will make contact with the Persai cruiser screen in thirty-four minutes."

"Understood. Please remind, Admiral Chavez, and, Force Leader Tolas, that the battle plan calls for them to draw the enemy away from the Sphere so no do or die last stands if they please."

The tactical officer gave John a wide-toothed grin and turned back to his terminal to comply with John's orders, however, the admiral, had already shifted gears and considered the next phase of the battle plan. The one that War Chief Vek was in the dark about.

◻ ◻ ◻

BUFFALO ASSAULT SHUTTLE | THUNDER FOUR

Philippa Papadomas grimaced beneath the sealed helmet of her Wraith combat suit as the area of her left calf demanded for the thousandth time that she give it a good scratch. Which, of course, was impossible. Not unless she wanted to strip out of her armor in front of her team and the three principles that they had been warned by General Egnorov himself were to reach their destination inside the Sphere without a single scratch or Philippa best pack her bags and grab some cold weather gear because apparently it was pretty cold on Uranus.

To get her mind off the interminable itch, Philippa, called up a feed from the Buffalo's cockpit repeater. Buffalo Four, her shuttle, lay in the middle of a loose formation of six other Buffalo's that were emitting as little detectable electromagnetic radiation as possible while they flew on a ballistic trajectory toward an area on the surface of the Sphere that one of her charges, a Saiph named Geoll, had indicted was the closest external bay to a local access node for the Sphere's artificial intelligence and it was that access node that was the troopers from Special Operations Unit 'Thunder' target. Sat between the troopers of Philippa's Team Nine were her other two charges. Captain Calan, Imperial Navy, and Commander Okal another Saiph, though Philippa had been assured that Captain Calan would keep a wary eye on him. She in turn would keep a wary eye on Calan.

"Seems quiet so far, Boss." Trooper 'Sven the Magnificent' Rintoul said in a bored voice.

Before Philippa could reply Staff Sergeant Semple was on the link. "You use that word one more time Sven and I'll space you myself. Understood?"

"Sorry Staff." Grumbled a suitably chastised Sven.

Philippa had never been one to believe in Lady Luck before joining the Marines but after her first combat tour she had changed her mind and one of the things Lady Luck did not like to hear was the use of the word 'quiet' in any shape or form.

"Bogey coming over the radar horizon at our three o'clock!" Called Buffalo Fours pilot followed a couple of seconds later by, "Hulls being pinged by radar." Philippa promised herself that she was going to kick Sven's ass up and down the running track if they made it out of here.

Any hope of the Saiph warship failing to detect their small group of shuttles was squashed a moment later by the copilots near screaming voice. "Radar lock! He's got us! Break! Break! Break!"

Philippa and the other members of Team Nine were pinned in their seats as their shock harnesses locked and Buffalo Four began a series of wild maneuvers to fling off whatever the Saiph ship had fired in their direction.

* * *

BRIDGE | CRUISER 167

Trakl could tell that his seething anger did not go unnoticed by the cruisers crew. The silence that permeated the bridge broken only by the most necessary of conversations may as well have screamed 'what have we done wrong?'

The Supreme Leader had personally passed on his condolences for the loss of Caretaker Geoll to the crew of the ship that he had once commanded. The whole thing had of course been broadcast live to every household and place of work in the Sphere for 1.8 billion Saiph mourned the loss of the man who, up until recently, had guided their daily lives.

The Supreme Leader had expressed his deep and painful heartache before launching into a tirade against the half-breeds who were at the very gates of their homes. Who threatened to destroy everything that they had worked so long and so hard for. To place the Saiph at the center of the galaxy as the prime race.

Trakl had been awarded a promotion in recognition of his tireless support for Geoll and then, as interpreted by the crew and Trakl, banished to carry out patrols on the opposite side of the Sphere from where the enemy fleet were hanging in space presumably contemplating their next move since the Supreme Leader had refused to sally forth and engage them in battle.

Urgent whispers from the sensor section caused Trakl to sit more upright in his seat. The whispers became more animated with the rating at the radar terminal gesticulating wildly for a senior officer to join him. When she did so the conversation restarted.

Trakl could bear to watch the huddled group no longer. "Would someone like to inform me as to what is going on?" Trakl's sarcastic tone was not lost on the junior officer who swallowed before she began speaking.

"Sir, we may have a sensor ghost. I have requested a technician from engineering make their way up here as quickly as possible to run a diagnostic on the equipment."

Trakl let out a tired sigh. "How many times to I have to remind this crew that we are actively involved in a war. All contacts whether you believe them to be sensor ghosts or not are to be tracked and treated as hostile until such time as they are proved otherwise." The officer's face was quickly going increasingly deeper shades of scarlet.

"Put it up on the main display and lets see what you have."

The officer spun away so fast Trakl thought they were going to screw themselves into the deck plating. On the main display the curved surface of the Sphere appeared as a solid block while above it and approaching at what would have been a crawl for a modern warship was a cluster of objects. Trakl counted seven in total.

"Enhance image and give me a thermal overlay." Trakl ordered as he leaned forward in his seat and his hand went to his chin and began rubbing back and forth as he concentrated. Each of the objects was returning a near exact same thermal reading.

If they were naturally occurring meteorites or other space body, then there should be at least a noticeable difference in thermal signature.

"Give me a lidar reading."

On the bow of the cruiser a metal cover drew back revealing the business end of a small but powerful ultraviolet laser. The laser fired seven short burst of coherent light each targeted at a specific one of the speeding objects calculating an exact distance to each. The cruisers tactical computer interpreted the result at nearly the speed of light and projected the results onto the main display.

Trakl gawked at the updated display for a few crucial moments before his training took hold and he began firing out orders. "Those are no natural objects those are stealthy ships trying to reach the Sphere!" Trakl's finger mashed down of the Action Stations alarm which began sounding throughout the ship including the bridge. Trakl had to shout to be heard over the wailing klaxon. "Weapons Officer. Lock bearings and fire all forward lasers on those ships then I want a missile salvo to knock down any survivors"

Seconds later the deck under Trakl's feet vibrated as the cruisers forward laser mounts poured thousands of terrajoules into space which impacted on two of the objects with pinpoint accuracy piercing the composite battle armor that was designed to resist heavy weapons fire but not the main armament of a cruiser. The thermal bloom engulfed the crew compartment incinerating all aboard before the intense heat caused the fuel tanks to fail. The two ships exploded less than a second from the laser striking their outer hulls. Debris flew out in all directions peppering the remaining ships with pieces of battle armor, engine parts and surviving hull pieces all moving faster than a speeding bullet. The closest shuttle suffered catastrophic damage as it was shredded by the expanding debris cloud. Another shuttle had a large section of its stern ripped away, the impact leaving it to tumble through space as the pilots fought for control. That left three shuttles all of which immediately lit off their drives and began performing intricate evasive twists and turns as they dove for the Spheres surface and safety.

Hot on the heels of the initial laser strike arrived Trakl's missile salvo. The Saiph missiles were equipped with proximity warheads which meant that there was no need for the missile to actually impact its target the tiny computer embedded in the missiles body used a millimetric radar mounted in the missiles nose cone to decide when it was close enough to its target to guarantee the maximum amount of damage.

The computers did their job as the salvo detonated their payloads in rapid succession sending a cloud of armor penetrating munitions in precise cones of death that engulfed two of the remaining shuttles. The specially designed penetrators punched through the shuttles armor like it was not there. Microscopic sensors bonded into the penetrators sensed that it had passed through a solid object and ignited the penetrators explosive charges. The effect was akin to exploding a hand grenade in a tin of tomatoes only the tomatoes were flesh and blood.

More by luck than design the seventh and final shuttle had been spared the effects of the missiles penetrators as it had been in the shadow of one unfortunate comrade when the missiles had exploded. This final shuttle dived at reckless speed for the surface.

On board the cruiser Trakl followed its course with his eyes. "Weapons Officer. Reengage that ship!"

The harried officer tapped furiously at his terminal before turning to face Trakl. "I'm sorry sir, the automatic safeties have locked me out. The ship is already too close to the surface for us to engage without a high possibility of striking the Sphere."

"Then why has the Sphere's surface defenses not blown that ship out of space?" Trakl demanded.

The cruisers helmsman faced Trakl but refused to make eye contact. "My apologies, Commander. In my haste to pursue the intruders I allowed us to wander into the inner discrimination zone. The surface batteries acknowledged our presence and deactivated."

Trakl burst out of his seat and grabbed the helmsman by the scruff of the neck. "Am I surrounded by idiots?" Trakl flung the helpless sailor in the direction of the bridge doors. "You are relieved. Get off my bridge before I shoot you myself!" Spinning he pointed an index finger at the Communications Officer. "Signal Ground Command. Warn them that we lost contact with a shuttle sized craft and it may have made a soft landing in quadrant three-nine-Gamma."

* * *

FLAG BRIDGE | TDF ITUS

"How much longer do you expect me to hold my position, Admiral Radford?" Demanded an enraged War Chief Vek.

John glanced hurriedly up to the clock which faithfully repeated the mission time. Thunder had gone communications dark the moment they had past the outer edge of the bubble John had ordered be put in place on the Combined Fleets initial arrival in the Sphere System. If everything had gone to plan, the Thunder teams should have entered the Sphere by now and be making their way toward the access node. Unfortunately, John had no way of knowing how the mission was progressing until it either reached a successful conclusion or..." John chose not to consider failure.

"Admiral! Do you read me?" The image of Vek shifted sideways before disappearing for a number of seconds before reappearing. Behind Vek, John could see growing clouds of toxic smoke.

"War Chief, have you sustained damage? Can you hold on a few minutes longer?"

Vek leaned in close to the cameras pick up and John could see blood trickling down the Turak's forehead. "Listen closely Human -" Vek annunciated slowly so John would not misinterpret his words, "Many Turak have died here today and more will sacrifice their lives while your precious Commonwealth spar with the enemy. My clansmen will hold the Saiph until their last breath but count my words Human. There will be a reckoning one day, and you will repay every drop of Turak blood with a sea of your own blood." Vek terminated the link and left John staring into an empty space. John shook off the feeling of foreboding that churned deep in his gut. He had bought Thunder as much time as he was willing to with the bodies of dead Turak.

"Comms. Signal all ships equipped with gravity nulling generators within effective range of the Turak battle line. They are to cease operation in precisely fifteen minutes." John switched his attention to Tactical without waiting for an acknowledgment. "Tactical. Initiate Dragon Breath at fifteen minutes plus thirty seconds. I want constant updates sent to Admiral Glandinning as to the position of the Turak fleet in relation to Force Alpha."

"Aye, aye, Admiral."

The next fifteen minutes would be the longest in John's life.

✳✳✳

LEAD CRUISER | FIRST WING | SAIPH FLEET

"The Turak die well, Supreme Leader, but they still die." Chortled Star Leader Foral as yet another of the enemy's largest ships broke apart under repeated bombardment from a combination of directed energy weapons fire, nuclear blasts and antimatter warheads.

The losses had not been all one sided. The Turak had learned early on in the engagement to concentrate their fire on a single Saiph cruiser at a time, battering down the cruiser's energy shields through sheer weight of fire alone. Twenty-eight Saiph ships had succumbed to the Turak though half the Turak fleet, over two thousand ships of all classes, were now nothing more than scattered irradiated fragments.

"It is time to finish this." The Supreme Leader said as his lips drew back and formed into a feral smile. "First Wing will close with the enemy and volley fire antimatter missiles. We will use crush their charred bodies under our boots before turning to do the same to the Commonwealth. Order Second and Third Wings to halt their retreat and form a blocking line. They shall be the anvil that we will use our hammer to smash the enemy!"

***

TEAM NINE | THE SPHERE

Philippa Papadomas ignored the pain of her left leg as she hurried down yet another unmarked corridor.

"Left at the next intersection then you should see the door to the access node." Geoll said softly from beside her. I sure as hell hope he knows where he's going thought Philippa as she sent the information over her Wraith suits data link.

Semple and Sven had point and the change of direction popped up on each of their HUD's at the same moment. A double tone in Philippa's left ear indicated that the troopers had got the message.

Captain Calan had the Alonan equivalent of a plasma rifle held loosely in his arms and the sight of the hulking form of Tai in his armored suit only served to emphasize Philippa's decision to pair one of her troopers off with each principle when they had set off from the crashed Buffalo. Both pilots had died on impact and they had only discovered that Browne was dead when he had failed to respond to Semple's team check. On closer inspection the staff sergeant had found a jagged hole in the back of Browne's suit. The hole matched one that penetrated the hull of the Buffalo directly behind Browne's seat. Strangely at the time Philippa realized that now she would never be able to ask him why his nickname was Dunkerdink. With no time to waste the team had left the dead where they were and moved off.

Philippa glanced at the countdown clock in the bottom left corner of her display. Six minutes fourteen seconds... thirteen seconds... twelve seconds.

"OK, people, we need to hustle it up." Turning her head to look down at Okal she turned the volume down on her external speaker so as not to deafen the Saiph when she spoke. "Are you armed, Commander?"

Okal looked up into the blank metallic face of the seven-foot soldier. "I don't think my Alonan friends trust me well enough yet to give me a weapon." He said with a wry smile.

A leg pouch popped open on Philippa's suit and she reached inside retrieving a PEP pistol her hand smoothly checking it before she handed it to the Saiph. "Consider yourself trusted. Safety's off so try not to shoot yourself in the foot, OK?"

The Saiph Commander hoisted the unfamiliar weapon and checked it for balance. "No foot shooting. Got it."

"Or shooting me." Interjected Leslie who Philippa had assigned to the Saiph.

Robb Bishop had noticed what was going on from his position beside Geoll. "You want me to arm Geoll, Boss?" He asked over the team link.

Philippa considered it for no more than a second before answering. "Negative, Bishop. Not until we are sure who's side he's on."

The sound of a plasma rifle on repeat echoed down the corridor at the same time Gavin's voice burst onto the link. "Contact rear! Quinn's down!"

On Philippa's HUD Quinn's name popped up blinking in red for the briefest of moments before going solid. Quinn was dead.

"I've got about a half dozen Saiph back here. Light weapons only. I'm coming in at the bounce."

"Understood. Out to you. Semple let's move out."

At the head of the small group Semple and Sven reached the intersection Geoll had indicated. Semple gingerly poked his rifle around the corner and called up the weapons electronic scope in his HUD. What he saw made him grimace. "Boss, by my count we got a dozen or so setting up some sort of weapons emplacement right where Geoll reckons we have to be."

"Push it across to me." Ordered Philippa and the image from Semple's rifle appeared floating in her view as she made her way down the corridor toward her two troopers. Semple was right thought Philippa, these boys were getting organized in a hurray so they obviously know that we aren't far away and the racket of Gavin's brush with their friends would have woken the dead. Well let's not give them any more time to get ready for us, eh?

Philippa checked the countdown clock again and her breath caught, and her eyes widened in alarm as it screamed three minutes twenty-eight seconds at her. With no time to lose Philippa activated her team link. "OK, Team Nine, we are going to have to do this down and dirty. No fancy tactics. We go around that corner at the bounce and run right over these guys. Leslie, I don't care what it takes but Okal gets into that room and does his thing. Got it?"

"Understood, Boss."

Philippa heard Okal let out a surprised shout as Leslie scooped him up in one power assisted arm and pulled him tight into his armored chest. Philippa used her eye movements to call up the medical drop-down list on her HUD. Selected the strongest pain killer she could take without putting her under and flexed her damaged leg. The pain that shot up her leg left her with stars floating in her eyes.

Gavin's plasma rifle barked again as the Saiph at their rear caught up with them. The sound of unfamiliar weapons fire reached her as the Saiph returned fire in ever rising volume.

"Team Nine. Go! Go! Go!" She shouted as she raced around the corner at the head of her team as fast as her damaged leg would carry her. Plasma rifle leveled in front of her as she went to rapid fire and swept the weapon from left to right laying down a withering field of fire. To her left Semple edged ahead of her mowing down Saiph with the precision of a trained killer. To her right Sven was knocked off balance by the impact of a heavy caliber round on his armored shoulder but he kept running and firing. Tai's name went red as she ran spurring her on. In seconds they were in among the defenders. Plasma rifles were swung like clubs pummeling bodies and cracking heads, the blood of the Saiph drenching their wraith suits until they looked like they had bathed in a swimming pool filled with it. Bishop was as good as his word. The trooper stopped for nothing. Blasting a route through the Saiph with his rifle before barreling through the half open doors leading into the access node.

"Grenade!" Screamed Sven as he dived atop a Saiph with a dull, metal fist sized object. The weapon detonated and thick, blue superheated plasma boiled up from beneath Sven's prone body. Philippa was physically lifted off her feet and flung through the now open door into the access node losing sight of Semple as she did so. Philippa hit the floor hard and skidded across it until the wall on the far side of the room brought her to a bone shuddering halt. Shaking her head, she found that her helmet had malfunctioned and the HUD and external camera was down. Wrenching the helmet off her lungs protested the choking air filled with death and blood.

Philippa's eyes fixed on Okal barely visible behind the armored figure of Leslie. The Saiph commander was working furiously at a terminal.

"Time?" She shouted.

"Two minutes dead." Replied Leslie, his voice sounding strangely robotic through his suit's speaker.

Chunks of wall blew off, Philippa ducked and scampered for cover as Saiph reinforcements fired through the open doorway. The instantly recognizable sound of plasma rifle fire answered and Philippa gave a small satisfied smile as she realized at least one of her team was upright and fighting. Scooting across to where her own rifle had fallen she scooped it up and smoothly popped the charge pack and replaced it with a fresh one from her belt, depressed the charging stud, she rolled into the open doorway and despite her protesting leg, went up on one knee and popped two attackers before dropping and rolling back into cover. For a moment the enemy fire slackened before resuming with increased intensity.

"Done!" Shouted Okal taking a step back from the terminal and colliding with Leslie's unmoving form.

"Time?"

"One minute." Replied Leslie.

Philippa closed her eyes and recited a silent prayer. Please let it be long enough.

The electronic consciousness that was the AI Chera raced along fiber optic and metal cabling until she reached her destination. The brain stack of the Sphere's AI. The AI attempted to resist Chera. To block access to its most critical command and control systems. In computers that think and work in microseconds the battle between the two artificial intelligences raged for days. In reality it was all over in under three seconds. Chera now had complete control and used that control to reach out to every Saiph vessel in the system with a single command. Disengage energy shields.

***

FLAG BRIDGE | TDF *ITUS*

The clock above the main holo cube reached fifteen minutes and exactly on time every gravity drive generator in the area of the Turak fleet went to standby. Seconds later the remains of the Turak fleet folded out of the system.

John Radford gripped the edges of his seat and slowly counted to thirty.

□ □ □

LEAD CRUISER | FIRST WING | SAIPH FLEET

"Supreme Leader, the Turak have folded out of the system." Exclaimed Foral in confusion.

"I can see that you idiot." Answered the Supreme Leader ignoring his fleet commander as he tried to comprehend what was happening.

The sound of raised voices in the Engineering Section caused him to turn and look in their direction, as he did so the officer in charge turned to face him, eyes wide with fear.

"Energy shields are down and the computer is refusing to reset them."

The Supreme Leader did not have time to react before a call from the Sensor Section drowned out the arguing voice at Engineering.

"Small craft! Dozens of them dead ahead... No, wait. They have folded out again, but sensors are registering something in our path" The Weapons' Officer's terminal screamed a warning at him; a missile had launched 300 kilometers ahead of the fleet. At that range flesh and blood could not react quickly enough and the computer was meant to take over and activate the cruisers close-in missile defenses. On this occasion the computer took no action; after receiving an override command to ignore the missiles.

The Supreme Leader had just enough time to realize he was about to die, before the 300 missiles ripple-fired from box launchers holding ten antimatter missiles, each ferried into the system by Fire Ant cargo ships, impacted on the unprotected hulls of First Wing.

There were no survivors.

□ □ □

FLAG BRIDGE | TDF ITUS

The mental sigh of relief that escaped everyone on the Flag Bridge was almost physical, and John gave a small word of thanks to whatever controlled the universe that his plan had worked.

The deep red icons representing the Saiph's remaining warships, which represented a potent threat, reminded John that he had business to complete. Clapping the palms of his hands together he shifted in his chair and prepared to make his next move.

"Comms. Open a link to those ships and tell them…"

"Admiral. Incoming signal from the Sphere." Interrupted the Comms Officer. "It's Caretaker Geoll, Sir." Not waiting for permission, the officer pushed the signal to the main holo cube and Geoll's face filled the display.

"Admiral Radford. The Supreme Leader is dead. With his passing I am once again the voice of the Saiph and my people will listen to me. I ask for an immediate ceasefire. I have ordered all our warships to return to port forthwith –"

John's eyes flicked across to the tactical display and, sure enough, the Saiph warships were moving once more however, they were shaping a course to return to the Sphere.

"Comms. Fleet wide flash signal. Weapons tight. Repeat. Weapons tight."

"My people will need time to adjust to their new reality however, with time and the assistance of Commander Okal I believe this to be possible."

"You understand Geoll, that decisions of that magnitude are not mine to make. I will have to consult with my political superiors, and they will undoubtedly wish to send their representatives to negotiate a more permanent peace accord."

In the display Geoll was nodding his understanding. "That is to be expected, Admiral."

"For my part though –," said John, "The ships under my command will honor the ceasefire."

"That is all I can ask, Admiral."

John was about to terminate the link when Geoll spoke again. "You have wounded here, Admiral. Perhaps I could arrange for them to be returned to you so they can receive more suitable medical treatment."

"That would be greatly appreciated, Caretaker Geoll."

Geoll nodded curtly one more time before the link terminated and John felt himself relax for the first time in weeks. The horn that sounded from the Tactical changed all that. On the tactical display five vessels emerged into normal space. In seconds the computer identified them as belonging to the Turak.

"War Chief Vek on fleet command link, Sir."

John felt the muscles in his neck constrict at the radical change of plan he was going to have to share with the Turak. "Put him through."

Vek's began speaking before John got a chance. "Ha! I see the cowards are running now we have cut the head off the beast. It is time for you to press the attack. Close with the enemy and finish them off."

"A cease fire has been agreed with Caretaker Geoll. The Saiph will be allowed to retire to the Sphere unmolested."

Vek's mouth snapped shut, the muscles of his cheeks rippled under the brown leathery skin and the red eyes burned with hatred. "If you will not eradicate these vermin from the stars then I shall..."

"You are under my command War Chief Vek. Need I remind you of that?"

"I do not recognize your command over me any longer, Human. You have betrayed the Turak and I intend to finish the Saiph blight once and for all!"

John rose from his chair and calmly walked over to the Tactical Officer. The audio and visual link to Vek still open. In a steady voice that betrayed no emotion John spoke loud enough to be heard over the link. "Tactical. Order the fleet to engage and destroy the first Turak vessel that makes any attempt to approach the Sphere." Turning to face Vek, John raised his chin and fixed his eyes on those of the Vek. "I outgun you, and I will not hesitate to blow you out of the sky. Leave now and there need be no more bloodshed today."

Vek continued to stare at John with hate oozing from every pore, until at last, the link disconnected.

"The Turak have folded away, Admiral, and we have a Saiph small craft on final approach to Landing Bay One. They say they have wounded on board."

"Thank you. I'll be in the Landing Bay One if you need me."

✳ ✳ ✳

John kept to one side as the medics rushed aboard the Saiph shuttle as soon as its ramp was lowered. It only occurred to John as he stood there that a single shuttle could not possibly hold the numbers of Thunder troopers that had accompanied Vladimir Egnorov on his mission to the Sphere. Raised voices at the top of the shuttles ramp drew John's attention. A large trooper, dressed in his Wraith armor minus his helmet was helping a female who was obviously in considerable pain down the ramp, any medic that got within the range of his free hand got pushed away.

"Come near us again and I'll end you!" Shouted the male trooper and, from the look in his eyes he meant it. Reaching the bottom of the ramp the pair went to attention as best they could as they propped each other up. As John watched on eight body bags on grav sleds floated silently past the troopers as they rendered honors. The grav sleds were lined up to await transportation to Med Bay. John walked across to the two troopers who looked like they were both about to fall over with exhaustion.

The female did not notice John until he had nearly reached her.

"Lieutenant Papadomas and Staff Sergeant Semple, Team Nine, Special Operation Unit Thunder and Captain Calan, Alonan Imperial Navy, report mission complete. All my troopers living, and dead are off the field of battle, Admiral."

John dropped his head as tears filled his eyes and his heart ached.

After the horrors that John had witnessed in the years that this war had raged from one end of the galaxy to another and back again this simple poignant ceremony conducted by two battered and bruised troopers on a cold metal hangar deck so far from home was the one thing that had finally pierced the hard shell that he had built around himself to ensure that he could make all those hard calls that had sent men and women under his command to their deaths.

Raising his head, he took his PAD from his blouse pocket and tapped a code by memory. The call John had placed was answered on the third ring.

"Marine Duty Officer, Major Murata speaking."

"Major, Admiral Radford. I need a detail to render honors. Landing Bay One."

There was a pause on the other end of link for no more than a breath before the major answered as any marine would to an admiral's order.

"Aye, aye, Sir."

John terminated the link and looked into the faces of the Thunder troopers. "Now get yourselves to Med Bay and get seen too." Both troopers hesitated before Philippa cleared her throat and spoke up.

"We would prefer to render honors until the marines can relieve us, Admiral. I –" Philippa flung a look to Semple. "We, do not want our men left on their own."

John realized the troopers would have to be dragged kicking and screaming away if he tried to have them removed before they could be properly relieved. John brought himself to the position of attention and saluted the troopers holding the position until they managed to return his salute as best they could.

"You are relieved Lieutenant Papadomas, Staff Sergeant Semple. It would be my honor and privilege to render honors to the troopers of Team Nine until relieved."

"I stand relieved, Admiral."

Satisfied her troopers would be not left alone Papadomas, aided by Semple, shuffled out of the bay.

Twenty minutes later a detail of marines in their dress blues marched slowly into Landing Bay One and relieved a five-star admiral who had stood at parade rest watching over the fallen.

EPILOGUE

NORSELAND | 127 LIGHT-YEARS FROM EARTH
A chill wind blew unnoticed across the wooden deck of the stone farmhouse the builder had hewn from the land surrounding the house. Admittedly he had had the assistance of machinery which had made the work easier, but he still considered the house to have been hand built and anyone who familiar with his volatile temper knew better than to argue with him.

The PAD lying on the wooden table beside the now cool mug of coffee vibrated softly and danced across the rough surface heading for an impeding fall to the deck. With a grunt Olaf Helsett lifted the PAD, the built-in biometric scanner matched his DNA to the one it held in its secure memory and activated the small screen.

"Must be Sunday." Olaf said aloud without expecting a reply for he was the only inhabitant of the small island that was surrounded by a dark green brooding ocean which crashed against the high cliffs of Olaf's self-imposed isolation.

Norseland had proved to be the ideal place for a man like Olaf who, even when Secretary of Defense in President Coston's government, Olaf had shunned the media preferring to get on with work rather than hog the limelight. The day he had left government Olaf had felt like a huge cloud had been lifted and he was free to enjoy life once more. When his daughter had none to subtly dropped him a brochure containing details of a startup colony financed by a private consortium who were looking for a number of hardy souls to make them up to the required complement to qualify for a mining license from the Bureau of Colonization. The promise of free land combined with a startup loan for a minimum commitment of ten years to the colony project was something which Olaf had found appealing. A divorcee of long standing and a daughter who had forged her own life and career there was little to tie Olaf to Earth. Putting his affairs in order had been a lot easier than he had thought it would have been and within a month he was surveying the island that would become his new home and digging the foundations for his house.

The PAD beeped reminding him that it was awaiting instructions. Olaf tapped the blinking download icon and the small device connected with the satellite in stationary orbit high above him that in turn linked into the planet wide data network. Each Sunday a comms drone would arrive from Earth and update the network with all the latest comings and goings of the distant worlds of the expanding Commonwealth. Olaf may have chosen to retreat from society in general, but he did like to keep abreast of events.

Another soft beep signaled the completion of the download and Olaf took a gulp of his now cold coffee before settling back to catch up with events beyond his island. The lead story was the ongoing deterioration of relations between the Turak and the Commonwealth. The media were bandying around words like 'crisis' and 'impending hostilities' however, the more level headed among them pointed out that the three way armistice agreement recently negotiated between the Commonwealth, the Saiph and the Alonan Empire guaranteed the free exchange of military technologies among other things. That meant the Commonwealth navies now had not only antimatter weaponry but energy shield technology that would keep any Turak aggression in check for the foreseeable future.

An article from a Garundan news agency concerning the securing of a deal with Caretaker Geoll of the Saiph to repatriate all refugees from their current quasi prison on Tanil to the Saiph Dyson Sphere caught Olaf's eye and he earmarked it for later reading. Olaf skimmed the remainder of the weekly update and was about to move on to his private correspondence when an otherwise innocuous entry in the business section caused him to pause. Opening the article, Olaf felt a sense of satisfaction fill him as he read the story. Zurich Lines, one of Earth's, if not the Commonwealth's, largest shipping conglomerates had been forced to call in the receivers. The business had made a number of bad investments under the leadership of Bryer Anderson and its creditors had pulled the plug. The journalist who had penned the article predicted that the business would be broken up and sold off to its competitors while Bryer Anderson himself faced financial ruin. Olaf's roaring belly laugh that rolled across the harsh landscape around his house caused a number of the local bird like creatures to take fright and flee into the heavy sky, with a flurry of loud squawking.

Chortling to himself Olaf called up his private correspondence. Among the usual heap of holographic images his daughter sent to him every week detailing the exploits of his grandchild's latest attempts to walk and crawl was a rather official looking email from the Office of the Commonwealth Combined Joint Chiefs of Staff. Olaf tapped the address line opening the message. Contained within was a personal invitation from Admiral Ai Jing requesting his presence at the Admirals Dining Out, the navy's way of saying farewell to a retiring officer. Attached was a second invitation to the Dining In of the new Chairman, Admiral John Radford. Both events were scheduled for three weeks hence.

Raising his eyes from the PAD, Olaf allowed them to scan the view before him. The not quite green grass covering the undulating ground before dropping away sharply at the cliffs edge. The water, its waves cresting to form the white foam that ancient sailors had called White Horses named after the mythical god Poseidon, king of the sea, who one day had created horses and the white crest of the wave was seen as the horses mane while the sound of the crashing waves resembled that made by a hundred horses hooves thundering across the ground.

No, decided Olaf, as he tapped on his PAD sending an auto reply declining the invitations. Let the outside world deal with the legacy of events. At long last he had found his place in the universe and he was happy.

Returning the PAD to the table he lifted his mug and went to get some fresh coffee.

Thank you for reading Legacy of the Saiph, Book 4 of The Saiph Series. If you enjoyed this book, would you please leave a review?

Would you like to know when the next book PP Corcoran book comes out? Sign up here: www.ppcorcoran.com/subscribe

ABOUT PP CORCORAN

AUTHOR OF THE AMAZON bestselling Saiph Series, PP Corcoran writes fast-paced military science fiction because he gets to mix his two loves; shoot em ups and science. A twenty-two-year veteran of the British Army, Paul began his writing career in 2014. After serving all round the world, this native of Scotland now lives in Northern Ireland and writes epic space opera for a living.

You can connect with Paul here:
Facebook: https://facebook.com/ppcorcoran
website: https://ppcorcoran.com

BOOKS BY PP CORCORAN

MOST OF PAUL'S BOOKS ARE available as part of Amazon's Matchbook program, which means: If you've already bought the paperback edition from Amazon you can download the ebook edition *free* or at a greatly reduced price. You can read more about the program here: www.amazon.com/gp/digital/ep-landing-page. Don't forget to visit www.ppcorcoran.com for the latest on PP Corcoran.

Military SF Series

The Saiph Series (4 book series)
The K'Tai War Series (3 book series)
Sinclair's Scorpions (The Four Horsemen Universe)

Anthologies

The Empire at War (4 Novel Anthology)
Explorations: Through the Wormhole
Explorations: First Contact
A Fistful of Credits (The Four Horsemen Universe)
The Stars in Flames (5 Novel Anthology)
Future Days (Short Story Anthology)
Alien Days (Short Story Anthology)

Short Stories

Beyond Apollo (SF)
Through Glassy Eyes (SF)
The Province, Ghost Soldiers 1 (Military Thriller)

AUDIOBOOKS BY PP CORCORAN

MOST OF PAUL'S BOOKS ARE available as audiobooks and many are available as part of Amazon's Whispersync program, which means: If you've already own the kindle edition, you can upgrade (at a much reduced price) and add narration, allowing you to switch seamlessly between reading and listening. Alternatively, you can download the audiobooks from the iTunes store or Audible.

Military SF Series

The Saiph Series, books 1 to 4 (Unabridged)
Invasion (Unabridged)
Sinclair's Scorpions (The Four Horsemen Universe)

Anthologies

Explorations: Through the Wormhole (Unabridged)
A Fistful of Credits: Stories from the Four Horsemen Universe (Unabridged)
Future Days (Short Story Anthology) (Unabridged)
Alien Days (Short Story Anthology) (Unabridged)

Short Stories

Haven One-Eight (Unabridged)
Beyond Apollo (Unabridged)
Through Glassy Eyes (Unabridged)
The Province, Ghost Soldiers 1 (Unabridged)

GET NOTIFIED OF FUTURE BOOKS

Sign up here: www.ppcorcoran.com/subscribe